Pretty People Are Highly Flammable

A Dirt Opera

GERRY WALKER

Published by SFE Books

New York

www.dirtopera.com
dirtopera@gmail.com

I am blessed. Thank you so much for sharing this particular experience with me.

My grateful thanks to Stacey Watson, Mark and Michelle Everetts, Don and MaryEllen Robertson, Elyse Adler, Reg Harper, Reginald Anglen, and those others who really desire me to succeed. Also, thanks to Nadja Deighan, Roger Atwell, and Lynn Del Negro for encouraging me to be myself to the *nth* power.

Coming in 2011:
Pretty People Make Great Projectiles

www.dirtopera.com

Part One: Catch Up

Episode 1

1428 Bakman Street, Nashville, 37206:
This cozy 1920's craftsman home was painted eggshell white just
last year by its owners, a young professional couple expecting their
second child next May. They've trimmed the windows in periwinkle
and installed a majestic mahogany wood front door for magnificent
curb appeal.

"*Smart look*," thought Xavier Jonson when he first laid eyes on it. One week later, on October 12th, the house was in escrow. Two weeks after that, it was his.

In order to settle into his new home, Xavier sliced out an entire twelve consecutive days of vacation – something almost unheard of at his firm. But he was the hot kid: two years in, twenty-seven cases taken, zero losses yielded.

So the big guys upstairs decided to grant his wish of a junior partnership appointment and ten days off to work on his new house – plus two additional days to draw up the preliminary outline for his upcoming ethics textbook.

While on break, Xavier dug up the grass in his front yard and planted new seeds. He also installed a new stone floor in his eighteen-by-eighteen square foot gourmet kitchen. He'd always dreamed of someday having a kitchen like this, because it might inspire him to learn how to be a great cook. He shellacked the dark hardwood floors in his living and dining rooms, and in his

office. He feng-shuied. He coated each wall in regal golds, brilliant blues, and robust reds.

All of these handy skills were learned at the orphanage where he grew up.

Xavier also installed new five-pronged chrome fixtures in his master bathroom. This, he thought, is what made the new house his home. If the walls could talk they would say, "*Show you right, baby.*" Counselor Jonson was proud of his new investment.

February 14th, 2010: 1:42 p.m.

Four months had now transpired since his vacation, and the kitchen floor was the last thing on his mind. The new grass outside did not matter. Xavier was terribly nerve-wracked about the day that lied ahead of him. He walked into the master bathroom, turned on the shower and placed his hand into the flowing water to circumvent any potential shock. He then dropped his towel onto the floor, stepped into the stall, and closed the door. He released a sigh that confessed, "*This feels so good… but how will I feel by the end of the day?*"

"Let's just enjoy this," he decided. The hot water upon his body was especially pleasing now: he had just completed a routine two-hour workout at the neighborhood gym and his tense hard muscles yearned to be loosened up. The water splashed onto his head, face, then trailed to his broad shoulders and sinewy back. Xavier loved his shower because its contents actually poured down upon him rather than shooting directly across onto his chest. Having stood six-foot-six since his final growth spurt at nineteen, he indeed welcomed this rare pleasure.

Episode 1

He lathered up his loofah mitt with a new shower gel that a coworker concocted in her garage and asked him to try. It smelled good, and Xavier had always been a sucker for pleasant scents. He massaged the mitt first over his well-sculpted arms, then across his masterfully-chiseled torso and up his back; next plunging down to his buttocks, his muscular legs and calves, then feet. He briskly ran a small brush under his manicured nails. His genitalia were always second to last in the regimen, right before his face – a ritual since childhood, no recollection why. The white lather against his bronze skin intrigued him, and for a moment, he just stared at it.

The steam was now so thick that he couldn't see his hands. It was a perfect time to release some of the tension generated by unbridled thoughts of his big day ahead. And being unable to see the deed would alleviate some of his inevitable Catholic guilt. He reached for that gel again.

Xavier slowly massaged his manhood as the water paved through his thick black tapered mane. "One day," he pondered, "I'll start locking it," but he was well aware that he had better first win about one-hundred-fifty more cases at work. And even then, he would most likely end up having to resign from the firm:

> ("Remember the time I wore a dashiki into the office on Christmas Eve and three people asked if I was upset about something?")

The law firm of Page, Seavers, and Markowitz, LLP just wasn't ready for any of Xavier's ethnic expressions. But he had always admired locked hair and its heritage, and knew that one day he would share it.

As he began to swell, his mind started to clear. Today's impending events vanished. He was alone. His eyes closed. His hand accelerated. His lips separated. His muscles mellowed. At any moment he would cry out in uncontrollable exhilarating ecstasy. And …

The water was bone cold.

"Aaaahhhggh!"

3

Xavier feverishly turned off the water. He jumped out of the shower and grabbed his towel. "*Drexel!*" Still wet and steeped in sweet-smelling lather, he thrashed open the bathroom door and squished hastily down the hall toward the kitchen.

"Drexel! Drexel!"

Facing the kitchen sink was a ruggedly handsome thirty-four year-old man rinsing off some boiled eggs. He was watching a talk show on a portable TV, and had not heard Xavier calling him.

"*Drexel!*"

The man looked up, then toward the doorway where stood a nearly naked Xavier in a pool of water and small clusters of Coco'-Nilla-scented suds.

"Huh?" he sluggishly replied.

"You're running the hot water again while I'm in the shower."

"Oh…" Drexel was aware that he had once again messed up.

"*How many times…?*" Xavier resolved to stop speaking right there. Speeches, he long ago learned, had no effect on Drexel. Maybe a little drama would work better, like in the courtroom. "Thank you," he huffed in conclusion, as Drexel watched him retreat back up the hall.

The one thing that 1428 Bakman Street did not yet have was a decent water heater. Xavier price-checked a few during his vacation, then calculated that replacing the present one could wait until next summer, when the price of having it installed would be cheaper. Besides, one person couldn't use that much water.

He had not anticipated Drexel knocking on his mahogany door.

Backstory: xavier and drexel

Stephen Drexel was Xavier's best friend growing up in the orphanage. Xavier always looked up to the three-years-older Stephen, who preferred to be addressed by his surname. Though Drexel was nearly one year old when orphaned, Wilson County

assumed that, being such a good-looking kid, he still had a reasonably good chance of being adopted by a loving couple.

The County was wrong. Drexel, like many children at St. Elgin's Orphanage and Day School in Mount Juliet, Tennessee, was multiracial. Most families preferred "purebreds", as the luckier ones were deemed by their peers. Being Black, German and Taiwanese, Drexel stood out, and was passed over again and again by parental hopefuls until it became evident to him that he was already quite at home.

Xavier was brought in two years after Drexel at the age of one month. There was much fuss over the new baby, and all the nuns just knew that he would be gone again within days. But Xavier had been born addicted to PCP, and still carried a habit that scared off every potential mom and dad.

But within only a few weeks of his arrival, the school nurses had completely detoxified his tiny body. And on June 5th, 1978, Xavier Nathaniel Jonson was adopted at the age of three months by an older Latino couple who appreciated his Dominican roots.

What they didn't appreciate was Xavier's constant crying. From dawn to beyond sunset, he would not stop. He had never behaved this way at the orphanage. His new parents did not know what to do. They tried everything: lullabies, vacuum cleaners, Elmo, nothing helped. Papa blamed it on the previous addiction, and Mama was convinced that Xavier had El Diablo in him. But when the exorcism failed to calm him down, the Saldevillas returned little Xavier to St. Elgin's after only three weeks, where he stayed until age eighteen.

Within days of the homecoming, Xavier and Drexel became fast friends. As they grew, Drexel took a grateful X – as he called his buddy because he could not yet say, *"ZAY-vyer"* – under his wing. It did not take long before the two began getting into trouble at school.

One Saturday evening when Xavier was ten and Drexel thirteen, a nun caught Xavier with eleven dollars which Drexel had only minutes before swiped from the Mass collection plate. He'd temporarily entrusted the money to Xavier since his own pockets were riddled with holes. Xavier spent the next four weeks

in two-hour detention after school, never revealing that it was actually Drexel who had stolen the money. The nuns knew the real story, though. They admired Xavier's selflessness and baked him a fresh weekly batch of chocolate walnut brownies, his favorite.

That incident introduced Drexel to the meaning of a true friend's love; he would never forget X's sacrifice for him.

Pretty soon, Xavier became known around St. Elgin's as the shy bookworm with a tendency to unwittingly mutilate the lyrics of 1970's pop songs. Drexel conversely flourished into the slick player with a way with the girls. Oh, how they all swooned over his fine curly hair, ice-blue eyes, milk chocolate skin and intense facial bone structure. And Drexel knew it. Just a few years earlier, these same physical features had proven to be his curse, but now he was a stud.

Sex had fast become his primary reason to greet the day, amplifying his already solid reputation as a troublemaker. He would engage in intercourse whenever and wherever he could: in the cafeteria, on the school bus, in the confessional, in his and Xavier's bedroom while Xavier lay right beneath him on the bottom bunk wearing headphones, writing book reports, and singing classic disco hits like the Bee Gees':

> *"Baldheaded woman –*
> *Baldheaded woman to me..."*

But when little Tammy Hendricks turned up pregnant at fourteen, all fingers pointed at Drexel. That was the last straw, forcing him to leave St. Elgin's for good at the age of seventeen. Xavier was crushed, for his oversexed friend was the closest thing he'd ever had to a real family. They vowed to keep in touch, and they did.

Father Milton used his community connections to secure Drexel a handyman job at a local apartment complex. In two short years, he emerged as manager of all two-hundred fifty-seven units. The gig paid him a nice monthly salary that supplemented the income he accumulated from other jobs. It also provided him

with a free two-bedroom apartment with which to *"entertain his ladies"*.

Xavier was proud of Drexel's achievements and wanted to be just like him, but Drexel would not have it. Xavier was going to college and Drexel would help him out financially by letting him live at the apartment for free.

Soon, things were back to the way they used to be: 3:00 a.m., Xavier studying, Drexel sexing. But one early September afternoon during Xavier's senior year at Belmont University, things changed, this time for good.

A resident of Building Three, the lovely liquor model Chantee Puirle (pronounced, *"Pearl"*, she enjoyed instructing), filed a rape charge against Stephen Drexel. Rather than fight it, he relinquished the job he loved. He reasoned that his promiscuous past would prevent him from winning the court case. And even if he did win, none of the residents would ever again view him in the same light. It would be better for Drexel to leave, so he did.

Xavier knew what really happened: it wasn't Drexel who raped Chantee. He had actually been in Atlanta with another woman – OK, three women – for the whole weekend in question. Chantee, who moonlighted as an escort, needed a scapegoat after her date with a famous golfer fell askew and threatened her career at Star Liquors. She chose Drexel.

That same week, Xavier switched his major to pre-law with a criminal defense concentration. He moved in with one of his classmates, and never heard from Drexel again until...

Ten years later, Drexel mounted Xavier's front porch. He was down on his luck and needed someplace to stay for a while. Nothing more had to be said. The two were roomies

7

once again. But this time something was different. Drexel was acting really weird and thoughtless. True, he had never been a genius, but he had always been mentally sharp. These days however, Xavier noticed that he was forgetting things and smelling bad. He seemed to be endlessly preoccupied, not present.

❦

February 14, 2010: 2:12 p.m.

After a final rinse, Xavier again exited the stall. He was now running late. Even more nervous than before, his mouth was dry and carried an odd taste. He walked into his bedroom, pulled a prepared formal ensemble from one of his two walk-in closets, and laid it on the California king bed. After pulling on a t-shirt and a pair of boxer briefs, he put on the crisp white shirt and looked at the grey suit lying before him. He sat down next to it.

"Should I really do this today?" he deliberated.

Too late now.

He stood up and stepped into his slacks. It had taken him two weeks, even with the help of his tailor, to make them fit onto his muscular bottom half properly. But Xavier was glad that he had persevered, for even he had to admit that they looked stunning on him. While he admired himself, his phone rang. He grabbed it while entering his armoire to find his wedding socks. "Yeah?"

"*Still in your drawers?*" a very deep voice replied.

"Who is this?"

"*Funny.*" It was Emil. "*Quit being such a wimp and get over to this church. Tergiversation won't get you out of this. And we aren't going to wait here all day for you to get pretty.*"

"Well, maybe if peeps would stop calling my house so I can get dressed," he laughed. He found the socks. "See you in fifteen."

"*All right,*" Emil said. "*Good luck today, man.*"

"Thanks."

Backstory: xavier and emil

Xavier met Dr. Emil Hubbard in 2000, the year before entering Vanderbilt Law School. New instructor Hubbard hailed from Afghanistan and taught church history at Vanderbilt Divinity School. He also taught French and Portuguese every other semester. Moreover a twenty-five year old ordained minister in the American Baptist Church, Emil was four years older than Xavier and seemed to have all of his shit together – a characteristic Xavier always admired in what seemed to be so few young men.

The two men were introduced by a mutual friend at Vandy's First Annual 'Young Leaders of Color' Conference – which Emil coordinated – after Xavier slipped and spilled Pepsi on the speech Emil had prepared to read before an excited crowd.

Xavier could hardly bear his own embarrassment. But Emil assured him that no real harm had been done. Later that evening, a lengthy conversation ensued between them. It would give birth to a strong friendship upon which they would heartily thrive; a friendship that for years would keep them laughing for hours on end and allay much pain lying in their paths.

But there was one particular anguish that not even their bond would hold at bay; a secret agony that Emil would hide from his

good friend until years later, during a Valentine's Day wedding weekend.

☙☙

Xavier hung up the phone and rested his head on his hands. "Shit!" He had forgotten to shave. He rushed to his bathroom door to find it locked.

A minute and two flushes later, out walked Drexel. "The other one overflows sometimes," he explained, then walked back to the kitchen.

"Not until your ass showed up here," mumbled Xavier as he rushed in and closed the door. Just seconds later he shot back out and stormed down the hall to find Drexel watching a different talk show.

"My bathroom," Xavier squeaked, attempting to restrain his infuriation. "It smells like…"

"Poop?"

"Man, how am I supposed to get ready for the wedding when I can't even use the bathroom?"

"I sprayed."

"Shit!" Xavier was now completely fed up. "It's all that horrible crap you eat!" he raged. "All those frozen burritos and enchiladas with their funky-ass preservatives – it's disgusting. That stuff is gonna kill you. And dude, what's with all the eggs – and that ancient TV? For the umpteenth time, please chuck it!"

Drexel gaped blankly at him.

Utterly exasperated, Xavier trudged back to his bedroom, grumbling ferociously. "Now my whole house reeks! Smells like your nasty dump was lodged up in you for a week. What were you waiting on, *a Pisces?*"

He slammed his bedroom door.

Episode 2

Charmaine Parker sat before her vanity attempting to style her temperamental shoulder-length mane. Her face toted a significant frown.

At five feet-eleven inches tall and measuring 48-29-44, Miss Parker was accustomed to routinely confiscating the attentions of either sex. Her almond-shaped chestnut brown eyes accentuated her luminescent ebony skin. And her thick, wavy black hair usually cascaded over her visage to complement her prominent cheekbones, inherited from her father.

But for today's wedding, Charmaine desired an up-do. In the last hour she had experimented with various buns and chignons, but none of them worked. Without her beautician, Mr. Moché, she was hopeless, and she knew it. "You know," she sighed, "Today, just this once, I want hair that stops traffic."

"Too bad, 'cause your hair *is* traffic," replied her best friend Karianna Cojoure from atop the day bed in the corner of the bedroom. "But we all have our crosses to bear, darlin.'"

"You juz' mad 'cause you ain't got my looong, byooliful, luxurious hayah," Charmaine replied in a mocked urban accent.

"...Which you can't do a thing with unless Moché is in town. Honey, flea markets sell plastic hair that acts better than yours. I keep telling you to try my conditioner."

Charmaine winced. "If I start putting that white folks' stuff in my head, it won't matter if he's in town because he'll be able to just mail it to me when he's done. Anyway, I think I'm gonna cut it all off just as soon as I..."

"...Get somebody to propose?"

11

"…Get that new job," laughed Charmaine. She then flung a platinum hoop earring at her friend. It landed in her cleavage.

Karianna threw her arms skyward. "Bullseye!"

"Cow's chest."

Backstory: *charmaine and karianna*

Charmaine Parker's family moved into 933 Akers Lane in the Bordeaux district on the coldest day of the year, January 22nd, 1987.

Little Charmaine was extremely peeved at what would be her new neighborhood while her father served at Fort Campbell Army Base over in Clarksville. She refused to speak to anyone – even her parents – for the entire day. Quite dramatic even then, she instead pouted on the swing chair on the front porch, sporadically executing violent sighs of adamant disapproval and even shedding the occasional tear for added effect.

Her mother, busy assisting and chastising the movers, intermittently swept by with a kleenex to soak up each tear.

But Mom's occasional morsels of attention were not enough to appease Charmaine. She needed her inner torture to be understood – absorbed, even – by all those around her. So, at 3:12 that afternoon, just as the movers took their break, Mr. Parker took another swig of beer, and Mrs. Parker took her water pill, Charmaine leapt up onto the porch banister and threatened to hurl herself to the ground, potentially maiming her pretty little face in the process.

"Girl, get down off of there before you rip your skirt! I paid too much for that outfit to have you rollickin' around in it like it was a pair of chaps," Mrs. Parker proclaimed. "Sometimes, sometimes, Howard; I just don't know what's wrong with that child. I think we should have her tested."

"For what? Your DNA? That girl ain't nothin' but you," Mr. Parker replied between swallows. He was a quietly intelligent man with

much patience, which often came in handy when dealing with the two ladies in his life.

Nine years his senior, his wife just looked at him: that look.

("Why did I marry beneath me? I shoulda just ran away with that mortician from Toledo – what was his name?")

Meanwhile, in the corner of her eye Charmaine was pleased to find someone staring directly at her. She turned to face the porch next door and saw a little freckle-faced white girl with long red pigtails and a smile presently awaiting the arrival of two new teeth.

Normally Charmaine would have been a little more self-conscious. Even at age six, she'd have immediately wondered what gruesome thing must be in her hair or teeth to provoke such a Chesirian grin from a total stranger. She would have therefore quickly performed what Mrs. Parker called, "The Check":

-pat the hair down then search the hands for lint;
-suck on the teeth to catch stray food particles; then
-complete a final outfit brush-off and pull-down.

But Charmaine was so happy to have an audience that she forgot her ritual. Good thing Mother was still leering at Dad (that look).

Charmaine continued to hang upside-down from the banister as the white girl next-house-over laughed encouragingly, clutching her nearly-one-eyed rag doll tightly.

Mrs. Parker was not as amused. "Heffah, git your black butt up into this house and take off your clothes. Git into your pajamas. You're going to bed. I've had enough of your little smart behind. Always wantin' some attention."

Charmaine knew that she would elude punishment. After all, it was only 3:21 and none of the beds had even yet been unloaded from the van. But she waved goodbye and smiled elfishly at the girl next door, whom she knew was now her friend in this God-forsaken place. The redhead smiled back and gripped her doll even more tightly as they retreated into their homes.

Over the next year, Charmaine and Karianna would become almost inseparable. They would do their homework at Charmaine's house, eat lunch together in the school cafeteria, and on selected occasions, skip school: something Charmaine loved because it felt like they were women living on the edge of danger. One March afternoon right before spring break, they would find out just how much danger was in store.

That morning, Mrs. Parker had, unbeknownst to Charmaine, rescheduled her weekly manicure to earlier in the day. That way, she could go pay some money on a coat she had placed on layaway (and you know those long lines) and get back home by the time her daughter arrived from a half-day at school.

While waiting on a green left arrow in order to turn into the Gant Department Store parking lot, Mrs. Parker spotted two little girls and a boy on the other side of the street. They were walking two blocks ahead and about to turn the corner. Was that Charmaine and Karianna?

Over the months, Karianna had grown quite irritated by Mrs. Parker's nosiness. "What's wrong with your mama?" she once badgered Charmaine. "Ain't she got *something* to do? Her eyes don't never miss nothin'. I bet if she tried hard enough, she could see Jesus."

Karianna was always chiding Charmaine about something. But since her observations were always so hilarious, Charmaine didn't mind. Her girlfriend's spicy candor delivered in that thick woodsy southern accent could always be counted upon to cheer Charmaine up.

But no amount of humor was going to fix what would happen today.

Mrs. Parker waited for all of the oncoming vehicles to turn. Then she slammed her foot forward and drove straight ahead from the left-turn-only lane, narrowly avoiding another driver exiting the parking lot.

Her car was a camel yellow 1979 Chevy Malibu coupe with a piece of twine fastening the trunk door shut, and emaciated threads holding together the foam bucket seats. It was the kind of car that you could always hear coming long before you could

see it. Its completely rusted muffler dangled beneath the rear bumper, igniting sparks wherever it trailed.

Immediately Charmaine's life began to flash before her eyes. "Oh, shit, Kari! What are we gonna do? *Kari!*"

She needed her friend to deliver a sassy remark to take her mind off of the trouble she was in. But Karianna not only remained silent; she became distant as well. Her plucky personality suddenly seemed to completely disappear. Edward, the boy they were playing hooky with that day, also noticed it. Karianna was now behaving very strangely.

The children continued moving forward. For some reason, the closer the car inched to them, the more slowly they walked. "Bu", as Karianna referred to Mrs. Parker's dilapidated vehicle, was now right upon them, directly to their right, creeping down the middle of the street. They dared not look over. Even Edward was scared, and he walked all over his own parents. Charmaine prayed for a blessing.

Just then, the muffler fell off of "Bu", and Mrs. Parker finally opened her mouth.

"Ohhh, my goodness! Lord Christ!" For the next few seconds, Mrs. Parker craned her head out the window, gazed at the downed muffler and spewed profanities between phrases with the word "Christ" in them. She could not decide whether or not she should just grab the kids and leave the thing sitting in the street. But given the fact that "Bu" was decrepit and now louder than ever, it looked like a getaway car, yes?

So she got out of the car and surveyed the damage. By now, Edward was bowled over with laughter and Charmaine was very delighted and relieved that her little prayer had worked. Maybe now she could work on getting other things she wanted as well, like a new CD player. After all, if her mother had the power to see Jesus, maybe Charmaine could actually talk to him.

Karianna remained voiceless.

"I told Howard this thing was a piece of junk when he bought it. *Now* look. See?"

Charmaine dutifully nodded.

15

"What a mess! Come on, Charmaine, help me put this muffler into the trunk."

"Yes, Ma'am."

After they retied the twine, Mrs. Parker and the children climbed into Bu and drove toward their own neighborhood. Charmaine knew that she'd just bought herself some time, and that was good. It is always wise to brush away as much initial parental fury as possible before an actual pouncing occurs: children are very keen to this fact. But the pouncing was still coming right now:

"OK, Little Miss Missy, so what the hell were you out here doing? Why wasn't your ass in school like it should've been? Wait 'til I tell your father. You're gonna end up just like his crazy sister. I can't believe this mess. What is wrong with you, girl? What gets into your hard-headed butt sometimes? They *told* me not to use Similac. And you, Miss Karianna Cojoure," she lectured to the rear view mirror, "You just wait until your father finds out about this."

Charmaine was worried about Karianna, who remained stoic and ghostlike, staring out the window.

"And you look at me when I speak to you, girl."

No change.

"And what were y'all doing out here with a boy?" Mrs. Parker continued. "Don't tell me y'all done started messin' around already, because I will stop this car and beat you both silly. With your hot asses. I can't believe it. *Hot asses*. Boy, where do you live? And git that smile off your face!"

"919 Creekside Road, ma'am. Just three streets over from your..."

"Hush. I know where it is. Where are your parents?'"

"At work."

"I tell you, we should've never moved into this neighborhood. Now my child is a hussy at seven, skipping school, trying to trick with a boy whose pebbles ain't even fell down yet."

"Huh?"

"Shut up and get out of my car, boy," she commanded while pulling up to his house. As he exited, she added, "And I'm tellin'

16

the principal what you did today. Be sure of that. What's his name, Karianna?"

Karianna offered no reply.

"I'm talkin' to you, girl."

Mrs. Parker noticed that while Karianna still refused to speak, there was now a torrent of tears rushing down her face.

"Oh, it's too late to cry now," she menaced. "Shoulda cried when y'all thought up your crazy idea to skip. And Charmaine, you'll be spendin' your whole spring break on punishment. You won't be leavin' the house for nothin'. And if your father has any sense, Kari, he'll do the same to you."

"If only he were so merciful," Karianna wished.

"Thank you, Mrs. Parker. I'll take care of it," said Beau Cojoure to the woman who had been trying for a whole year to get into his house.

She was sure that today's achievement would grant her entry, and was rather excited.

"Um-hmm, you're welcome," Mrs. Parker promptly replied through the skinny crack in the doorway. "I just don't know what's going on with these kids today, my Lord… Um, say… do you have a cup of sugar I could borrow? After all this mess, I really don't feel like going back out to the store…"

"I'm sorry. I just ran out. But thank you again for informing me of this matter. I don't know what got into Karianna. I apologize for any trouble that this may have caused you."

"Oh, no trouble," assured Mrs. Parker, beginning to feel uneasy about his eerily placid demeanor, as well as that of his daughter, who had now not yielded a sound for almost a solid hour. "You know kids… Well, don't go too hard on her, all right?" she smiled sheepishly while retreating back down the porch stairs.

With no reply, he closed the door.

Mr. Cojoure was a slight-statured man, about five feet and five inches tall, 130 pounds, of French and Welsh descent. He had moved his daughter to Nashville from Lafayette, Louisiana when she was just two. As far as Karianna knew, her mother was deceased.

"So, you're out here running around with boys, eh, Petite?" he interrogated.

Karianna grabbed her tear-dampened doll and clutched it fiercely.

"Answer me!" he yelled with a force that made her knees buckle. "What were you doing with that boy?"

"N-nothin,'" she whispered.

"You know, I oughta shine your tail right now for skipping." His attitude suddenly changed. "But I forgive you, ma sucre!" He noticed her body clinch as he walked to her. He held out his hand. "Ah, now, ma sucre. You know I'm not gonna hurt you. Come on over here with me."

Karianna, panting furiously, shook her head "no", her tears now flooding the creaking old hardwood floor beneath her.

"Now stop that, Kari. Don't make Papa angry. You don't want to do that, right? Now come with me. Maint-nawnt." He escorted her to the enormous pink lounge chair in the next room. It was aged and knotty, but quite comfortable. "And put that down. You're too old to still be playing with dolls, hon."

She placed the doll on the floor.

He sat in the chair. "Come sit down right here in front of Papa, OK?" he gently urged.

Hesitantly, Karianna obeyed.

"Now darlin', you know you're not supposed to be hangin' around boys at your age, right?"

"Yes."

"So it'll never happen again?"

"N-n-nooo," she sobbed.

"C'est ma Petite Fille," he smiled. "Elle est une belle fille, aussi, eh?" He brushed his sharp rough knuckles across her cheek. Then

Episode 3

"Ashley?"

"Here."

"Justin?"

"Here."

"Megan?"

"Here."

"Karianna? …Karianna? Karianna Cojoure?"

The following afternoon on the bus ride home, Charmaine decided to head straight over to Karianna's to find out why she never made it to school that day. Boy, would she be jealous if her friend were able to play hooky again so soon, and without even inviting her. Upon reaching the Cojoure house, she found three local news vans perched on their front lawn. She also found her own mother, who was in the midst of being interviewed by each of them.

"…And when I got back home," Mrs. Parker expounded, "I saw that his car was still in the driveway, and I thought that was odd because on Friday mornings, he's always gone to work by 9:45. So I knocked on his door to see if he was ill and needed me to bring him something, but he wouldn't answer. Then, when I called him on the phone he didn't answer that either and that's when I really got worried. So I went back over and peeked in the side window. That's when I saw him lying on the floor, just wrigglin' around, looking like he'd been shot or something. So I called the police and they came, and that was it."

After being hospitalized and treated for a thirty-two caliber gunshot wound to his chest, Beau Cojoure was immediately taken into the custody of the Metro Nashville Police Department. There, he was subjected to intense questioning regarding the rape of his daughter on the day before she shot him.

Over the next twenty-three weeks, numerous debates would ensue as to whose hands in which to place Karianna now that her father had been found guilty of first-degree rape. He would dwell inside the penitentiary for at least the next fifteen years.

It turned out that her mother, Greta, was indeed alive and well, living in Tucson with her husband of five years and their two sons JoJo and Salvador. But Greta could not fathom the possibility of disrupting their lives by taking in this other child whom she hardly even knew. Beau had abducted Karianna years before and moved to Nashville because of Greta's aggressive former drinking habit. She still attended the AA meetings. But bringing a daughter back into her life now would be too overwhelming. Too much bad history.

So Karianna's only remaining options were the Metro Nashville foster care system or an orphanage. At the court's ruling, on September 7th, 1988, Karianna was sent to an orphanage in Mount Juliet called St. Elgin's.

On her first day there, an obnoxious boy with chocolate skin and crystal blue eyes walked up and stomped her foot. He then said he was sorry, but she kicked him in the groin anyway. That landed her in detention with another sweet boy who was doing hard time for stealing eleven dollars from the collection tray. The boy confided to her that he didn't really do it, and she believed him.

So the next time Karianna saw the blue-eyed kid, she kicked him again – this time harder – thereby becoming his first crush. But he would have no time to act upon it, for Karianna's violent behavior had now landed her a one-year sentence inside the Davidson County Juvenile Correction Hall.

Right after Karianna said her goodbyes and exchanged phone numbers with the blue-eyed kid and his angelic friend, she began the dreaded walk to the white Metro van driven by the man in the orange uniform.

But before she could fasten her seat belt, into the St. Elgin's parking lot drove Mr. Parker, Mrs. Parker, Charmaine, and Bu. That day, initial measures were taken toward what would

eventually become the Parkers' legal guardianship of Karianna Cojoure.

February 14ᵗʰ, 2010: 2:00 p.m.

"Thank you," Karianna said in a gravelly-sugared drawl. "I knew you had my earrings. You're always takin' my stuff. Where's the other one?"

"Somewhere on this table," replied Charmaine. "I was thinking about wearing them to my interview tomorrow, but I don't want them to think I'm pretentious."

"I still can't believe you're interviewing for a job on a Sunday. You're supposed to keep the Sabbath holy."

"Girl, I know *you* of all people are not trying to talk to me about anything holy. All I know is that I'd better get this job or I'm a goner. My new landlord is trying to get rid of me."

"Why?" Karianna inquired.

"I pay three-hundred dollars a month less than everyone else in this complex."

Karianna pulled in more closely. "OK, so who ya fuckin'?"

"You make it seem like I don't have legitimate skills. Hand me my brush, please."

Karianna lifted the hairbrush off of a tangerine-scented pillow and placed it in Charmaine's hand.

"My apartment became eligible for re-leasing last month," Charmaine explained, "Because they found out that I've been unemployed for over ninety days, and they have a three-page waiting list."

"Can they legally do that?"

"They can do whatever they want when the vacancy rate in this building is zero. You definitely did the right thing by buying.

If I don't show proof of full-time employment by Monday, I'm out. So I guess I'll just have to walk into that interview and dazzle 'em."

At once tickled and astonished by her friend's game plan, Karianna rose from the bed and walked over to the mirror to give herself a brief once-over. She was a beautiful and petite woman with full lips, long legs, lightly tanned skin, dark green eyes and a reddish-blond closely-cropped and layered do. She dabbed a bit of stray lipstick from the corner of her mouth before speaking. "You've always had to have your drama. But you'd better hope this one works out, honey. Moché's not goin' anywhere near your hair if rats are droppin' their babies in it on skid row."

"You're coarse," Charmaine smirked. "But don't you worry about me – I'll have that interviewer eating out of my hand." Then she briskly turned to her best friend. "And as far as men are concerned, I already have one, boo. A doctor, thank you. We may even get married."

"OK, so if he's the one, why are you still scourin' those icky online personals?"

"Oh, please, Kari. *You're* the one who always has to have a man in her life, on her arm, in her boudoir…"

"Wait a minute: I've been on sex sabbatical for almost eleven months now, C. You know that."

"Um-hmm."

Karianna lay back on the bed. "Dear, believe me: these days, the only thing deader than my sex life is *your* credit."

Charmaine attempted to push a bobby pin into her hair but it would not fix. "Are you sure? Because going by your past…"

"Just a minute, darlin', my recollection states that your bed sheets aren't exactly lily white either."

"They were just dates, K. A girl's gotta eat. Very few of them ever got past dinner and a movie." She turned back to the mirror and silently contemplated wearing a hat to today's affair. "But you know, I'm just not feeling all these tired men anymore."

"Well, what about that one guy? The massage therapist – Phil? He was beautiful."

"He should've been," Charmaine scoffed while finishing off her eyes. "He wore more Maybelline than you do."

Karianna's jaw dropped. "Girl, shut up! But he was fine!"

"Correction: he was fake. Those thick black gorgeous eyebrows? Penciled in."

"Whaa?!"

Charmaine laughed. "Look, I can't deny I love men. But the ones who perpetrate like they're something they're not, I have a real issue with that."

"But Xavier..." Karianna commenced, only to be abruptly halted by a warning glare in the mirror.

"You ready?" Charmaine asked.

"I've decided I'm not going."

"What?"

"I'm really heavy this month, C. I can't risk a wedding. That would be ornery."

"Come on, Karianna," she begged. "You'll be fine. I have something you can wear. It'll be over really quick. You may even find someone there to plug it."

"Now who's coarse? I oughta call your mama right now but don't feel like hearin' her mouth."

Charmaine patted down her new French roll and whispered a small prayer for it to stay in place. "It wouldn't matter if you called. I think their phone is disconnected or something. I keep getting a busy signal."

"Oh?"

"Emil will be at the wedding."

Karianna looked up, unaware of the urgency imbedded in her gaze.

"It's Valentine's Day, Kari. And we're invited to a wedding. Please don't make me go through this one alone."

"You have a bobby pin sticking straight out of your 'long luxurious hair', luv. Leave it just like that and I might go."

Charmaine grinned. "Girl, please. You are the only ghetto chick in this room."

Episode 4

"…Oh, yeah, and that guy from Brazil? Yeah, him:
already wants to get married. He introduced me to
all his friends, took me to meet his folks, and now he's
tryin' to sign me up on his gym membership – now, wait:
I might actually do that because his gym is fiyah,
and you have to be cute to get in; I am not lyin'!
Miami is a mess.
…Anyway, I'm supposed to be spending Easter at his cabin
in Santa Barbara, but I also got invited to three other cute
guys' houses that weekend, and I want dinner from all of 'em.
Now, how am I gonna work that out?
…You're right, the Lord'll make a way.
…Oh!
…Did I tell you? Listen to this: I've been
kinda datin' a dude over in Lauderdale.
He's OK, but he is just too tall, even for me —
almost seven feet. Now what am I supposed to do with all that?
Plus, he's tacky. I mean, he wears all the right gear:
Versace, Armani, K.C., you name it. But he combines it all
into the wrong outfits. Don't you just hate that?
It happens a lot with tall and fat people.
And he don't even stand up straight when he walks.
He just kinda bounces up and down, draggin' his
knuckles on the ground like a big ol' lanky yellow
orangutan, lookin' like Rudy from Fat Albert.
…And he needs a new barber, 'cause his 'fro looks like
a helmet."

Andrew Freeman Niles, known to the world as Drew Niles: stand-up comedian, actor, rising star, and one of People Magazine's "50 Most Beautiful People of 2010", was flying from London to Atlanta. After landing, he would fly up to Nashville, the city where he grew up. But this was no pleasure trip. He hated Nashville.

A thin boyishly handsome baby-faced young man with light brown skin, freckles, sandy hair, hazel-grey eyes, and deeply penetrating dimples, he had only agreed to go there today to perform at a wedding reception as a favor to an old friend. After that, he was hopping right back on the first flight to Miami the next morning.

Andrew, whom everyone called Andy as a child, turned twenty-four today. He was the youngest and most outspoken of his friends, challenged only by Karianna, with whom he was closest. He looked forward to seeing her today. She might make this trip almost bearable.

Almost.

But Andy was already a ball of wrecked nerves, because:

-The stray hairs from his freshly faded cut irritated the back of his neck;
-Not only had the plane been an hour late getting off of the runway, but it did not have one single bag of chocolate macadamia nuts on board (he had the staff conduct a search);
-He had not had a cigarette in nearly ten hours;
-His seat wouldn't recline far enough (*"I thought this was first class!"*); and lastly, because...
-Nashville harbored a multitude of hideous memories he left four years ago to try to completely forget.

Back**andy**ory:

By twelve years old, Andy was fat. Period.

Frequently teased by schoolmates for his hearty appetite and stout form, he secretly vowed to one day become the most famous person in the world (fame is power) and then return to Nashville to rub his accompanying glory in everyone's face. But what was his talent? What could he actually *do* to escort his glory into fruition?

He was awful at fractions, so math was out. And had it not been for the school principal tampering with students' test scores to meet a quota that expanded the athletic program, Andy would have miserably failed his ninth grade reading comprehension exam.

Not that he would have expected anything different. Labeled a learning disabled student since age ten, Andy deciphered early on that he wasn't just humongous; he was also "slow". Maybe even stupid. In fact, compared to his big sister, Aniah, Andy believed himself to be only mediocre, if that.

Eight years his senior, Aniah Renée Niles was a force to be reckoned with. Strikingly beautiful and exceedingly popular, she would receive her Bachelor's degree in Physics from the University of Tennessee, paid in full by her track and field scholarship for being the state's number one placeholder in the 100-yard dash and number two in the 250-meter hurdles. She would then graduate Summa Cum Laude from Vanderbilt with dual Master's degrees in mathematics and statistics, before serving on the research team of a highly lauded textbook on supernova.

Andy would watch from the sidelines as his big sister excelled at academics, athletics, then vocation, while he struggled to just get through the day without becoming the victim of yet another beat-down. Because he wasn't just forty-nine pounds overweight and stupid. Somewhere between fourth grade recess and sixth grade homeroom, Andy realized that he was also gay. And so did everyone else.

At first he attempted to conceal his random effeminate mannerisms from the other kids at school. But his efforts generally only provided them with further fuel for ridicule. It was the girls who were most merciless: laughing at him for what he was – and wasn't; inventing a new, more colorful and insulting nickname for him each week.

The boys were much kinder: they would just hit him. At least the predictability of their abuse would extract some of the sting from the whole ordeal.

So Andy began to eat even more. Sometimes, until his jaws literally hurt from chewing. He dipped his pain in creamy white filling. He quenched his hurt with a ham sandwich. Then another. And one more before dessert.

By seventh grade, he would skip school at least once a week to avoid the certain heartache dispatched unfailingly by fellow students. But one day, in Mr. Yubani's tenth grade English class, Andy awoke to find a dead gerbil inside his backpack with a note hanging from its broken neck:

"Until you can find somebody pathetic enough to stick his dick up your faggot ass, try this you fat bitch."

Andy was mortified. He ran into the boy's restroom and remained there for the next two hours, bawling inside the handicapped stall until a janitor forced him to exit. Waiting for him outside was the crew who made his life miserable. Kevin Bulen, their leader, stepped up and slapped him on the head, prompting the usual giggles from the others.

"I hope you catch AIDS and your fat ugly ass dies, shithead." Then Kevin slapped him again. And again.

Andy, in tears, wanted to die.

Then, a moist gelatinous substance hit Andy's eyebrow, fell past his eye, and dripped down upon his nose. It was Kevin Bulen's phlegm.

And that was it.

"Then I'd better get back over to your daddy's house so he can finish what he started!"

What?

Kevin and the group were stunned. Andy wasn't supposed to talk back.

"What did you say?"

"You heard me," Andy cried. "But don't worry. I won't drain him completely dry. I don't mind sharing if you don't."

The gaggle of distraction-starved teenagers surrounding them guffawed gratefully. Kevin was embarrassed, and that satisfied Andy immensely. But before Kevin could clobber him, the vice-principal trudged over and broke up the crowd.

Andy had finally gotten the final word, and the last laugh. And he quickly discovered that he was good at it. It seemed his mouth had special powers. And he would now wield it like a weapon.

Whenever someone spewed nasty remarks about him, Andy would make sure that his response would be even more banal. Once, when a girl in music class called him a "fag", Andy's retaliation was to declare her mother a "welfare ho", then immediately spit out the names of each of her known clients, male and female.

The other teens were still laughing, but no longer at Andy. They were laughing *with* him, *at* the other kids. His victims. He was finally in the driver's seat. He distributed the pain, designed the doom. He manipulated the sheep-like opinions of the flaky adolescent masses. He could give the people something to laugh at, at the expense of whosoever dared attempt to make him cry.

Pretty soon, his ego-shattering comments began to materialize on their own, with no solicitation from his counterparts. A runaway train determined to destroy anything in its path, Andy Niles was angry, hurt, and desperate to be heard. And finally, he had found a way to express it.

Meanwhile, Aniah was jumping over hurdles.

Andy's catty wit forced him to now play hooky even more than before in order to avoid certain assassination. He chose to spend those days in the Midtown district of Atlanta, because there, everyone was so self-involved that no one cared about his portly form. And it only took three hours to get there by bus.

During his visits to the ATL, he took lessons from the local derelicts on how to steal. One morning, while attempting to lift

a LaVerne Baker CD from Jessie's Record and Tape Den, Andy was caught by a sales associate, and arrested.

His first thought was, *"Aniah wouldn't have gotten caught."* He could already hear his parents reassuring him of that certainty later on that evening.

"Why weren't you in school? Hell, why weren't you in the state of Tennessee? And you wonder why you can't read."

"They tease me at school. I don't like it there."

Andy's parents went into the den to discuss The Andy Problem in private. By now they did this often. What they did not know was that he could hear them loud and clear through the wall, and many times he would have preferred to hear the girls at school.

"Helen," his father would plead, "We have to send that boy away before someone else does. He needs to learn self-discipline. I'm tired of all the trouble he gets this house into."

"No, Jack," she would reply. "We've already discussed this. He is not going to some military school. He's not ready. They would eat him alive. There is no way I'm going to send my baby…"

"See, that's just it. He's not a baby, Helen. He just keeps behaving like one because we allow it. Hell, we're enabling him."

Drs. Jackson and Helen Niles were child psychologists with a joint practice in Brentwood, Tennessee. Being a biracial couple – he Nigerian-American and she Hungarian-American – they had moved there from Mississippi while in their mid-twenties in search of a friendlier environment in which to someday raise their children.

Helen and Jack really tried to be good parents: they never cursed at, or around the children. They let them "express their feelings". They issued "time outs". They discussed *"why"* with the kids. And they never, ever spanked. They did everything right. The problem was, it worked. On one of them.

The Doctors Niles hadn't contemplated that different parenting methods might be necessary for their very different children. No college professor had ever taught them that. It wasn't that Andy was gay (They studied "Gay". They *knew* "Gay"); or slow (This was not a problem: they each took four graduate courses on

"Developmentally Impaired Children"); and they didn't mind his obesity, much.

But sometimes, Andy was downright mean to people. And, though his parents' affluence afforded their family a life of great comfort, he stole things from random establishments, only to later throw them away in the trash bin behind the house, unopened.

His behavior was a solid mystery to his parents. They could not find their son anywhere on any page of any psychology text they opened. And Dr. Spock – damn him – had forgotten to list "Andy" in his table of contents.

Truth be told, he was just plain weird in his parents' eyes. They actually understood why he was not well-liked by others his age, for they had a hard time liking him themselves. Nevertheless, despite their son's lack of a promising response to their clinically-proven parenting methods, they continued to lovingly push harder and harder.

Finally, on Andy's sixteenth birthday – Jack, exasperated and near tears, asked him, "Why aren't you like other children?" Andy decoded the question to mean: "Why can't you be like Aniah? *The one we wanted?*"

He never told them he knew.

One morning when he was thirteen, Andy decided to snoop through his parents' closets for loose dollar bills, something he did often while they were away at medical conferences. After opening a green metal filing case, he learned the truth about his birth.

He already knew that he had been conceived during the same year that Jack and Helen launched their new practice. But what he learned from a piece of folded paper, is that because of the untimely pregnancy, initially his birth was to have been aborted. Helen, however, had become a skeptical candidate for the surgery

due to a small rupture in her uterus created during his older sister's birth.

So in essence, Andy owed Aniah his life, too.

What couldn't that girl do?

Jack and Helen loved their son, but they could not understand him. So they finally began, unwittingly, to just ignore him and focus all of their time and energy on Aniah, their one good child. She was so smart. And thin. And heterosexual. And tall. And pretty. And nice. And…

For his entire life, despite all of his sister's accomplishments and all of the praise bestowed upon her, Andy never envied her. He believed that she deserved it; that she was just superior to him, so why be upset about it? He never became jealous.

…Until *him*.

During Aniah's senior year at the University of Tennessee, she befriended a gorgeous young instructor from Afghanistan. She met him while attending an annual event he coordinated called the 'Young Leaders of Color' Conference at Vanderbilt University. His name was Emil Hubbard.

During her final semester, she and Emil began dating. By her third month of graduate school at Vandy, the beautiful researcher and the newly promoted assistant professor were engaged. Emil introduced Aniah to his friends Xavier and Charmaine, also a couple. Aniah introduced Emil to her baby brother, Andy.

And Andy fell in love.

It was not enough that she had to be skinny, smart, and elegant. Now, Aniah even had the perfect man. Handsome, eloquent, intelligent, amazingly built, and well-mannered, Emil seemed to be perfect; the antithesis of the youngest Niles. How

Andy wished this man would, just for a moment, look over his way and want him.

The two fellows would converse lightly while Emil waited for his fiancée to finish dressing for a date. Emil would sometimes take him to lunch, where they would discuss life, dreams, and plans for the future. Andy enjoyed that Emil – even though he was an associate minister at New Israel Baptist Church – did not talk down to him as others would.

Emil also refused to insult or reprimand Andy's shameless flirtatious gestures. Instead, he would politely decline each one, citing his allegiance to Aniah.

The fact that Andy desired Emil but couldn't have him propelled him to resent the one person who could – TBA: "That Bitch Aniah". She had everything. All he wanted was a tiny morsel of her grand existence. But she was not going to hand it over to a fat dumb gay delinquent, even if he did happen to be her brother.

So one day, she would pay as well, just like all the others. He would see to it that his accomplishments would outshine even hers, and then everybody – even Dr. Emil Hubbard – would have to see him, acknowledge him, love him.

But what could Andy *do*?

Episode 5

By eleventh grade, Andy was sent home from school regularly for his behavior; that is, when he even bothered to show up. One November morning, he decided to leave all on his own, and never come back.

The next day, while casing a drug store on Atlanta's Peachtree Street, he noticed a rather odd-looking bald, middle-aged man staring at him. The man walked over.

"Hello, I'm Richard. You have a very pretty face."

"You don't. Get the fuck away from me." Annoyed with the man for disturbing his concentration, Andy scurried away.

But the odd man followed him down the next aisle. "You know, you don't have to steal to get the things you want," he sweetly whispered. "Stealing doesn't befit you. You're such a beautiful boy."

Andy prayed to Anyone Listening that this man would not recognize that those five words were exactly what he had yearned for years to hear somebody – anybody – say to him, even if they were untrue. "What do you mean?" he timidly investigated.

"You're so good-looking; you could do many other things."

"Like… model?"

"Yes, kind of," Richard replied. "Except that you would do it privately, instead of on a runway."

"I'm fat."

"We can fix that… what did you say your name was?"

"Andy."

"Work for me Andy, and you can have anything you want." He handed Andy a sheet of miniature tablet paper with a cell phone number and the words, "*Richard M., Dream Maker*" printed on it. "I want you to call me. I'll be waiting."

Richard walked over to the counter and handed the cashier a fifty dollar bill. "This should pay for whatever that young man over

37

there buys. You can just give him the change." He smiled once more at a mesmerized Andy and walked out of the store.

Later that night, after his family retired, Andy called Richard, who told him stories of other young men like Andy who were making their own money, buying their own designer clothes, and living their lives on their own terms because of their affiliation with *"Richard M., Dream Maker"*. It got his attention, and they arranged to meet each other the next morning.

He took the train to Richard's well-appointed home in Ansley Park. There he was introduced to five young men, all within three years of his own age. They had cute faces and wore brands like Armani, Hugo Boss, and Dolce and Gabbana; brands that did not manufacture clothing that fell within Andy's dimensions.

Beginning to feel uncomfortable and out of his league, he crept toward the door in order to make a quick exit. But it would not budge. Andy was locked in, and Richard, who had suddenly disappeared, had the key.

"What's the matter? We not good enough for you?" called a voice from immediately behind him.

"I, I..." a worried Andy stuttered, before turning around to notice a young blond individual wearing a khaki plaid outfit by Ralph Lauren.

"He won't hurt ya," smiled the blond. "I'll admit he's weird, but it's only 'cause he's trying to protect us. We can't risk some stuff happening, either by our doing or theirs."

"Theirs?"

"You know."

"No, I don't."

"Our clients, man."

"Oh."

"I'm Joe."

"Andy."

"So, Andy, judging by how you look..."

"What's wrong with how I look?" Andy quizzed.

"Nothin'. Chill, man. I was just going to say that you're probably from the 'Ville."

"Brentwood."

"Oh, yikes!" Joe smirked.

Andy laughed. "I hate it there, though. I wanna leave… so I take it you guys have sex with people for money?"

"Hey, don't judge, man. It pays the bills. I'm only doing it because my girl and me got a kid comin' and we need the money to get a nice place to live and stuff."

"You're straight?" Andy said.

"Look, I do this for money, nothin' else. I love my girl. Got nothin' against your kind, though. Just don't get any ideas, OK?"

Andy chuckled again. "Does your girlfriend live here with y'all?"

"Nah. Right now she's in a shelter downtown. But when she starts showin' in a few weeks, they're gonna kick her ass out, so I gotta be ready." He stealthily brushed up beside Andy. "Don't tell anybody, but I already got almost four-thousand saved up. All I need is a little more, and I'm outta here, man."

"I thought you said it was nice here."

"Look, it could be the fuckin' Taj Mahal, but I don't wanna be suckin' dick for a livin' when I'm thirty, OK?" Joe declared.

"So I would really have to… suck guys off?"

"Don't tell me you've never done it?"

Andy remained silent.

"Oh! Richard really outdid himself this time." Joe momentarily studied Andy's person, caringly cocked his head leftward, then consented, "Well, don't worry about it. I'll show ya the routine. Stick with me. We'll go out on doubles at first. You can follow my lead and watch what I do, then do your own thing when you're ready."

"I'm still not sure I want to…"

"Well you better decide quick, 'cause here comes Richard. See ya." He walked out of the room.

Richard M., Dream Maker scooted up to Andy and presented him a glass of iced tea of which Andy did not take a sip. "I see you're becoming acquainted with our personnel. That's good. Joe is wonderful. A little hard-headed, but good at what he does. Stick with him. You'll make a lot of money."

"Look, I don't know if I wanna do this."

"What?" Richard exclaimed.

"You said I could model."

39

"Oh, but you will," he assured. "Privately, for your clients. These are very rich and powerful men who only want to be around someone young and good-looking like you: the 'you' that we are going to create. "Believe me," he continued, "I know what you want, Andy. And I'm the one who can help you get it. Just give me a few weeks, and you'll be just fabulous. But you've got to do exactly what I say, with no cheating. And one last thing: you'll have to move in with me and the other boys as soon as possible..."

"Move in?"

"So that I can better monitor your progress," Richard explained. "It's your decision. But you'll have to make it quickly, because there are dozens of young men out there whom I could invite into our family. But I chose you. We run a very high-tier service here. I only want the best, and cannot risk any defaulters." He rested his thin hand on Andy's shoulder. "Face it, if you were already satisfied with your life, you wouldn't have been in that drug store yesterday trying to steal baby laxative. Let me make you happy. Let us give your life some enjoyment."

For the next two hours, Andy weighed Richard M., Dream Maker's proposition. Then, later that afternoon, he rode the Greyhound bus back to Nashville and dropped his toothbrush, a wash cloth, and a week's worth of clothes into his backpack. Before leaving his parents' house, he left a note on the dining room table explaining his departure, but not disclosing his future whereabouts.

Over the next two and a half months, Andy was restricted to a low-carbohydrate diet on which he averaged a weekly loss of four pounds. At its near-conclusion, he found himself able to – for the first time ever – wear the clothes he just knew that he had been born to. He saw the change in how his naked body looked in a full-length mirror, and he liked it. Random people on the street noticed him now. He received compliments. He mattered.

<u>Fat is evil</u>
<u>Thin is love</u>

And whatever he had to do to stay that way, he would. He began to sustain himself on carrots, chocolate milk, and the

occasional box of caffeine pills to help him through the plateaus. He started smoking to help overcome food cravings. Andy was determined never to return to his former girth. Ever.

It had now been twelve weeks, and the evening had arrived for him to go out on his first date. To commemorate the occasion, his pal Joe presented him with a brand new Armani ensemble that included a blue wool sweater and a pair of tan jeans, size thirty waist.

S i z e t h i r t y w a i s t

They fit Andy perfectly. Unable to withhold his joy, he ran into the bathroom to cry. What a friend Joe was.

During the taxi ride to Buckhead, Joe briefed him with last-minute pointers on things never to tell a client (i.e.: "*I love you*"), things always to tell a client ("the price, upfront") and a few other miscellaneous tidbits of the trade. The new information, however, did little to lessen his angst.

At the hotel, he watched Joe and the two men for forty minutes. Finally, one of the men asked him to join them. The concerned Joe looked up at Andy, not wanting him to do so if he wasn't willing. But Andy felt good. Confident. Thin. And that night, he and Joe made four-hundred dollars.

Backstory: *andy and emil*

"OK, one-fifty," Andy recited, while rising from the floor to put on his pants.

"A hundred and fifty dollars?" scoffed the skinny man sitting on the bed. "Hell, no. You better get back down here and finish what you started, punk."

"I did. You nutted. What do you want me to do now, play with it? Learn how to control your bodily functions. And gimme my money, please. I gotta go."

"You little bitch motherfucker!"

The skinny man jumped up and grabbed something in his coat pocket which Andy, in a sudden panic, assumed to be a knife, or worse. So Andy grabbed the Gideon Bible off of the nightstand and thrashed it at the man's head, knocking him out cold. Standing there for a brief moment, he felt like Coffy, one of his all-time favorite movie characters. He took all four-hundred eighty-seven dollars out of the man's wallet. He then fled the building and phoned Joe, but could not get an answer. Joe had suddenly for some reason disappeared. Scared of repercussion, Andy never called Richard again. In fact, he avoided Ansley Park altogether after that; it had now been nearly a year since that first assignment with Joe, and he didn't want to trick anymore. But he still needed "things". And he wasn't going to crawl back home to his family, at least not until he was certain that he had exhausted every other option.

After relocating to downtown Atlanta, he was able to stretch out the skinny man's paycheck for nearly nine weeks by taking showers in gyms, sleeping in college lounges, and eating most of his meals at Sammie's Subs. He made certain, though, not to ever go overboard on the honey oat bread. But one night, when all the money had finally been depleted, Andy headed over to Midtown.

He knew what he had to do.

———————————

It was "Open Mike Night" at Crush, a local gay bar off Peachtree with a strict "twenty-one and over" policy. Being only nineteen, Andy hoped that if he found a way in, some dude might slip him a ten or a twenty for his services. So he climbed through the bathroom window and scanned the smoky tavern for anyone who looked like he might desire a somewhat different breed of company than what the bar was able to provide.

Meanwhile on stage, a man in his early fifties was finishing up the final chorus of "*Piano Man*" on an old Yamaha upright piano. Upon his last note, everyone applauded while Andy continued to scope the room.

And then, something happened that would change his life forever.

"Thank you, thank you boys," acknowledged the man. "And I would especially like to thank Emil back over there in the corner…"

Andy turned around.

"…For being such a good friend, for being so damn hot, and for giving me the guts to finally get up here and do this. Thanks, man!"

Yes.

Yes, it was. Dr. Emil Hubbard. Aniah's man. The Divinity professor. The Baptist minister. In a gay bar. Yes, it was.

Suddenly, Andy hatched an idea rooted equally in desperation and naughty abandon. He walked up to the bartender and asked to be placed on the night's roster.

"So what's your talent, cute stuff?"

"I believe you just answered your own question."

"OK, where's your ID?"

"Uh…"

"Go ahead," the bartender conceded. "But tonight you're twenty-one, if anyone asks."

Ten minutes later, after another singing performance, the name "Drew Niles" was announced for the first time ever from the microphone behind the bar. And up onto the portable card box stage stepped Andy.

"Excuse me, excuse me everybody," he began, "I'm sorry to bother you, but does anybody here happen to have a twenty I could borrow?"

A few people giggled curiously at the cute guy up on stage. But behind them, in a corner, a young college professor felt his heart begin to pound brutally.

"I'm serious," Andy escalated. "I've recently run out of money and I'm willing to do just about *anything*…"

The enthusiastic audience's cat-calls and whistles reverberated throughout the bar.

Then Andy shifted his focus to Emil, who was hurriedly preparing to leave. "How about you, dear sir?" he called out. "Could you spare a young brother a dime? We've all heard what a great guy you are, and I promise, I'll make it worth your while."

The audience squealed their mischievous appreciation of Andy's candor and natural command of the stage. They were unaware that the sequence taking place in front of them was actually not very funny.

Emil stood in the spotlight that had found him, his face totally flushed. He did not attempt to feign amusement, for he had too many other things on his mind. How to get out of this? How to shut Andy up? How not to lose Aniah's love and respect? How to disappear?

Andy soon transferred his attention to the rest of the room, flirting with some, cattily insulting others to the point of exuberant glee. All eyes and ears were on him, and they liked what they saw and heard.

"Oh, here's a gentleman I might be able to get some hard cash out of! Look at him: he's short, bald, overweight, and probably has an itty-bitty wee-wee! Do you know what I call men like that, folks?"

"What?!" howled the lively and inebriated audience.

"...A cab."

After ten minutes, Andy exited the stage to a standing ovation. He tremendously enjoyed the high it gave him, and while taking it all in, bumped into a loud, curly-haired man who shook his hand.

"Do you want to make a lot of money?" the man asked.

Andy was leery. "...Doin' what?"

"This! What you just did. It was brilliant. With your look and that act – polished up a little bit – you could stand to become quite wealthy and famous."

"I'm listening."

"My name is Sid Eschleman," he said. "I'm a promoter, new here from St. Louis. I need an act to get going in this city, and you're it.

Here's my card. Let me take you to dinner in a few days and we'll discuss it, OK?"

Andy made a strained effort not to reveal his excitement. "OK."

The man left, only to be replaced by more who desired to shake Andy's hand and congratulate him.

Emil waited patiently in the rear hallway for Andy's conversations with his new fans to end. Once they did, he grabbed his arm and dragged him through the back door into the alley and threw him against the brick wall.

It hurt Andy's back, but it also turned him on a little.

"I should rip out your throat for what you did to me in there."

"What? I was just having a little fun. And I was the hit of the night. Look," he exclaimed while revealing Sid's card, "I may have even gotten a job out of it, Em-"

"Listen, I don't know what you're trying to pull, but you had better not say a word to anyone about seeing me here," warned Emil, his nose dripping and eyes blinking rapidly.

"Do you have a cold? If so, you shouldn't be out here. We need to get you back inside."

Emil pushed him several inches up the wall. "I mean it, Andrew. I cannot risk a scandal spreading its way up to Nashville. So don't play around."

Andy's body suddenly swelled with anger and disgust. "Look who's tellin' who not to 'play around'. Shut up, Emil. You're 'playing around' behind my sister's back! In random cities! *With dudes*! So get outta my face with your shit. Hey, you know what? I *am* gonna tell her! So you can beat me up all you want. You think it would be the first time?" his voice cracked. "Hell, kill me. I don't even care." He fell limp against the wall.

Sorrow subdued Emil as he lowered Andy to the ground. "Look, man, I'm sorry. It's just... I don't think that Aniah would understand this. She's so..."

"Perfect. I know." The burst of triumphant energy which had only seconds ago radiated from the nineteen-year-old had now completely evaporated.

"She talks about you a lot," Emil said. "She misses you. I know that you trick, Andy. A friend of mine says you approached him

45

tonight before your performance. You don't have to do that. You've got a great family back home that loves you."

"Wait a minute," Andy retorted. "What I do is my own damn business. I don't need Prince Pakistan telling me how to handle my shit. I'm fine." He studied Emil's washed-out complexion and sweat-soaked bald head. "If you ask me, you're the one who's lookin' tore up. What have you been up to?"

Just then, a faint silhouette appeared beneath the yellow light at the far end of the foggy alley. "Oliver! *Oliver!*" it cried in an agitated tone.

"Ain't no 'Oliver' out here. Leave us alo-…"

"Hang on," Emil said as he ran to the man.

After the two conversed quietly under the yellow light, the mysterious man dropped something into Emil's coat pocket and speedily vacated the alley as Emil walked back over to Andy.

"So, all I'm saying is that there is help for you…"

"Who was that?"

"No one."

"Mm."

"OK, look: I'll pay you," offered Emil. "In order to retain your silence and to keep you off the streets, I'll give you a hundred a week."

"Do I have an alternative?"

"Expiration, perhaps." He wiped his nose again, then pulled five twenties from his wallet and handed them to Andy. "I cannot stress this enough: please do not tell her that you saw me here. I will do that myself when the time is right."

Andy slipped the cash into his right sock. He wasn't broke anymore, but something else was wrong. He continued to inspect Emil.

"…Oh, and by the way, I've never cheated on your sister, with anyone. Just because a man is attracted to other men, doesn't mean that he's hooking up with every single one he meets, despite what our unconversant society would have you believe."

"You can start droppin' off my money at my parents' house every Friday," said Andy, nonchalantly. "I should be there at four o'clock, but I'll be headin' back out before six, so that don't give you much of a window."

46

"That's fine. Thank you. And you promise to return to Nashville tomorrow?"

"Yeah."

"Great. Aniah will be very happy."

Andy walked to the curb to hail a cab to the bus station. Truthfully, he would have kept any secret for Emil, and he would have done it for free. But he was now experiencing a hodgepodge of emotions:

> Excitement: he may have finally found his calling as a stand-up comedian.
> Relief: he's got some extra cash flow now coming from Emil.
> Confusion: who was that strange man?
> More confusion: who is 'Oliver'?
> Wonderment: why, despite the secret Emil is keeping from his sister, did he still care so deeply for the bald, goateed Adonis?
> Even more confusion: what the hell is *unconversant*?

He went back to Nashville the next morning.

Episode 6

Six days later, Andy caught the 2:05 Greyhound back to Atlanta to have dinner with Sid Eschleman at Sardi's Grill while Andy's parents attended medical tests for Aniah at Baptist Hospital. She had taken strangely ill just two weeks prior.

At dinner, Sid offered Andy the opportunity to perform in Atlanta the following weekend at a small club for an eighteen and over crowd. "I have some friends from Miami who are dying to see you."

"But I don't have an act."

"Just do exactly what you did last week. That was great. We'll worry about the other stuff later. It's next Saturday night at seven. Can you do it?"

"How much money will I get?"

"If my friends like you, we'll both get a lot, in the long run."

"Well, are you at least going to pay for this dinner, or should I have worn my Nikes?"

The next nine days were terrifying for Andy. He desperately wanted to make a good impression at his first official gig, and he worked really hard to come up with a good routine. He wished he could ask Aniah's opinion of some of his jokes, but these days she was feeling too weak to help him out.

The Saturday gig in Atlanta turned out to be, to Andy's amazement, an absolute success. And it put him in touch with

49

exactly the right kinds of people: well-connected middle-aged gay men with lots of money to invest in a promising young talent. They had Hollywood ties, and were sure that Andy's was just the right face to finally catapult gay men of color into the hearts of mainstream America.

Weeks later, he and Sid found a manager, Daniel Neesen, who was looking for a new project to nurture. Andy became that project. Over the next four months, the men worked together to create an entire stand-up comedy act from scratch, as well as a fresh, stylish and sexy new alternate persona for Andy. His natural talent for insulting others while keeping them in stitches and even turning them on, was the base upon which they built.

They started out in Atlanta, then journeyed into the Greater Miami area, and back up the East Coast. After creating the necessary buzz, they then trekked out west to do some high-profile shows there. Andy was learning industry tricks quite competently and becoming more polished each time he stepped out on a stage. It fast became evident that their plan was working.

One night after a sold-out show opener for Margaret Cho, he looked up in his dressing room to find his old friend Joe in the mirror. Excited, he spun around. "Hey, man! I thought you died or something. Where did you go? And did you guys have the baby?" They hugged.

"Yeah," said Joe. "A year and a half ago. I ran into some trouble, but I'm better now. We moved up to Nashville. I hope you and I can catch up if you still live there."

"Hell, yeah! I missed you," Andy admitted.

"Me, too. Sorry I didn't keep in touch. I had to take care of a few things before gettin' myself back on track."

"I understand. No worries."

"Well, this is certainly a long stretch from Richard's," smiled Joe.

"You know, sometimes I wonder. If I've learned anything these last couple of years, it's that we're all just hustlers searchin' for our next pimp."

"Hang in there, man. I was so stoked when I saw your name in the paper. You're gonna be huge, I can feel it."

"Thanks. So, what are you up to now?"

"I got a job at a clinic up in the 'Ville," Joe began. "We help recovering addicts: booze, drugs, sex, you name it. We also do conjunctive work with clinics in Atlanta, New Orleans, Memphis and Houston. It feels good to do something meaningful with my life. Hey, are you gonna be up there at all this week? If you're not on the road you should stop by and we can maybe have lunch?"

"That's wassup," replied an excited Andy. "How about Friday at noon?"

"Perfect. There's someone I want you to meet. She actually kinda reminds me of you. I think you'd like her."

"Cool. What's the address?"

The next Friday, Andy walked into the Northside Addiction Therapy Clinic on Trinity Lane where Joe introduced him to his boss, clinic director Karianna Cojoure. Within three minutes, the two were laughing like old friends, comforted by each other's freedom with ribald humor. They ordered in Chinese and gabbed nonstop for hours.

Andy could have talked for at least a few more, but it was Friday, and he had a 4:00 appointment with Emil down in Brentwood. He had to go.

"Well, it was wonderful meeting you! I hope you come around here again soon," said Karianna.

Andy did not want to leave. He really liked this woman, and had missed Joe a lot. "I'll be back, don't worry."

"Oh, look at you, hanging your head like a little puppy," she said. "Don't do that. Just come on back whenever you feel like it. And I really mean that."

"OK."

As he stepped into his taxi, Andy felt more sadness infiltrate. He did want to see Emil, though not because of their agreement. But he feared that if there ceased to be a monetary transaction between them, their weekly rendezvous would also dissolve. And besides his club dates, their secret meetings were the highlight of Andy's weeks. Emil's kind voice would always make up for the fact that Andy could only understand about three-fourths of the words that came out of Emil's mouth.

God, he loved that man.

But he also noticed that Emil was looking stranger each week. His skin was becoming yellow and he was beginning to lose some of the muscle tone Andy so enjoyed ogling. And he was relinquishing some of his trademark neatness. It was time to investigate.

"Can I come over to your place?" Andy asked in his parents' driveway. "I just don't feel like seeing my folks yet."

"I was going to hook up with some friends, but sure, you can come hang out."

"You'd give up your friends for me?"

"Well, you're a friend too, so…"

"Still just a 'friend', huh?" Andy clarified.

"You should be flattered," Emil chuckled. "Blackmailers don't generally progress to that echelon in their victims' rolodexes."

"You offered me the money. I would've kept your secret for free, Emil."

"Yeah, right. I know you, man. You're evil."

The quip punctured Andy. "No, I'm not, really!" he asserted. "Don't you see? That's only what I need people to think." He scurried up to Emil with the hope of a puppy yearning to bond with its master. "Look, I know that I'm not all super-duper-maxi-fantastic like my sister, but I think you really ought to consider me. I'm older now. I'm not a kid anymore. And in a minute, Aniah won't even be able to compete with me. I'm on my way up, so you'd better catch me."

Emil's laugh hurt Andy more than he would ever know.

"I love you," Andy uttered faintly to the ground beneath them.

"Hey, I love you, too. Look at how you've turned your life around, and in such a short time. I'm very proud of you. Seat belt, please."

———————————

"Would you like something to drink or eat?" Emil offered.

"Yeah, I'll get it myself."

"OK, I'm going to take a quick shower. I'll be out in a flash."

"Take your time." Andy opened the refrigerator. It was smelly and riddled with mold. There were foods that had never even been opened, spoiled inside the wrapper. Emil normally ate like a horse in order to support his massive physique, so that would explain his recent weight loss.

Andy was now quite suspicious. He walked down the hall into the bedroom. He opened drawers and searched through them, looking for answers, but coming up empty-handed. Dumbfounded, he reached into his pocket for a cigarette but dropped it beside the bed. Right beneath it was a shoebox. He picked it up and opened it. What he found made his stomach turn.

Emil walked into his living room to find Andy smoking a cigarette.

"I'm sorry, this is a no-smoking inhabitance."

"Whatever."

"Excuse me?"

Andy held up a vial containing white powder. "What is this, Emil?"

Emil's heart stopped. "...Huh?"

"Are you doing heroin?"

Caught off guard, Emil was unable to produce a reply that would make any sense. "What are you talking abou..."

"Don't insult me even more than you already have today, Emil. I *know*, OK? Contrary to what you guys may all think, I'm not an idiot. So that guy in the alley was your dealer, huh?"

Emil stood speechless.

"Can't you see what's happening to you? You look a good mess, you're not eating... you need help. And now it's my turn to do you a favor."

"You don't know what you're talking about," pressed a fearful Emil. "You should go. Right now, please. I should not have brought you here. I'll call you a cab."

Andy put on his coat, removed a card from his wallet and placed it on the coffee table. "When you're ready to admit you're not Superman and you might need some help dealing with your problem, call this number and ask for Karianna. She's cool, you'll like her. But leave your shit at the door, 'cause she don't play around." He walked to the door and opened it. "I love you, Emil. Do whatever you want with that, but don't destroy yourself. I don't know if I could handle that. Oh, and no need to call a cab." He threw the five twenty dollar bills onto the coffee table. "I got it."

He was gone.

Within the next twelve months, tickets to Andy's shows were selling well, and he was now able to headline small tours and relocate permanently to Miami where he and Daniel could concentrate on securing television and film roles. Five years later, small tours had become big tours, and big tours became talk show appearances and movie offers. Everyone now wanted Drew Niles to share his gift.

◎◎

Episode 6

February 14th, 2010: 2:24 p.m.

The gift was on prominent display today aboard British Airways flight 0227. He chatted on the phone with friend and gardener Monica Shackley about *"this man who wanted me"*, *"this woman who wanted to beat my ass for talkin' to her man"*, and *"this man who couldn't bone to save his ass"*.

By now several passengers aboard the cabin had requested a seat further away, though each of them made sure to obtain his autograph before relocating.

> *"...Now here's the crazy part. Are you ready? Why is*
> *ol' dude a point guard for the Heat? Yeah,*
> *I found out when he was on the cover of the sports page.*
> *I mean, I knew he was really tall, but damn, you know?*
> *Anyway, there's more: I was buyin' groceries*
> *about three months ago, when I saw him*
> *with some woman. She was not cute.*
> *When he peeped me, he snuck down the aisle I was in.*
> *So we started talkin', but then*
> *that woman came lookin' for him.*
> *She rolled her ol' crossed eyes at me—*
> *and for one split second, I had the nerve to feel cheap.*
> *Can you believe that? I just walked away.*
> *...Well, I know: maybe I shoulda said somethin',*
> *but I don't know what that bitch had in her purse*
> *and I ain't about to get shot over no man who can't dress.*
> *I don't need that kind of stress,*
> *especially since I got back my EKG and blood work.*
> *Yeah, Danny's been whinin' for me to take a break.*
> *But I feel fine. I'll get some rest at my hotel.*
> *By the way, the Fox deal is on hold right now because they "don't*
> *know if America is ready for 'a Black gay lead' in prime time".*
> *Now ain't that a bitch?*
> *But that's OK because ABC is lookin' real hard at me.*
> *Uh- huh, I have a meeting with them in two weeks.*

Pretty People Are Highly Flammable

I'm young, I'm rich, and I'm about to be really famous.
Hey!
What did you think of my picture in 'People'?
Do I really look that good?
…Do you mean it?"

"*Attention, passengers: we are now beginning our descent into Atlanta International Airport. Due to current heavy winds and for your own safety, we ask that you remain seated even after we land, until the plane comes to a complete stop. We'd like to thank you for flying with British Airways…"*

"…Yeah, well never again," Andy snorted to the nearest flight attendant. "I could've Sea-Doo'd here faster than this."

"*…Look, boo, I gotta get off this phone. They finally decided to land the plane. Yeah, I guess they got sick of my mouth. Either that or the smell of this man's feet in front of me, damn! I gotta call and let everybody know I'm in the States. OK. Bye.*
-Feed my fish!
Bye."

He hung up the phone and redialed.

"Hey, it's me – why aren't you picking up? Anyway, my plane was late getting in so I'm taking the next Nashville flight I can find and then coming straight over to the church. I'll have my stuff sent to my hotel. And please, no drama, OK? It wasn't my fault."

Two hours later, Andy peered out the window of his second plane as it dropped into the cool atmosphere that was

Episode 6

Nashville, Tennessee. "Shit," he ruled minutes later while lighting up a cigarette and advancing through the sliding airport doors. He pulled his jacket closed and cringed slightly at what was in store for him. "They need to be happy I came back at all... *Taxi!*"

Episode 7

There was a wedding today.

Sometime today.

But an hour had now passed since its scheduled starting time. And one half of the betrothed still remained missing in action.

Some attendees were starting to exhibit their impatience. But while restless toddlers galloped about the aisles and tempers flared, Charmaine perkily jotted down perfect phrases to insert into her newest online personals ad.

Karianna sat next to her, wearing the most discontented facial expression she had on file.

Meanwhile, around the corner from the church, a metallic blue Mercedes E63 AMG sedan swerved onto the curb and parked. Seconds later, the door opened to reveal an irritated, though impeccably dressed, Xavier Jonson.

He ran up the church walkway and scampered into the chapel, adjusting his tie while struggling to cram his jingling keys into his jacket pocket. The squeak of his new shoes immediately captured the attention of the congregation. Some commented as he shuffled past the altar and into the pastor's study to join Emil, today's presiding minister.

"Is that the groom? Girl, he's worth the wait."

Xavier closed the door behind him. "Hey, E."

"Well, we're all thrilled that you could finally make it. What happened?"

"I swear, man, I was all dressed and on my way here," Xavier explained. "But I had to do something to get rid of this tension. The whole day's been crazy. I was just brushing up on my Japanese."

Emil was confused. "How does it take someone over an hour just to masturbate?"

"I was so stressed out that instead of lube, I accidentally grabbed my after shave – the one with alpha-hydroxy acid in it."

"Ouch," Emil marveled. "You must have one heck of a healthy glow right now?"

Xavier nodded. "I practically glow in the dark."

Emil's terrific bass-baritone echoed valiantly from the walls as he threw back his head in robust laughter. "Wow! You know, Charmaine is a nurse; she may have gauze in her purse…"

Xavier perked up. "Charmaine came?"

"Don't look now, but she's in the third row on the left."

Xavier swiftly pulled open the study door and scanned the left side of the church. Upon locating Charmaine, he also found his good friend and confidant Karianna, temporarily lapsing her protest in order to wave to him.

Charmaine, however, turned away the instant her eyes connected with Xavier's. It had now been nearly seven years since they had last spoken, and they both knew why.

"She didn't have to come today," Xavier said softly. "She's being so great about all of this."

Emil agreed. "Despite what happened, she wanted to show her support. What can I say? The girl's a saint."

"Yeah," he sighed. "A true saint."

Backstory: *xavier and alex*

On an unseasonably warm December morning during his senior year at Belmont University, Xavier opened his mailbox to find a small postcard asking him to report asap to the academic

counseling office. He did not understand what could possibly be wrong, but prayed that no one had finally found out that he had plagiarized half of his freshman history term paper directly from an obscure 1960's textbook.

"That's all I need when I'm about to graduate, is to get kicked out," he mumbled as he threw on a pair of jeans, a football jersey and a pair of flip-flops, and dashed out the door.

"Hello, I'm Xavier Jonson, here to speak with..." He looked down at the postcard. "...Alex Young. I don't have an appointment, but the card said *'urgent'* so I came right in."

"No problem at all, Mr. Jonson," replied the woman behind the desk. "Just have a seat for one moment, and I'll check to see if someone is able to see you now," she chirped.

Xavier could not sit. He began to panic. "All that hard work, all the struggle, just to be kicked out for one little mistake?" Now prepared to beg for mercy, he had only two weeks ago been accepted into Vanderbilt University Law School, and would die if something were to prevent his attending in the fall.

The lady waltzed back out front. "Alex can see you now. Go on back, and it'll be the third door on your right."

Xavier walked down the long grey corridor assembled with carpeted cubicle walls connected by screws and hinges. He heard a buoyant friendly voice call his name, and realized that it had come from the cubicle that he had just passed.

"Xavier Jonson? Is that you? I'm Alex Young. You can come on in and have a seat. I'm just finishing up this call. Won't be a second."

Behind the desk sat the young academic counselor, about five-foot-eight, with freshly gelled short black hair, wearing a new purple shirt and khakis, swiveling back and forth in the chair and playing with the phone cord.

"She looks younger than me," thought Xavier as he walked in and sat.

"Hey, we'll talk about it later, all right? I've got a student in my office. OK. I'll call you... yeah, me, too. Bye." Alex hung up the phone, reached upward into a lengthy arm stretch, then leaned forward on the desk, perusing Xavier with a feigned air of suspicion.

Though worried, Xavier could not refrain from staring at the attractive woman in front of him. The uneasy feeling already in his stomach suddenly shrank to make room for something besides his potentially threatened academic fate.

"Hello, Xavier. How are you doing today?" Alex exclaimed, attempting to break the ice by flashing a spectacular grin with a small gap between its two front teeth.

Xavier, immersed in befuddlement, offered no reply.

"Hey, you in there, dude?"

"Oh!" he yelped, his now heart palpitating fiercely beneath his jersey. "I'm sorry... what?"

Alex, a new graduate student from China working in the office of Academic Affairs to satisfy an academic requirement, reached for Xavier's academic file.

Xavier noticed that her skin appeared unusually bright and supple.

After quickly reviewing Xavier's file, she looked back up. "Well, Mr. Jonson, I have to be honest and tell you that there's a problem here..."

"I'm sorry!" Xavier squealed.

Alex inquisitively stared at him.

"I didn't mean to do it. Really, I didn't! I didn't want to copy from that book but I was really tired, and I didn't know what else to do."

"Whaa?"

Xavier jumped up and began pacing frenetically about the cubicle. "I had four exams and two papers due in three days. I was freaking out!"

"Like, right now?"

Xavier looked at Alex's face. "Yeah! I mean, no..."

Episode 7

(wow, your lips are perfect)

"...Miss Young," Xavier begged, "Please..."
"It's *Alexia*. But please call me Alex."

(Alex... Want a kiss, Alex?)

Xavier sat and leaned forward in order to plead his case more comfortably. "Alex, please – I'm so sorry. I've never cheated before or since, I swear. I just got accepted into Vandy Law, and..."

"I know," she congratulated. "Good work. You're gonna do great there, I'm sure of it."

"...And I've worked four jobs to get myself to this point, but if you kick me out now, I..." He paused momentarily to absorb her statement. "...What?"

"I'm sure you'll be a great student at Vanderbilt, and become a fantastic criminal defense lawyer. That's your concentration, right? Criminal Law?"

"Yeah..." replied a still-dumbfounded, ruby-faced Xavier. "So... you're not kicking me out?"

"No," Alex laughed. "How could I pluck out such a brilliant and promising student? Water?" she offered, already dispensing a stream from the cooler behind her desk into a clear plastic cup. She handed it to Xavier, who was now finding himself more at ease with this beguiling figure.

"Thanks." He took a sip. "I can't be much younger than you. How old..."

"Twenty-three."

He wanted to know more. "If you don't mind my asking, where are you from?"

"Beijing."

"What happened to your accent?"

"It got lost along with my luggage. Now back to you. Apparently you've got some secrets, Xavier Jonson."

(if only you knew)

63

"It's OK," she reassuringly parlayed. "We've all got something, huh? But that's a later conversation. We asked you to come in because we've noticed that you're scheduled to graduate this spring. But you still have not fulfilled one of your primary education requirements."

Stymied, Xavier sat up and placed his fists on the desk. "Which one?"

"Arts."

"But I took Chorus."

"Which counted as an elective," she explained. "But that alone wasn't enough to fulfill your arts requirement. You need two more credits, and you need them quickly… more water?"

"No, thanks. What are my options?"

"Uh, sorry: 'option'. Since spring registration has already closed, every class is full, except one."

Xavier was hesitant to ask, "Which one?"

"Ballroom dancing."

"What? Ballr-! You're kidding, right? This is a joke? Look, I can't dance…"

Alex reached over and poked Xavier's left fist with her right index finger. "I believe that's the point of the class, dude. To teach you?"

Xavier glanced at her. What was it about this woman? Why was he so fascinated with her? For years he had assumed that his painful shyness would preclude him from ever achieving any kind of sexual awakening.

But he sure felt mighty sexual around Alex.

"Hey, if it makes you feel any better, I took Cha-Cha lessons in high school," she said, her dimples in proud exhibition.

"They have the Cha-Cha in China?" he blurted, just before realizing how ignorant he sounded.

"Yeah, that and indoor plumbing. And we're about to get electric ovens, so we'll finally be able to cook our cats before we eat them," she chuckled boisterously.

He joined her, hoping it would camouflage his attraction, and moreover, hoping his attraction would just go away. "Look, the way I'm acting, I'm sure you must think I'm some sort of crazy person."

"There's nothing wrong with crazy," she replied. "You are what you are, and I happen to think you're pretty cool. So let's get you signed up for that class so you and I can go grab some lunch if you have time. I'm starving."

"Me, too."

"Great. Because I've got some leftover cat in my locker."

xavier and alex... and charmaine

By spring, Xavier and Alex were good friends, taking weekend hikes, shooting hoops on warm breezy weeknights after class, catching a new movie every now and then at the local cineplex and grabbing a cup of coffee afterwards at the popular café beside it.

He acquainted her with the Middle Tennessee area. In turn, she helped to expand his limited social scene by bringing him to various functions like Vanderbilt University's First Annual 'Young Leaders of Color' Conference. There, she introduced him to her pal Dr. Emil Hubbard.

Xavier never ventured to inform Alex of his attraction to her. He was unsure of what results such a confession could bring.

But every now and then, Alex would make it difficult to stick to the plan. Intermittently interchanging back pats with hand caresses, and *"Yeah, Dude's"* with *"I Love You, Baby's"*, she coerced him at times to wonder if she was actually flirting with him. And increasingly, he found himself unsure of how to respond.

Alex was very open about her attraction to women and she even had a girlfriend down in Columbia who visited often. Did Alex hug *her* this much? Or was Xavier overreacting? Was this just her way of displaying her friendship? Maybe she just comes from a really affectionate family?

Or, was she trying to tell him something? And if she was, what would be his reply?

Xavier decided that maybe it was time he found himself a girlfriend.

There was a really pretty woman with big hair in his ballroom dance class named Charmaine. He had noticed her eyeing him at the beginning of the semester; she had even managed to partner off with him during Merengue week. He recalled how much he really liked the sensuality of her moves, and the way she smelled. He also admired her vivacious personality, something he himself wished he had.

OK: he would ask her out on a date at the next class.

"Well it's about time," Charmaine smiled. "I know you've seen me watching you, because I've certainly caught you enjoying it. But Karianna did say you were shy."

Xavier's mouth opened. "Wait – you know Kari?"

"She's only my best friend in the whole world. We're practically sisters. You and I have actually met a couple of times. I'm Char."

Xavier was stunned. "Oh my God – Charmaine! You grew up. You look great."

"Thanks. I guess a lot can happen in a few years."

"Well, now you have to have dinner with me this Saturday," Xavier said.

"I'll have to check my book. I'm a busy gal, you know. How about you give me your number, and I'll call you?"

Xavier laughed. "I really hope you'll be able to pencil me in. I have tickets to the Me'Shell NdegéOcello concert at the Exit/In."

Charmaine's eyes lit up. "Really? I love her!" she beamed while devising a plan to ditch her current Saturday date. "I'll call you tomorrow, OK?"

"OK."

Four days later, Xavier's phone rang.

"Hello?"

"Hi. Is this Xavier? This is Char."

"Hey. I thought you weren't gonna call, but Kari said you're always running behind schedule."

"So..." she purred, *"You talk to Kari about me, huh?"*

"You've come up," Xavier smiled.

"Good… well, um, I wanted to let you know that if you'd still like to go out tomorrow, I'd love to."

"Great. I'll pick you up at seven. Which dorm are you in?"

"I'm actually at Hillside."

"Cool," piped Xavier. "See you then."

A pleased Xavier hung up the phone. Then he began to worry. It suddenly occurred to him that he had never been on a date. Not a real one, at least. Back at St. Elgin's, there were annual dances, but the boys and girls were never even allowed to touch each other. He wished that he could call his old friend Drexel, the Mack Daddy Extreme, to get some quick pointers. But he did not know where he was hiding these days.

His breaths sharpened as the worries mounted. Then the phone rang.

"Hello?"

"You sound winded. What are you doing?"

It was Charmaine again.

"Oh! Nothing. I just… nothing."

"Well, you wanna do something tonight?"

"I thought you had a date?"

"I do. But I'll cancel if you want to have a cup of coffee with me or something. Unless you already have plans…"

"Oh, no. I'm just studying."

"Studying? *On a Friday? Boy, you better get your fine butt over here,*" she laughed. "*I'll be ready in twenty minutes, cool?*"

"Cool."

Xavier glanced at the mirror on his closet door. No time for panic now. He brushed his hair, washed his face, brushed his teeth, gargled, sprayed on some Calvin Klein, pulled on his Vanderbilt Law sweatshirt, and ran out the door. When he arrived at Hillside Apartments, Charmaine was already perched on the front stoop.

"I expected to be the one who'd have to wait," he said.

"I'm an enigma. How are you? I didn't see you in class yesterday."

"I had to work a little overtime at the Ed library, so I skipped."

"I missed you."

"You did, huh?" Xavier blushed. She was definitely making him more at ease.

They walked to Cyber Java on Twelfth. Charmaine asked him what his favorite coffee and pastry were, then ordered and paid for them, while Xavier ogled his wonderment.

"I know," she referenced as they found an outside table. "'Smart, pretty, and generous, too'. I'm just too much, huh?"

Xavier laughed. Yes, she was.

"So," she began, "What's with the Vandy Law shirt?"

"I'll be going there in the fall. It was a gift from them."

"Yay! Congratulations!"

"Thank you." He could tell that she really meant it.

"That's wonderful! Your parents must be really proud!"

He wasn't sure if right now was the best time, but felt like he could tell her just about anything. "I... don't have parents."

"Oh..." Charmaine was embarrassed. "That's right. Kari said you were an orphan. Shit. I'm so stupid. I'm always doing that, speaking before I think. I get it from my mother."

"It's OK, Charmaine. I don't mind."

"Thanks."

"So, do you ask men out a lot?" he inquired.

"Never. You're the first."

"Really? I'm honored. Why me?"

"Well, first of all, you invited me to the concert and didn't get all ugly when I called you back after I said I would. That scored you some points from jump. And secondly..." She thought for a few seconds in order to retain accuracy. "I don't know, Xavier. There's something about your spirit: it's just so big and wide and beautiful. I've noticed it for a while. Most of the guys I date..."

"So this is a date?" he clarified.

"Yes. Most of the guys I date just wanna hit it. They don't really feel me, so they get the boot. But for whatever reason, I feel like you actually understand what I'm really about, and that's so refreshing."

Xavier was touched and grateful that this earthbound goddess had chosen to exhibit a moment of vulnerability in his company.

"You don't talk much," she smiled. "...Remember that."

Episode 7

As they sat in the temperate night under a half moon sipping coffee and gulping cake while watching passers-by head off to their respective worlds, Manfred Mann's *"Blinded By The Light"* began to play over the speakers. Xavier sang along what he thought were the words:

"Nine dead by the light –
Wake up by the douche or want a runner in the night…"

Charmaine watched in spine-tingling merriment as he minced the whole song. Xavier seemed to inhabit his own happy little world; a world she wanted to visit, soon.

As he walked her home, they talked about the orphanage, his plans to one day open his own law firm, and her dreams of someday becoming a doctor, or a trapeze artist, or a nun, or something. They were amazed at how much they had in common, her being such the social butterfly, and him the consummate wallflower. A comfort was discovered between them that neither had ever felt before with the opposite sex.

Before long, they were back at Hillside.

"Well, thank you for a great evening, Xavier."

"And thank you for the coffee and conversation. I owe you."

"Now, are you sure I didn't talk your head off, because I know I tend to…"

Just then, Xavier grabbed her right hand and planted a soft kiss where her palm met her wrist.

A liquid warmth sprayed through her.

"I'll see you tomorrow night, OK?" he said.

"Uh-huh."

Xavier couldn't resign his smile for the entire trip back to his apartment. He definitely liked Charmaine and could feel it was mutual. Things were looking up. And not once the entire night had he thought about Alex.

At 7:00 the following evening, Charmaine answered the knock on her door. She was exquisite.

At twenty-two years old, Xavier was a virgin. But by no means was he ashamed of it, for he believed the lack of sexual diversion provided more drive to succeed at his studies. Besides, being such a loner, he didn't have many friends around to set him up on dates. He had, many times in the past, seen a girl and wanted to say hi, but his tied tongue would crush every possibility. And whenever someone showed any particular interest in him, he was generally too preoccupied with something else to even notice it.

But tonight, Charmaine Parker would not be overlooked. Halfway through Me'Shell NdegéOcello's performance of *"Mary Magdelene"*, she pulled Xavier to her and slowly kissed his warm lips, making her interest in him quite clear. He liked it, and reciprocated her affections for the duration of the show.

Later on, while eating dinner at Lola's on West End, Charmaine became curious. "So… how come you and Kari never hooked up? Or did you, and she just didn't tell me? She can be sneaky."

"Oh, no. Kari and I are like brother and sister. I couldn't think of her in that way. We've known each other since St. Elgin's."

"It must have been rough all those years, huh?"

"You learn to deal. I'm glad your family was there for her, though."

"Me, too."

"Hey, who's she dating now?"

"Please, you know Kari," laughed Charmaine. "What time is it?"

"Aw, that's not nice," he jested.

"I'm not telling you anything that I haven't told her a million times. Kari is my girl and I love her. But I'd be lying if I said that I don't worry about her sometimes. She's got a heart of gold, but she really doesn't take relationships too seriously and endangers herself with guys. And some of those men she meets when she's competing in those beauty pageants are just disgusting."

"It's looking like she might go all the way to Miss USA this time, huh?"

"Yeah. I'm so proud of her. I might give her flack about it, but the truth is, her pageants paid for her education, and if she gets a

USA sash next year, that's going to pay for grad school. But Xavier, some of those nasty judges, my God."

"You really love her, don't you?"

Charmaine sipped some mango tea. "Yeah. I just don't want her to get hurt. Some guys can really be jerks, you know?"

"Well," Xavier pointed out, "Given what happened to her, who could really blame her for not respecting what men represent?"

"Amen …as if I can talk about anyone, anyway," she giggled awkwardly. "I hope you don't think that I'm loose."

"Why would I?"

"Because I practically accosted you at the concert."

"Well, I'd hardly say that it was all you," he adjusted. "Besides, I enjoyed it."

"It's just… I believe that if you want something, then you should go for it, you know? And I like you, Xavier. I've never met anyone like you. I don't really know exactly how to say this, but I feel like… like I can trust you, you know?"

His responsive grin summoned to her surface a self-consciousness more intense than what even she was used to.

"Do I sound like a lunatic? Because I know that sometimes, I tend to…"

"Come home with me tonight, Charmaine."

"…Call me Char."

———————————

She scanned his apartment. "Whoa. It's so clean. I knew I liked you. Do you have a roommate?"

"Yeah, Jabaar. But he's in Portugal this semester. Otherwise it would never look like this. He's sort of a slob sometimes." He walked to the kitchen. "Would you like some wine, or Pepsi, or I've got room-temperature water…" He turned back around to find…

Charmaine stood in the middle of his living room clothed in only a beautiful burgundy bra and panty ensemble that unbound the fiery highlights in her radiant chocolate skin. Her cotton dress puddled her ankles. She smiled at him.

"Come here."

Episode 8

Xavier dropped the ice tray to the floor and advanced to her. He kissed her neck softly, then lightly pressed his lips behind her ears, upon her shoulders, her arms, her hands. She smelled of Victoria's Secret jasmine body lotion, and he wanted to consume her.

As he navigated her velvet exterior, she could feel his presence pressing vibrantly against her torso. She lifted his t-shirt up as far as she could reach. He accommodated by pulling it completely off of his body. Her mouth, now level with his enormous moist bronze chest, kissed, gently sucked and nibbled both of his nipples as he cried out his gratitude.

She reached to unbuckle his belt, but found that he had somehow already beaten her to it. So she unzipped his pants and let them fall to the floor, noticing his ample sex now protruding over the waistband of his black boxers.

"Damn. Someone's happy."

Xavier lifted her into the air, then carried her into his bedroom and placed her delicately down upon his bed.

("She looks like an angel.")

("This feels like heaven.")

But suddenly he grew pensive. He sat down next to her. "Charmaine, I… I've never…"

"It's OK, Xavier," she smiled. "You're doing great. Don't stop."

And they made love for the first time.

Over the next few months, Xavier would become quite the capable lover at the sole teaching of Charmaine, who had finally found what she'd dreamt of: a paramour custom-made for her body. One whom under her tutelage, learned everything he

knew: how to awaken her every crevice; how to navigate every single curve; how to please her in every way imaginable.

Xavier in turn found someone to love, one with whom he was completely at ease; a smart, funny, sexy, vivacious sista who made him feel like his being alive actually mattered. He was no longer alone in this world, for Charmaine was his bridge to life waiting outside for him.

They double-dated with Emil Hubbard and his fiancée Aniah Niles at campus games, concerts and plays, sometimes bringing along Aniah's brother Andy until he suddenly disappeared one afternoon, leaving only a note.

Xavier and his "girlfriend" (he loved saying that) would study together during the week and go dancing on Friday nights. They savored the stares of others as they set the floor aflame with their phenomenal salsa moves – which helped them both earn A's in that class.

Sometimes they would just sit and gaze at each other underneath the star-filled blue Tennessee night sky, sharing their deepest innermost thoughts, dreams, and desires. They would fantasize about the future: the lawyer, the doctor, and their three kids. Almost like the Huxtables.

They would enjoy each other's bodies, each feeling as if it had been specifically crafted to the other's touch. Their bodies, which fell into one another appropriately.

They were in love.

And Xavier was on top of the world. His second year of law school was progressing marvelously. His great new one-bedroom apartment in Hillsboro Village was a steal. He had also recently sealed a clerk internship at Steele and Webber, a Green Hills law firm, and they liked him. They'd even invited him and Charmaine to their upcoming corporate holiday dinner party. Things were finally going exactly as he had always wanted.

But there was also Alex.

On a chilly mid-November night, as an exhausted Xavier was preparing to turn in after an extended study session at the law library, he received a phone call. It was her. Sounding distressed and bordering on tears, she pleaded to come over to his place immediately.

"Please, Xav, man. You're the only one I can talk to, and I really need to talk…"

"OK, no problem. Come on through."

"Thanks, man."

Alex arrived clutching a near-empty can of Coors Light. She pulled another from her coat pocket and placed it on the coffee table before slouching down on the sofa.

"That one's yours."

Xavier noticed a fresh tear on her face. He sat down beside her. "Hey, Al, what's wrong? What happened?"

"You're so lucky, man," she sobbed. "You have Charmaine. She understands you and loves you unconditionally. I have nothing. Nobody."

"What's up with you and Deborah?"

"Ohh, God…" she wept.

"Alex, what's going on? Talk to me." He couldn't remember having ever witnessed such beauty in so much pain.

"You're a good guy, Xavier. I'm so lucky to have you in my life." She brushed her hand across his face. It both surprised and exhilarated him.

"Did she… break up with you?" He took a gulp of beer.

"I told her I like guys."

Xavier struggled to keep from spraying his beer across the room. "Huh?"

"Yeah, and she left me. I honestly didn't think it would be a big deal, you know? But when I told her, she called me a fucking whore and started screaming and crying and shit, and…"

"You're *bisexual*?" he pronounced.

"Then she said that all men are assholes, and I'm a liar and she never wants to see me again…"

"Wait, Alex. You are *bi*-sexual?"

She appeared perplexed. "Yeah. Didn't you know?"

"Unh-uh."

"Oh, my God, Xav, what am I gonna do? She's everything to me. She's all I have." She turned to cry upon the arm of the sofa.

Xavier embraced her. He hadn't anticipated doing so, but it felt right. "No, she's not. You've got me."

Alex smiled and hugged him. Then she kissed his shoulder. Then she kissed his left bicep. Then his neck. Then his chest. Then his stomach.

Xavier sat completely motionless, with the exception of the next place she kissed.

So many questions now raced through his mind. And he had just downed almost an entire beer, which wasn't helping any. He knew all he had to do was say, "No, Alexia. Don't." But he did not. He had always wondered, even fantasized, what it would feel like to be with her this way.

But what about Charmaine, his "girlfriend"? He loved her.

Still, he kissed Alex back.

She removed her jeans to reveal her well-proportioned lower physique. Then she removed her flannel shirt and athletic bra to reveal other proportions.

Xavier stared in amazement. *"She's almost as big as Charmaine,"* he thought.

Alex noticed his approval. "How many times have I told you not to believe everything you hear about Asians?" She pulled Xavier's sweatpants and briefs down to his shins. Then she descended to glide her lips up and down Xavier's avid member while he closed his eyes and relished every moment of it.

She coaxed him to the floor where they now lay, excitedly groping and caressing each other's naked flesh. She sprawled forward to place her nipples at his lips. Right on cue, he began to suckle one, then the other, harnessing her shapely hips as small random streams of his warm saliva trailed between her breasts, prompting her progressive pants of appreciation. She climbed to her feet and walked into his bedroom. He followed her.

Five minutes later, they were cuddling playfully on the bed.

Ten minutes after that, they were naked.

Within ten more minutes, Xavier was fucking Alex like a wild animal in near-epileptic frenzy.

Two minutes later, Charmaine stood in the bedroom doorway, her mouth wide open, her key to Xavier's apartment fallen to the floor, tears in her eyes, devastation to her core.

Noticing that Alex's attention had somewhat shifted, Xavier turned around. What he saw stopped his heart.

"Char!"

"Shut up! Shut up, just *shut up!*" Charmaine bounded for the door.

Xavier quickly wrapped himself with a sheet and stumbled after her. "You... you weren't supposed to come 'til tomorrow!" he exclaimed.

"You either, muthafucka! Obviously neither one of us could wait!" She threw open the door. "Bye, Xavier. And don't you ever even *think* of calling my ass again!" She slammed it behind her with such venomous force that the picture they took in Vegas leaped clear off of the living room wall, shattering onto the floor below.

Xavier was terrified. His eyes welled over as his knees rigorously quaked, preparing to give way at any moment.

Alex ran over to comfort him.

"Get out!" he screamed.

"But Xav, I..."

"I don't want to hear anything you have to say! Please, just leave. I'm sorry. Just go..."

Though greatly concerned for her friend, Alex reluctantly dressed, then exited the apartment.

Xavier hadn't cried so hard since his arrival at the Saldevilla home twenty-four years earlier. He was once again an orphan, naked and alone, rocking back and forth on the floor beside the broken picture.

And there he stayed until morning.

February 14th, 2010: 5:04 p.m.

Xavier turned to Emil. "Hey, did you see Karianna out there? She's sitting right next to Char…"

"I know where she is," Emil heaved.

Xavier knew that he was treading on a minefield. Nevertheless, he itched to explore: "So… you do know, right?"

"Know what?" Emil asked, examining his watch.

"She's not seeing anyone right now. As a matter of fact, she hasn't been with anyone for eleven months. She's been completely abstinent."

Emil did not reply.

"Well, I think it's great," Xavier tweeted. "She says it's really helped her to focus on what she really wants. And it must be working, because she looks fantastic, huh?"

"I see you've been duped by her sophistries. But I know her: that woman couldn't go even eleven hours without humping something. Not 'Carnival.'"

"'*Karianna*'. Be nice. We're in church."

"No wonder she looks uncomfortable."

Figuring it time to change the subject, Xavier looked at his watch and then wondered, "Where's Alex?"

"I don't know," replied Emil. "But she'd better hurry up. Some of her guests are looking a little irascible. Are you still nervous?"

Xavier adjusted his tie. "I haven't seen her in seven years. Now all of a sudden I'm the best man at her wedding. What do you think?"

"All that unfinished business… I have to admit I still don't fully understand why she invited you and Char to be a part of her big day."

"Well, you know Alex: terminally optimistic. Who else on the planet would forego a wedding rehearsal?"

"True… hey, maybe she got cold feet and she's waiting for you outside on her Harley," Emil chuckled.

"I recommend reality," Xavier smirked. "See you out there, Reverend Hubbard." He walked to the altar.

"Ooooh, girl, there he goes," squeaked Karianna. They were the first words she'd uttered since being dragged, while on her period, to a wedding she'd had no desire to attend in the first place. "Looking fine as ever, huh? He misses you. You know he was just promoted to junior partner and he got a textbook deal with the Witherton Group…"

A perturbed Charmaine rolled her eyes then slammed her pad and pen into her purse. "I know about his book and his promotion, Kari. We all knew it would happen for him one day, and it did, and-I'm-very-happy-for-him-*when-is-this-stupid-wedding-going-to-start*?!"

Andy Niles tiptoed cautiously through the church's side door. Expecting the ceremony to be nearly over, he determined it best to remain in the anterior hall until after it was finished. He didn't want to risk his celebrity stealing any of the happy couple's thunder. But seconds later, a tuxedoed Alex Young flew in and slammed the door. "Hey, Drew!" she hollered. Then she grabbed his hand, pulled him into the chapel and charged down the aisle.

The confused congregation was now in a total uproar. A newly-robed Emil entered the chapel to investigate the source of the commotion.

> *"How many grooms are there?"*
> *"Isn't that a woman?"*
> *"Start the organ!"*
> *"Is that Drew Niles?"*
> *"Where?"*

As the behemoth pipe organ introduced "*The Wedding March*", Andy broke away from Alex and searched for somewhere to

79

quickly hide. But when he reopened the chapel door to make a clean getaway, there the bride stood.

"Oh, my God: Drew Niles!" she exclaimed. "Alex told me you might show up but I didn't believe her. Oh, please, Mr. Niles, my father didn't come today; would you please give me away?"

Unable to deny the beautiful bride's wish, Andy gently took hold of her arm. She ushered him, to the one-two beat, down the long lily-lined aisle to join Alex, her spouse-to-be. The crowd buzzed in amazement. One man walked up and asked for Andy's autograph.

And, though still a bit disoriented, Andy could not hide his satisfaction once he spotted Emil standing in up the pulpit, his scarlet minister robe alloting him even more sex appeal than normal.

Emil, on the other hand, cowered slightly at the sight of Andy. But he snapped out of it once Alex reached the altar. He pulled her aside to talk privately.

"Alexia, you're over an hour late for your own wedding, and I'm not even going to inquire as to why," he declared, still expecting to receive an explanation.

"I'm here now. Let's do it. I'm ready."

"Here, something's wrong with your collar." Emil inspected more closely, then stepped back. "There's lipstick on it. What'd you do," he smirked. "Bed some girl on the way here?"

"No," Alex whispered. "And keep your voice down, will ya? There were two of them. A guy and a girl."

"You're kidding."

"Look, Sherri's not into that kind of stuff and … well, I promised her I'd never cheat on her after we get married, so…"

"So you had a three-way when you should've been here reciting your vows?" Emil attacked.

"Alex looks really good," thought Xavier as he watched their conversation. He was getting a kick out of the two friends, and figured that whatever they were discussing was juicy: partly because of how red Emil's face had become, and partly because everyone knew that whenever Alex was involved, there was also bound to be some sort of controversy, at least for all concerned but her. She played by her own rules and never understood the fuss everyone made over it. To her, she was just living life. Xavier loved that about her.

But today after the ceremony, he would have to face her again after many years of avoidance, for he still had some unanswered questions. Had she planned that incident years ago? Had she just preyed on his naivety in order to get what she'd wanted all along? Was today's wedding invitation an attempt at a truce of some sort? And would she finally admit that she was wrong for what she did – the vixen?

He had almost considered not coming to her wedding at all, much less being her best man. But he owed her at least that. Meeting Alex changed Xavier's life in many ways. Unfortunately, much anguish accompanied the outcome. He had no idea what would finally happen when they'd meet, and that heavily concerned him.

Meanwhile, Emil came to a conclusion. "I'm sorry, Alexia. I cannot preside over your nuptials today."

"What? No, E! Don't do this!"

"You're crazy. You obviously shouldn't be getting married, so I will not facilitate this union. I can't contribute to a lie. You need help, not a life partner so you can mess her up, too." He took a deep breath and grasped Alex's shoulders. "Listen, I know of a very good therapist…"

"Emil, she knows."

"Huh? Who knows? What?"

"Shhh, it's all right. Sherri knows exactly where I was. I got her permission first."

A thoroughly bemused Emil looked at Sherri, the youthful Caribbean beauty now standing in front of him, ready to vow herself forever to the woman she loved. Her smile seemed especially intended to console him.

"That's why I'm marrying her, E. Who else in this world could understand me like that? I've finally found someone who won't punish me for who I am. It took a long time but I'm in love again. I've got a great partner and I'd think that you of all people would understand how important that is."

Emil looked away momentarily to process what he'd just heard. Upon doing so, he found Andy staring right at him.

"Please stay," Alex pled.

Emil smiled at her.

And they wed.

Following the ceremony, the attendees clapped, cried, whistled, and hurrahed as the newly married couple skipped back up the aisle and out the front door.

Again, Xavier caught Charmaine's glance. This time, however, her eyes did not retreat as before. It was now he who had to look away, for standing in front of her he still felt completely unveiled and apologetic.

Charmaine, aware of that fact, promised herself right then that she would avoid him today at all costs. Where had Karianna run off to so quickly? Please, let her get back soon so they could just leave. She knelt down to grab her coat. Just then, a familiar voice broke through the cacophony of activity surrounding her.

"There you are!"

She turned around to hug her dear friend. "Emmy!"

"Hey, Sweetness! Happy Valentine's Day. You're quite lovely, as always."

"Thanks. You, too. And you were fabulous up there today! You should call me before the white lady starts answering my phone."

Emil's eyebrows levitated. "You're still unemployed? Char, you're way too talented and connected to be sitting around jobless. But if I know you," he scrutinized, "You're probably just remaining the pendulous wonder, building up as much drama as possible so that at the last minute you can emerge from your cocoon with a great new job. You'll never change. But I love you, anyway."

"Thanks," Charmaine replied, "But I'll have you know that I've got an interview tomorrow and things are looking really good. I just didn't want to settle for just anything this time, you know? I had to wait until something really nice came along. And this one feels perfect for me."

"I keep telling you that what you should do is…"

"Yeah, yeah, *'go back to med school and get the stupid M.D.'* "

"Charmaine, you only had one more year to go."

"Emil, *you* may be the eternal student, but I got sick of school," she stated. "My heart just wasn't in it anymore. I got tired of just making A's. I needed to start making some money instead."

"Well, I can understand that," he replied, "Because all of my friends have far more baronial bank stashes than I. Even you, and your phone line is about to be disconnected."

"What's going on with the French Embassy thing? Have you called them back yet?"

"I need to give that opportunity a little more thought. A lot has happened in the past few years and… you know how much I love teaching, Char. It really stimulates me."

"Yeah, I know."

Charmaine felt something bump her shoulder. She turned around to find Karianna now quickly gathering up her things.

"Oh, Emil, of course you remember Karianna…"

"Hi."

"Hi."

Karianna firmly pulled Charmaine aside. "I'm going to go change my pad and when I come back, we're leaving.

"Weren't you just in the ladies' room?"

"No. I was looking for Andy. I'll just have to call him later."

"But Kari, I…"

"You promised, Char! I'll be right back."

Karianna nodded good-bye to Emil, whipped another sharp glance at Charmaine, then walked to the restroom.

Emil shook his head and smiled remorsefully. "She's still quite the raging heifer, I see."

"Emil, stop." Charmaine sighed. "God, why do you two always have to give each other such a hard time?"

"Let's end that here." He embraced her and began guiding her to a remote and quiet corner outside. "Let me tell you the *real* reason why the wedding started so late…"

Then he heard a voice call out:

"Emil Hubbard."

It was a voice from his past, stopping him cold in his tracks.

Charmaine could feel the weight of its impact upon both her shoulders, upon which Emil was leaning. And it hurt, so she turned around to see who it was.

"Andy! Baby!" she yelled. They hugged and kissed, then she examined him. "Look at you, big star! What's goin' on, boy? And happy birthday! See, I didn't forget! Did you get that new movie?"

"We're still in talks," Andy replied, without taking his eyes off Emil. "Hey, Emil. What's crackin'?"

"Hello, Andrew. How are things in Florida?"

"Hot."

Just then, five loud fire engines sped past the church.

Andy turned to Charmaine. "Where's my boo?"

"In the ladies' room. She'll be out in a minute. She's gonna be so happy to see you! How long has it been? Like, four years?"

"Something like that," he said, continuing to peripherally monitor Emil. "Xavier called and asked me to do the reception."

"Yeah, Kari mentioned you might come," she faintly replied. "Hey, I bought that new magazine with you in it!"

Emil quietly interjected, "I'm going to check on a few things..."

Andy grabbed his arm. "Hey, we gotta sit down and chat real soon. I wanna catch up with you. Alright?"

Emil nodded then hugged Charmaine before heading into the crowd.

"So, Charmaine, tell me for real: how did I look in that magazine..."

"OK, I'm back. Let's go," commandeered Karianna.

Charmaine stepped over to reveal a beaming Andy Niles.

"Puppy!" Karianna screamed as they smooched. "How are you? I'm so happy you're here! You look so good!"

"So," he asked, "Are you coming to the reception?"

Karianna looked at Charmaine.

"You better come watch me work these bitches," he warned.

Almost unnoticeably, Karianna shrugged. "Yeah, we'll be there."

"Oh, good," smiled Charmaine. "This is all going to be so nice!"

"Hi, Char."

Charmaine's
heart
sunk

Xavier was now standing behind her, waiting to be greeted. But what was she to say? She'd had something clever and witty prepared, just in case she would be forced to talk to him today. But it all vanished the moment he spoke her name in that soft dedicated baritone. So she turned around and said:

"Hello, Xavier."

She couldn't think of anything else and hoped that someone would say or do something to break the silence; even for another one of those god-awful fire trucks to blast by, but alas, nothing. She would have to perform again. "Congratulations on your book deal and partnership."

Xavier turned to Karianna. "You told her?"

85

"Actually, she already knew. So are you coming to the reception, luv?"

"I'll be a little late," he said. "I've got some personal business to tend to first, but I won't be long." He looked to Andy. "Thanks for coming today. I got your voicemail. I was a little busy when you called."

"Cool," Andy saluted.

"We'll save you a seat at our table, then," confirmed Karianna.

"Thanks. See you all there," Xavier replied before departing the deep silence that immediately followed.

"Why is everybody looking at me?" Charmaine questioned.

"Don't flatter yourself, darlin'," Karianna deadpanned. "It's that damn bobby pin."

Episode 9

Alex and Sherri Reed-Young's wedding reception began right after the ceremony at the Eunice Angley Center Main Ballroom across the street. Gigantic red and silver balloons, strung together to create a giant valentine, garnished the east wall, while a sea of white balloons carpeted the ceiling.

The room was packed with friends and who drank, ate, laughed, and danced to old-school jams interspersed with fresh new joints.

At 7:30, Ludacris' latest hit faded out, and comedian Drew Niles was introduced to the room.

Toting a freshly-lit cigarette and a cocktail in one hand, and a microphone in the other, Andy glided onto the stage into the soothing cradle of a standing ovation. "Thank you, thank you," he said. "Y'all obviously know a good thing when you see one. So I'm sure you won't mind paying me individually once I'm done. And yes, I take Visa."

The crowd laughed as each person shuffled to find strategic locations to sit and watch.

"Wait, didn't nobody tell y'all to sit down! Get the hell back up!" he playfully chastised.

Emil and Charmaine watched him from their table in the far north corner of the room.

"Andy looks good, doesn't he?"

Disregarding the topic, Emil asked, "So, are you going to continue not to speak to Xavier when he arrives?"

Charmaine smoothed her 'do before imbibing a hefty swallow of merlot. "What do you mean? I said 'hi'."

"You two are so funny, even now," he laughed. "Just get over yourselves, already. Life's too short. Talk to him. You know you want to."

"OK," she anteed, "I'll make a deal with you: I will if you will. Whaddaya say?"

"I say she's on her period and she's going to really hurt someone if you don't get her out of here, pronto."

"You know she hasn't had sex in eleven months…"

"Damn it, Char," he spat. "Was it on the five o'clock news? Personally, I don't understand the effulgence of it. When most people abstain, they just aren't getting any. Kari does it, and people want to give her the bronze. But let me tell you something: if you think that woman's been celibate for eleven *days*, let alone months, then you be her fool. I'll pass."

Charmaine recoiled. "Emmy, *why* do you dislike her so much? She's such a wonderful person. You know that better than anyone."

"How about we change the subject?"

"Whatever you say." She monitored some of the guests before recalling, "Hey, did you hear that guy at the next table saying that all gays and lesbians are going to hell?"

"Why did he come here, then?"

Just then, Karianna sashayed to the table, her second Dark and Stormy of the evening in tow. "Maybe it was God trying to tell you something."

Emil scowled. "He should've told you to wear a darker skirt."

"Oh my God," she squeaked while attempting to scope her person without spilling her drink. "Am I…?"

"Shhh!" exclaimed a guest.

"You're fine, honey," assured Charmaine. "Sit down."

Emil stood up and pulled out a chair.

"Thank you, Thing."

"Listen, you…"

At that moment, Andy broadcast a name that made Emil shudder.

"…His name was 'Oliver'. Oh, let me tell y'all about that man!"

Charmaine laughed, "Emmy, isn't your middle name 'Oliver'?"

Emil's heart fell to his knees. Andy was at it again. What would he do this time?

As the crowd roared, Andy continued:

"OK, now, can I get a little personal wit'ch'all for a minute, now that we're friends? Oliver was my ultimate dream: tall, with these amazing eyes, skin like honey butter, and a body by none other than the Creator. And he was amazing in bed. Y'all know what I'm talking 'bout!"

The laughter crescendoed as Emil, now staring at the tablecloth, grew more consumed with dread over what might next fall from Drew Niles's lips. Karianna sympathized, for she was cognizant of the cruel deed her young loudmouthed friend was committing on that stage. She knew the whole truth, as well as how painful it must be for Emil to be reminded of it.

Andy continued:

"...But there was just one thing wrong with him."

"What?" yelled an inebriated woman from the south side of the room.

"Well, folks, he smoked... crack."

The audience exploded into laughter and applause, with the exception of Emil, whose eyes moistened and skin brightened to the hue of a delicious apple.

*"No wonder he was so good in bed: he was
probably pretending I was a pipe."*

Emil peered down at the business card Andy placed on the table before walking out of the apartment. On it were the words: "Northside Addiction Therapy Clinic. Karianna Cojoure,

89

L.C.S.W., Director". He pitched the card into the wastebasket. "I don't need therapy. I'm a highly revered pedagogue at a world-renowned learning institution. I can stop using whenever I'd like."

But Emil knew he was in trouble. Over the previous ten months, he had become addicted to heroin, and was now vigorously struggling to keep it a secret.

The mere thought that someone else was now privy to his growing habit both terrified and embarrassed him. He'd overheard the growing buzz at work: colleagues were beginning to inquire about his increasingly frequent absences from classes, or about why he would just disappear from campus in the middle of the day, subsequently missing faculty meetings, speaking engagements, and the like.

Some of the staff over at New Israel were talking, too. The current rumor was that he might have cancer.

Even the senior committee for Young Leaders of Color – the very organization Emil founded just five years prior – was engaged in discussion as to whether he should be replaced by a new faculty advisor. It had been over twelve weeks since he'd come to a monthly meeting, and he had not returned any of their phone calls.

He had begun to deteriorate physically as well. He was losing weight and layering his shirts in an effort to conceal it. He'd begun purchasing more heroin each week from a man who only knew his middle name: "Oliver". He felt ashamed for not reaching out to his good friends Xavier and Alex, and for allowing such a large, hairy monkey to mount his back. What would happen if Aniah found out? Especially now, when she's experiencing problems with her own health?

He pulled the business card out of the wastebasket and stared at the phone number on it for a few minutes. Then he picked up the phone.

"Uh, yes… Karianna Cojoure, please?"

Backstory:
emil and karianna

Thursday, 2:00pm: Emil's appointment time had arrived. He walked into the building to find, to his surprise, quite a reposed atmosphere.

A young woman was reading a story to a group of eight preschoolers. And a twenty-year-old blond sat at the receptionist desk typing up a certificate of completion for a recently matriculated twelve-stepper celebrating one year of sobriety.

After finishing up the document, he ran the letter to the upstairs loft, where sat a leggy beautiful petite woman in a sleeveless caramel-colored mini dress and two-inch-heeled sandals. She offered the young man encouraging suggestions to improve the overall look of the form, and smiled while asking that he bring it back to her once he had followed them.

"Thanks, Kari," he said while jaunting back down to the reception area. "Hi. Welcome to Northside. How may I help you?"

"Hello, my name is Emil Hubbard, and I have an appointment to see Ms. Cojoure."

The young man scanned the schedule, then handed Emil a questionnaire. "Please fill this out and return it to me once you're done." He then buzzed Karianna on the intercom.

"Yes?"

"Emil Hubbard, your two o'clock is here."

"OK, Joe, send him up when he's ready."

Five minutes later, Emil was back at the desk.

"You can go right up and take this with you. That's her," he pointed.

"Thank you." He walked up the stairs.

Karianna stood at the top waiting for him. He could not help but be awed by how lovely she was.

"Hi, I thought your name sounded familiar," she smiled. "You're Xavier's friend, right? I'm Kari." Then she hugged him, whispering, "Don't worry, anything that goes on here is completely confidential. Xavier's my boy, but he understands and respects my professional

91

obligations." She smelled of lilac, and possessed a cool positive energy and a comforting gleam in her eye.

"Thank you," he sighed, relieved. "And thanks for seeing me on such short notice."

"Oh, thanks aren't necessary, Emil," she said while ushering him to the sofa, about six feet from her desk. "So can I get you anything? Meth? Crack? Cheap, meaningless unprotected sex?" she asked, while heading toward the small refrigerator next to her desk.

Had Emil heard her correctly?

"Or how 'bout a root beer? I've got one of those, too."

"Oh… OK," he laughed, realizing he had just been teased by the stunning redhead.

"All right, Emil," she declared while handing him the soda. "Here are the rules if you're going to play in my yard. The first thing you have to do is trust me at all times. Around here, I'm The Diva. I run everything, and I am always right. But please know that I will only have your best interests at heart." She sat in the easy chair across from him. "I am all-seeing and all-knowing. But I only use my powers for good – and I will teach you to do the same. One thing, though: you will have to be honest with me and with everyone else here, because we're your family. We're the only ones who know exactly what you're going through. Face it, if you actually had somewhere else to go, you'd probably be there now."

Emil nodded.

"Yeah?" she demanded.

"Yeah."

"Good." She quickly studied his questionnaire while sipping cranberry juice. "OK, so you're an extremely good-looking PhD recipient with two steady incomes, a great body, and absolutely humongous hands and feet. How on earth did you come to the decision that you somehow needed heroin to complete the picture?"

Emil blushed. He hadn't expected the therapist to be so forward… or so gorgeous.

She smiled and crossed her long bare lightly-tanned legs. "In order for this to work, Emil, you have to at least talk to me."

"OK, Kari. It's just…I've just been under a lot of stress recently."

"Um-hmm. Go on."

"Well, work can get to you after a while, as I'm sure you're quite aware… but don't get me wrong, I love Vanderbilt. And I also enjoy being a minister; it's just… it can be difficult at times juggling them both…" He felt as if she were looking right through him and had not yet believed a word he'd said, because he sure didn't. "I'm attracted to other men."

Emil was astounded by the words that had just escaped his tongue. But it sure felt great to finally say them out loud after all these years.

Karianna sat back in her chair. "Oh, please, *is that all*? Are you seeing anyone?"

"Why? Would you like a date?" he shyly joked, for she made him comfortable enough to do so.

Karianna's giggle was music. "Sorry, can't date the customers. It's in the rule book. Besides, what would I do with a heroin addict? I already have enough dating issues. We've gotta get you sober first; then maybe we can talk."

Emil had forgotten what it was like to enjoy a good laugh. Her unabashed vibrancy soothed him. "I like you," he said. "And I don't say that to just anyone, believe me."

She rested her soft hand upon his muscular thigh. "I know, Emil. I can tell."

Emil could tell something, as well: she liked him, too.

"The reason I asked if you were seeing anyone, is because I'd like to know if you've discussed this issue with her."

"No, I haven't told her."

"Why not?"

"Because she might not appreciate hearing it at this point in our relationship. We're engaged."

"Are you cheating on her?"

"You sure do ask a lot of personal questions, Kari."

"And you're going to answer them. Go."

"No, I'm not cheating. But I feel as if I am. I go to bars – not to cruise – but just to be around others like me. I don't know if she would understand that. She comes from a really good background."

"And being bisexual isn't 'good'?" Karianna queried.

"It's not that. I just don't want to raze her plans. She's got a great future ahead of her and she's already come so far. She doesn't need me coming out to her right now."

"OK, Emil, wait a minute. You mean to tell me that you were so stressed about messing up your fiancée's life with your 'bad' little bisexual tendencies, that instead of trying to talk to her about it, you chose to take up heroin instead?"

"It's not quite that simple – please allow me to elucidate…"

"Yes it is, and you already have," she retorted. "Emil, I like you, so I'm just going to say it: you're stupid."

"What?"

"You're letting someone who loves you crush you without even trying. I'd thought that your problem might have something to do with your role in the church, but you don't seem conflicted in that area. Turns out it's all about her."

"This isn't her fault."

"You're damn right it's not her fault. It's yours. Like I said, luv, you're stupid. But you know what the silver lining to all of this is?"

Emil, shaking his head, dropped his eyes to the floor.

"The good part – no – the *great* part is that you've found The Diva. Come over here. I wanna show you something."

She escorted him to the balcony overlooking the clinic and pointed to the young woman reading to the children. "You see her? That's Leila. She lost her three month old son to foster care when he accidentally turned over a boiling crack pot and got second degree burns. Stupid, huh? But that was nearly two years ago, and now she's in her third semester at Volunteer State, studying child psychology, and you know what? She's going to get her son back. She's been clean now for thirteen months because she came to The Diva."

She next peeped over the banister to the reception desk. "And that down there, is my boy Joseph!"

The blond man grinned up at her.

"Joe introduced me to your friend, Andy. They used to trick together sometimes. Then, Joe's girlfriend, who had an acid habit, got pregnant. Shortly after that, they learned that their child could

be HIV-positive. It was just a mess. But then, by God's grace, they found The Diva. And now Joe works with me, and his girlfriend's in beauty school. Both are off that crap. And their little girl is just fine: no trace of the virus anywhere in her body. Of course, I had nothing to do with that part. Even I have my limits."

Emil was mesmerized by Karianna's heartening words.

She looked up at his face. His sad, glorious face. She did like him, more than she wanted to. But composure and professionalism had to be maintained.

"You see, Emil," she explained, "You will get over this. Your life will continue. And you will no longer have to hide who you are from anyone. I may go on about the whole 'Diva' thing, but the real reason why what we do here works, is because we don't shoot blanks. We only deal truth, respect, and love. *'Face the truth, live respectfully, and love yourself.'* Everyone here – myself included – was saved from certain doom because somebody loved them. And here, we celebrate that. You don't have to jump through anybody's hoops in order to receive assurance of your own worth. Everybody else has to either accept you and love you for who you are, or just step off. And that's their only choice to make, because you've already made yours."

She could see that Emil was quite moved. The honesty in his dark hypnotic eyes was melting her. But she wasn't going to show it. "So, how about it?" she asked. "Do you want to get better?"

"Yes, Kari, I do. Please help me."

Emil signed up for Monday and Thursday evening group sessions for addicts, plus a lunchtime session every other Friday. There, participants would discuss their current situations and what led them to start using. Emil attended every meeting faithfully, each time arriving early, grabbing a chair over in

a corner, and listening to others' stories. But he would never volunteer his own.

He was careful to not let anyone catch him gazing at Karianna at every available opportunity. He loved to hear her speak, empowering group members with just the right mix of wise words; giving them the confidence to take on the world, and the compassion to embrace it. He loved her smile. He loved her sense of humor. He loved…

Kari

After four weeks, Karianna became concerned about Emil's reticence to share his journey in group. She was also, to her dismay, curious about what lay behind the mask of the handsome tortured soul in the corner. So she came up with an idea she hoped would satisfy both urges. At the next meeting, she asked him to wait afterwards to chat for a spell. He leapt at the invitation, and within thirteen minutes, the room had cleared.

"Hey, I'm glad you asked me to stay. I have to tell you that all of this is doing wonders for me. Thank you, Kari."

"Oh, you're very welcome. But I've noticed that you don't say too much during groups. May I ask why?"

"I'm not very comfortable discussing my private affairs with most. I hope you can understand."

his eyes

OK, she would not push. Besides, it was none of her business until he decided to make it so. He was just a client. A *client*, dammit.

"Rest assured, no pressure," she complied. "I just wanted to make sure you're alright, that's all. I hope you'll stay with it and then down the road, participate with us. We've got good people here. I guarantee your nightmare will pass if you continue to let us help." She smiled. "All right, that's all. You can go now."

"When can I see you again?"

"Well, your next group is Thursday, but there's another one before that if you'd like to come…"

"No, I meant, when can I see *you* again, Kari?"

"Tonight. My place. Au natural."

The thoughts this man pushed into her mind! She'd always had a knack for becoming attracted to the wrong men, but this was the one thing she had promised herself she would never, ever do. She knew much better than to fall for a counselee. There had been other ones in the past whom she found cute, charming, or even downright hot, but Emil Hubbard was a different entity altogether, truly unlike any other man she had ever encountered. She felt helplessly bound to his gentle, bottomless soul; so much so, that she wanted to touch him, hold him, right now.

In light of that, she decided it best to refer him to another reputable therapist in town. That's why it came very much as a surprise to her when she replied:

"You can come back here tomorrow to join me for a cup of tea if you'd like. Around five, after we close."

"How about 5:30? My last class ends at 4:45."

"Good, see you then. Oh, and Emil – bring along something that's really important to you."

"Why?"

"It's part of your recovery."

"OK, until tomorrow," he gleamed.

Clutching her notebook to her bosom and sighing majestically, wearing the hint of a lingering smile upon her lips, Karianna watched Emil walk out of the Northside Clinic and up the street, until he turned the corner.

"Uh-oh."

Episode 10

At 5:30 the following evening, Emil shuffled into Northside with a smile, a daisy, and…

"A dictionary?" exclaimed Karianna. "This is your dearest possession? Hmm…"

"Do you think it's odd?"

"It doesn't matter what I think – but no. I'm just glad you didn't bring a needle or a spoon or something."

Emil laughed. "My grandmother gave me this dictionary when she sent me over to the states from Afghanistan where I was born. She took care of me there after my mother fled the country in order to stay alive after having me out of wedlock. My grandmother couldn't read, but wanted to make sure that wouldn't be a problem for me. She worked three jobs to provide food until she injured her back, and had to rely on the local government for aid. That forced her to find my father, who was in Iowa. She sent me to live with him, figuring he could give me a better life there. But just in case he couldn't, she gave me this dictionary and told me that with it, I could build my own better life. She died four months after I left Afghanistan. I promised her that I would learn one word a day until I graduated from high school. But I lied. I've been out of school for quite some time now, and I still do it."

"So where is your mother now?" Karianna asked.

"I don't know; we've lost touch."

"And your father?"

"Still in Iowa with his American wife and his two American children, living the American dream. He finally got it right, I guess," Emil lamented.

"So, you feel that you were a mistake?"

"Oh, I'd say I was something more like a crisis."

Karianna sneered. "You sound almost as dramatic as my best friend."

"Well, what else would you call the product of a one-nighter between a rich twenty-four year old Harvard grad student and a dirt poor fifteen year old who can't read? A gift?"

"OK," Karianna conceded.

Emil shrugged. "I'm sorry. I suppose I'm still a little touchy when it comes to my history."

"It's fine. I see you have lot of passion. You probably throw yourself completely into whatever you do."

"Yes, sometimes to my detriment."

"How about your relationships? Are you as devoted to your fiancée as you were to your dealer?"

He chuckled. "You're horrible."

"Yeah, well…" she smiled. "So tell me about her, Emil. She must be an incredible woman. What's her name – if you don't mind?"

"Her name is Aniah, and yes, she is incredible. She's also intelligent, beautiful, thoughtful, honest, and compassionate. Everything I'd always hoped for in a companion."

"…But?"

Emil began to feel warm. "Could I have some water, please?"

"Sure." Karianna rose from the sofa.

"No, don't bother. I know where it is." He filled up a glass then sat back down, about three inches further away from her than before.

Karianna noticed the distance, which seemed more like yards. "If you'd rather not talk about this now, we can move to something else."

"It's not a problem."

"I ask because you said a few weeks ago that you felt that your relationship with her was an integral part of your addiction."

Emil took a sip, then stared at her intensely. "Is that the only reason you ask?"

Karianna shrunk. She hoped that he hadn't noticed. At this point, it was absolutely imperative that she regain control of their conversation. She could not let this fallen angel's radiance continue to knock her off balance, for either of their sakes. "I'll ask

the questions here, Dr. Hubbard. Now, let's change the subject. Do you have any..."

"Oh, I'm sorry, Miss Cojoure," tittered Emil. "Did I upset you? Because the last thing that I would ever want to do is to upset 'The Diva'..."

"Look," she charged, "If you're just going to play games, then you should leave, because I've got better things to do than sit around here going back and forth. I have a clinic to run, damn it, and I've got budgets to turn in and client charts to review and paychecks to sign, so you can just go." She walked to her desk and shuffled some papers around in hopes of finding composure, but it didn't work.

Emil followed her. He placed his massive hands upon her petite shoulders. They numbed her.

"I'm sorry," he said. "I was way out of line. I don't know what's gotten into me lately. I'm never like this. I just... things aren't as clear as I thought they would be. I think I... I'll go."

Karianna turned to him. "No, please don't leave. I apologize." She wished his eyes would look away and give her an opportunity to resume normal breathing. His eyes, which now somehow held her body erect, since her knees had given away only moments earlier.

Emil then gently grabbed her waist and pulled her to him, lifting her out of her sandals. She was breathless, suspended in the miraculous depths that lurked behind the eyes of this dark prince before her. Then...

– he kissed her –

And her body ignited with unbridled lust. She pressed her hands upon the face she had wanted to touch since she'd first laid eyes upon it. Upon the terrific bronze chest chiseled to perfection. Upon the ass so round and firm that it seemed impossible to sit upright upon.

He pushed his large fingers underneath her blouse, up her spine, exciting her. He unclasped her bra to experience her firm golden breasts. He kissed them greedily.

Then suddenly, she tore open his shirt.

What was this? Emil had never been this turned on. He had never met such an alive, forceful creation. She pulled down his pants and boxers and guided him back onto the sofa. Climbing up onto his thighs, she threw off her blouse. She was making love to him and he enjoyed it. He watched in pleasure as each contour of her body kissed the next while she maneuvered herself on top of him.

"Kari, I... don't have a condom."

"That's alright." Without a single lapse in performance, she reached into her desk drawer and pulled out a string of three Trojans.

"You're assuming a lot," he smiled.

"I'm just hoping they fit."

Emil unzipped her skirt then picked her up and flipped her onto her back. Looking down upon her, he dropped his knees to the floor to admire her more closely. He stretched his dexterous fingers along the waist of her thong, witnessing her body writhe more heavily with each successive heave, taking in her excitement and anticipation of what might come next.

Slowly, he inserted his left index and middle fingers into her. He massaged her flesh quietly, precisely, beckoning her to *"come hither"* as she shamelessly moaned her overwhelming endorsement. No move was made without her communicating to him that it was now time. Their eyes never parted, until...

He pulled the front of her thong aside to reveal her swelling femininity. He then perched his lips upon her. He began to lick her. As his excitement advanced, he began vibrating the threshold of her engorged flesh with his talented tongue, pushing further inside her until her pelvis fully surrendered, welcoming each increasing invasion.

She could feel the hot, aroused air from his nostrils tickle the growing pool adorning her pulsating crevice. Then...

"Fuck me, Emil," she gasped.

Emil was a brick wall.

Karianna grasped his magnificent member and tugged him to her. It was now right in front of her eyes. She unwrapped a condom and rolled it onto him, retracing the slow trail of latex with her full, wet lips.

Emil was at once aroused and amazed. Sex with Karianna felt nasty, but not dirty. Bad, but sweet. Carnal, but pure. He'd never experienced anything on this level with Aniah, nor anyone else.

After a few moments, Karianna began to insert his peak inside of her.

"This may take a while," she said.

"I'm yours for as long as it takes. Maybe this'll help." He rolled down onto the floor and guided her on top of him. He then kissed her sculpted arms, stomach, and navel while softly pinching and rubbing her stiffly protruding nipples. "You are so beautiful."

He was inside of her. He admired with gluttonous pleasure as she allowed her body unprecedented titillation. She wasn't ashamed to show how much she enjoyed him. She wasn't afraid of her own desires. Submerged by hedonistic greed, she cried out while slowly vacillating atop him, her toned abdomen flexing upon every inch.

Emil could feel himself losing control over his body like never before, and it injected even more excitement into him, along with a hint of fright. The force of his two-hundred-fifteen pound frame conquered him as it began rapidly shaking with an intensity all its own.

Karianna felt him swell even larger inside her. It pleased her. She oscillated atop him faster and faster, firmer and firmer as he began to scream. She leaned forward and kissed him, rewarding his tongue for its previous unselfish deeds. Then she began sucking and nibbling his earlobes, and his neck. Upon arrival at his collarbone, she watched in full respect as each of his sleek solid torso muscles churned at record-setting speed.

"Are you ready?" she asked.

"Yeah! Y-y-yeah…" he yelled, his heavenly form now completely drenched in sweat.

"Come in me, baby."

"Oaaaaaaaaaah! Ooooooahh! Aaahohhhh-ahh!"

Karianna climbed down to rest her head on Emil's torso. She could not understand why she was so at peace in his wake. As she held him, she noticed a tear stream from his left eye. While kissing it, she came to grips with the truth she had been fighting

for weeks: she had finally found the man with whom she wanted to grow old.

She pointed to the plaques, degrees, and certifications decorating the wall behind her desk. "I'm gonna lose my license," she frowned.

"Well, we can't let that happen, because you have to get me all better."

"Emil, you're already better," she said, trying to remain upbeat. "And you have Aniah. I'm sure she can help you continue your healing process."

"She could never help me like you can."

Karianna stared inflexibly at Emil. "Listen, you can never tell anyone about this. Please."

"Don't worry. I'll never hurt you, Kari."

She knew he believed it.

Over the next fourteen weeks, Emil kept attending Monday and Thursday groups, followed by intense lovemaking sessions with Karianna after everyone else left.

He had not taken one hit of heroin since the day they met. At Vanderbilt, his colleagues gladly mentioned that they were noticing huge improvements in his performance. Rumors at the church ceased, and he had once again started attending the Y.L.C. meetings, helping to recruit speakers for their next conference. He was also a regular at the gym again. He credited Karianna and the clinic for helping him change his life back into something he could once again be proud of.

Nine more weeks flew by as a giddy Karianna and Emil continued dating on the down-low, rejoicing in every moment they spent together. But that was about to change.

One nippy Monday afternoon, Emil stopped by the clinic. He looked very troubled and seemed to be in an enormous hurry.

"Hey, there," smiled Karianna, as she walked down the stairs. "You're early. Maybe you could help me set up the chairs again tonight?"

"I need to talk to you. Can we step up to your office?"

"Sure." She knew something was wrong.

"It's Aniah."

"Oh my God, does she know?"

"No, it's her health," he replied. "She has lymph cancer, and it's eating at her fast. She's dying, Kari."

"Oh…"

"I'm going to have to spend more time with her and her family over the next weeks. I hope you understand."

"Of course," Karianna said. "She's your fiancée, and I would expect nothing less of you. Take all the time you need, Emil. Really." She felt horrible for Aniah. But she was also ashamed and angry at herself for resenting that Aniah's terminal diagnosis would pull Emil from her arms indefinitely.

He kissed her. "I'm so glad. Thank you, Kari. I will call. I promise."

"OK. Now go to her. And keep strong. We'll all be here when you get back."

As Emil walked down the stairs and out the door, Joe noticed the sad dim look in his boss's eyes. Karianna had always feared that one day, it would finally set in that she was not officially Emil's woman. She had wanted to believe that he would someday leave Aniah. She now saw that it would never happen. And she dared not hope for Aniah's demise to be a quick one. She hated herself for the thoughts that were starting to creep into her frozen psyche.

Emil Hubbard swept into her life and made her fall in love with him. And now he was gone.

Backstory: *...and Andy*

"Didn't expect to see you here," Andy said as Emil walked through the Intensive Care Unit door.

"I was just about to say the same to you," Emil scorched. "She's been at this hospital for months now, Andrew. Why'd you finally decide to show up? To pull the plug?"

"Shut up, Emil. We both know that if there's anybody who wants my sister out of the way, it's you."

"What's that supposed to mean? Look, don't you have a gig to get back to or something?"

"She's my sister and I'll leave when I'm good and ready. Um, by the way, how are things down at the clinic?"

"Actually, they're good." Emil was grateful for Andy's seeming concern. "Man, I have to apologize for the way I behaved when you gave me Kari's card. You were only trying to help me and I shut you out. Thank you. She's incredible."

"You're welcome. So, uh… just how incredible is she?"

"I beg your pardon?"

"Guess who showed up at one of my gigs the other week? Joe! From the clinic. Well, as you undoubtedly know by now, we go way back. And you'll never guess who he saw skipping out of Kari's clinic way after midnight a few months back, all huggin' and kissin' and gigglin' and shit? Guess!"

Emil glanced at Andy, wondering how someone so small in stature could be the source of so much of his torment.

"OK, so why don't you just tell her," Emil surrendered, pulling Andy into a vacant nook. "Isn't that what you'd really like? To hurt her? That way, you could get your revenge on both of us: her for being so goddamn perfect, and me for not wanting to fuck your brains out. So go ahead. The shock might just kill her, if you're lucky."

"Shut up!" Andy roared, punching Emil as hard as he could. "I hate you! I helped save your life and you *still* have the nerve to look down on me? When are you gonna see I am grown? Hell, I already pull in more stacks than you! You'll see: I'm gonna be

big! And I don't care what you say anymore because you're no better than I was. *You're a drug addict Baptist minister cheatin' on your dying fiancée with your muthafuckin' therapist!* So you can't play that 'holier than thou' card anymore. At least I have a damn conscience. What the fuck do you have?"

Emil felt enormous shame. Until now, he had thought he was OK – having just kicked a drug habit– but the truth was, he was still doing wrong. And it had taken Andrew Niles of all people to point that out. He felt terrible, because he lied. Because the young man who stood before him, who used to adore him, had now lost respect for him, and even seemed to pity him as well. He hugged Andy. "My God, I'm so sorry. Please forgive my words."

"You know," Andy sobbed, "There were times when I used to want her to just go away. And now, when I'm finally ready to move on and try to get over all my stupid shit, she up and gets cancer. Why does she always make it so hard for me?"

Emil wanted to ask Andy the same question.

"Come on," Emil invited. "We'll go visit with her, then I'll drive you back home, because I'm sure you still haven't bothered to acquire a license."

"OK."

———————————

Two hours later, they arrived at Andy's large loft in Nashville's trendy Five Points district.

"I'm gonna move somewhere even nicer next year, maybe buy a house in Franklin. Cash. My accountant says I'll be making enough money by then."

"Great."

"Want something to drink?"

"Nah, I should probably get going," Emil said. "I've got an early morning meeting."

"Not even one little glass of wine?" coaxed Andy.

"Nope, I'm totally clean. One-hundred percent substance-free."

"Well, Karianna must be supplying all your needs. That girl ain't told me nothin.'"

"We both promised not to say anything to anyone. And we haven't been together lately. I haven't seen her in over two months now."

"So, tell me… is she better than my sister?"

"I don't want to talk about that."

"She is, isn't she?" Andy cackled. "She's a freak! Everybody knows. Now don't get me wrong – that's my girl and all – but I'm twenty and I wish I had *her* stamina… she's told you about her past, right?"

"Yes, Andrew. Now can we just drop it?"

"OK, OK… but you're looking really good again, so she must be doing something right. You never looked like this with Aniah."

"Thank you, I think. You're looking pretty good these days yourself."

Andy's eyes instantaneously reflected an intense jolt of self-esteem. "Really?"

"Yeah. Looks like life in the spotlight agrees with you. I'm still very proud," he smiled while patting Andy's shoulder.

Andy took a large gulp of his pinot noir and stood up. It was now or never. The decision made him very nervous, but Emil did not notice.

"You've at least gotta have a Coke or something?" Andy asked.

"Got anything a bit softer?"

"Wow, you are clean. Let me see…" Andy pulled a pitcher of orange punch from the refrigerator and filled up a glass. While Emil sat on the sofa flipping through a magazine, Andy stealthily pulled a small pill from the corner drawer, crumbled it between his thumb and index finger, and dusted the powder into the glass. He then swished it around vigorously to mix the contents. He gave the glass to Emil, who, without even looking up from the magazine, chugged down the whole concoction in one gulp.

"Thanks, buddy." He flipped the magazine closed. "Well, I'd better be getting out of here…"

"No!" Andy jumped. Attempting to calm down, he appealed, "Just wait... I mean stay, a little bit longer. I enjoy your company, and it has been a while, right?"

Emil was convinced. "OK. You're right. But just a few more minutes. It's a school night."

Three minutes later, Emil began to feel strange. Good, but strange. Andy, now monitoring his every move, carefully pulled in more closely to check out his condition.

"Hey, how are you feelin'?"

"Good. Really good," Emil chuckled.

"I'm glad. Are you warm? Here, let me just take your coat."

"Oh, that's OK..."

"I insist." Andy pulled off Emil's tweed sports jacket and placed it on the night stand. "You still look a little uncomfortable. Let's get you out of this tie." Andy pulled it off and unfastened the top two buttons of his shirt. He then walked into the bathroom and returned seconds later wearing only a silk orange brief, a recent gift from a Williamson County judge with whom he was secretly messing around. But the judge would not be the first to see him in it.

"Hey, man, where are your clothes?" Emil sluggishly questioned.

"It's just so warm in here..." He then dimmed the lights and turned on the stereo.

"Oh... OK."

Andy slowly unzipped Emil's fly, being careful not to make any sudden movements. Then he began to stroke Emil's penis. "How's that feel? Good?"

"Yeah... Wait, you shouldn't be doing that."

"Shhh. It's aight," Andy whispered. "It's all good, bruh."

As Emil firmed up, Andy pulled down his suspenders and his pants with one hand, while continuing to stroke him with his other. Then Andy went down on him.

"Hey... what are you doing?"

"What does it feel like I'm doing? Now just relax and let me do all the work... You know, I still love you."

"I love you, too. I mean..."

Andy paused soberly. "I know what you mean, Emil." He reached into his nightstand and pulled out a tube of ID Glide

lubricating gel and a Magnum XL condom. He placed the condom and a large helping of the lube onto Emil's rock-hard nature. Next, he climbed onto Emil. He then tried to push Emil into him. It was a very difficult undertaking, but Andy was determined to make this happen now.

Once penetrated, Andy, in formidable pain from Emil's titanic girth, took in long deep breaths and began moving his hips around in order to become better accustomed to the intrusion. Finally, he was. Finally, he was having sex with the man he wanted more than anyone. He kissed Emil, who lay almost motionless, conscious of pleasure but oblivious as to the rest of the specifics.

Emil passed out immediately after coming. Andy used that time to crawl down beside him, cradle Emil's smooth bald head in his arms, and lay his own head upon Emil's chest, pretending that they were lovers; pretending that Emil really wanted him, really needed him, really loved him. Just for a few hours; then he would get up, clean up the scene, and vacate before Emil woke up.

Six minutes after 4:00am, however, Andy's phone rang. He reached over to answer it, awaking a groggy, disoriented Emil in the process.

"Hello? Hey, Ma, what's wrong?" After a long silence, Andy began screaming at the top of his lungs.

Emil jumped up to find his open pants soiled with random drops of his own dried semen, a dull ache in his head, a dry mouth, and a hysterical Andy crying and beating the walls, prompting his neighbors to scream obscenities. It did not take Emil long to decipher what had happened:

Last night he and Andy had sex. And this morning Aniah was dead.

Emil pulled on his pants, grabbed his jacket, and ran out of the apartment. He would not see Andy again until four years later, at the wedding of Alex Young.

He headed for Baptist Hospital.

Episode 11

Emil was greeted by Jack and Helen Niles, their niece Delphine, and a beautiful big-haired medical intern.

"You're not a relative of the deceased, are you?" the intern said.

"No. I'm her fiancé. What happened?"

"Her heart failed about three hours ago. I'm so sorry," she uttered, sensing his devastation. "Look, if you need to talk or anything, just let me know. I finish my shift in fifteen minutes. I'm a good listener."

"Thank you…"

"Charmaine. You don't remember me, do you? You guys have horrible memories. We met back when I was dating your friend, Xavier."

"Charmaine! Yes! I'm sorry, my mind is fried. Hello, I'm…"

"Emil. Yes, I know. She pulled him discreetly aside. "I also know the *whole* story. Kari and I are really tight. And right now, I may be the only person around here you can really chat with, if you get my drift."

Emil exhaled a long, deep sigh. "I'll be waiting."

Twenty minutes later, Charmaine joined Emil in front of the hospital. He briefed her on his relationship with Aniah, his addiction, his falling in love with Karianna, and the guilt and hurt intertwined throughout all three circumstances. As they walked, Emil noticed the wealth of attention she received from total strangers, and furthermore, how much she seemed to enjoy it.

"You sure are popular," he joked.

"Not popular, just pretty," she argued, "And eventually that'll fade. And trust me, there's nothing more pathetic than a 'used-to-be-young-and-pretty' person with nothing to show for it. So I do this," she said, modeling her hospital uniform. "Gotta have a brain

and a career. Hopefully they'll both hold up when the boobs decide they can't anymore."

"Well, you certainly have excellent bedside manner. I've just divulged my entire screwed-up life to you. Contrary to what Kari says, you do know when to shut up. You'll make a great physician one day, Charmaine."

"I wish I had your faith in me. Sometimes I just don't feel like I'm cut out to be surrounded by all this death. I started in medicine because I wanted to save lives. Now it seems that all I do is keep bodies breathing until the families either give up or run out of money."

"So what might you like to do instead?"

"See, that's the thing," she said. "I've never really wanted to do anything else. Aniah's brother suggested that I might want to consider the theater, but I couldn't tell if that was a compliment or an insult. I know how I can come across to people sometimes. I'm just my mother's daughter."

"Well, knowing Andy, the comment might've come forth in a vitriolic manner, but that's just how he is. He makes a living being crude."

"Yeah… where is he, anyway? I haven't seen him yet."

"Actually, I don't know, and I honestly don't care."

"Ouch. What'd he do to you?"

Emil thought carefully. He had just relayed his whole private life to Charmaine, and it felt really good to talk to someone who would listen without prejudice. But should he tell her about last night? Even she may not be able to process that. He decided to remain tight-lipped. "Nothing. He's just a nuisance at times."

"I can definitely see that," she agreed. "But I like him. I think he just might make it big. So does Kari. How are you and she doing, by the way?"

"We're good. I'm sure it's been hard on her these past few weeks, though. I miss her so much. Has she said anything about me?"

"Actually, that crazy girl hasn't called me in almost two weeks. I'm beginning to get a little worried. She's not returning my phone calls."

"Mine either," Emil said. "After this I'm going to drop by the clinic to say hi. You're welcome to join me if you'd like."

"No," she insisted. "I'll let you lovebirds catch up. But tell the wench to call me."

Emil laughed.

"So," Charmaine posed, "You're not going to ask me about Xavier?"

"I figured you'd bring him up when you were ready. I know what happened, and I understand why you left him. But Charmaine, I have to say…"

"Call me Char, please."

"Char, Xavier is a good person, but as you know, he's a tad complex. And back then, he was still really confused about a lot of things. I see it often in my students. He just needed to explore. That's no excuse, but I know for a fact that he did love you, very much."

"Thanks, Emmy – can I call you that? The whole thing just hurt so much. How's he doing these days?"

"He's good; still at Steele and Webber. And he still mentions you. I could give you his number?"

"I already have it. Kari's always saying I should call him. I just don't know, though."

"I understand."

"Please tell him I said hi, though, will you?"

"You got it," Emil promised. "I know he'll love that."

Charmaine looked at her watch. She was running late for her spinning class. "I like talking to you, Emmy. You're cool. And you haven't looked at my butt once since we started walking."

"As if you're not insulted," he quipped.

She giggled while pulling a business card from her purse. "Here are my numbers. Call me."

She then entered her red Honda Civic and waved good-bye as she drove off. What a breath of fresh air she was. And what a terrific friendship this was to become.

It was starting to rain. Emil was anxious to confront Andy about last night, but after sitting with Aniah's family for nine hours with still no sign of him, he decided to head over to Northside to check up on Karianna.

He walked into the clinic, greeted Joe, then ran upstairs, where Karianna sat at her desk in the midst of a phone conversation. Emil smiled and waved at her, and though she waved back, she made no attempt to end her call. He assumed that she was discussing an important business matter and sat on the sofa to wait for her to wrap it up. Thirty minutes later, however, it had become obvious that this was not a business call, but a personal one – one which involved flirting. What was going on? Was Karianna really setting up a date with another man, right in front of Emil?

After a few more minutes, she hung up. "Hi, Emil. What brings you back?" she said briskly, while grabbing a cherry seltzer from the refrigerator.

"Aniah passed on. I thought you might like to know."

"Oh. I'm so sorry to hear that. Char did say that she wasn't doing too well. How are you?"

"I'm fine, thank you. Are you OK? And if you don't mind my asking, why haven't you returned any of my calls? Or even Char's, for that matter?"

"Oh, I see you two have gotten reacquainted – that's great." She gazed momentarily at the clock on her desk. "I've just been busy. You know how that is."

Why couldn't she look into Emil's eyes?

"Are you seeing someone else?" Emil hesitantly inquired.

Karianna crossed her legs and took a sip. "Well, darlin', you *would* say that we have an open relationship, right?"

"I just thought that now, we might attempt to advance to a more solid arrangement…"

"Oh, is that what you thought?" she sneered. "That's cute. *'Little Kari is just going to sit around and wait for the Big Man From Afghanistan to come running back to her, once his fiancée finally dies?'*"

Emil could not believe his ears. Was this the same woman?

"Kari, I don't know what's going on, but believe me, whatever it is, we can talk about it…"

"But you see," she interrupted, "That's just it. I don't want to talk to you about anything." She paused briefly, then stood up. "You know what? I'd like you to leave."

Emil was paralyzed. "Kari, I love you," he cried. "Why are you doing this? What's wrong? Please tell me. If you're incensed with my actions of late, that's OK, I understand why. But don't shut me out."

"Emil, our whole relationship has always been about you, hasn't it? *Your* addiction, *your* dying fiancée, *your* needs and *your* wants. Well I'm sick of it, and I'm sick of you. So just get out. Here's the number to another clinic. We share the same nurse practitioner. They're very good over there, and they're expecting your call."

Emil was completely crushed. His worst nightmare was now playing out in front of him. He grabbed her. "Kari, I'm so sorry. Please…"

"Get the fuck out of here right now, or I will call security. I mean it, Emil. I have to get ready for my next appointment, anyway."

Totally stunned, he turned around to find Joe staring up at them. "…Charmaine says to please call her," he mumbled while running down the stairs and out the front door.

Once outside, he rested his unstable weight upon the trunk of his car as a fresh dark cloud poured mercilessly upon him. A few minutes later, he climbed inside. His throbbing head fell to the steering wheel. In the last twenty-four hours, he had been the victim of sexual assault. He had once again fallen prey to drugs. His longtime companion had died. And the love of his life had dumped him.

He wanted to die.

February 14th, 2010: 5:05 p.m.

"...Well, I should've just let him go," Andy continued from upon the stage, *"But the sex was just so good!"*

The audience, still in stitches, was riveted to the story.

"But I knew I had to get rid of him... when I came home and found him trying to break into my crack stash."

The crowd burst into thunderous laughter and applause, much to Andy's satisfaction.

"Thanks, everybody," he concluded. "You've been great. Congratulations to the newlyweds. God bless. And somebody get me a refill." He presented his glass to a waiter and strolled into the assemblage to sign autographs and mingle with star-struck fans.

Emil remained engulfed in a thick daze. It took Xavier, newly arrived at the reception, to knock him out of it.

"Hello again, everyone."

"Hey, Sugar."

"Late again, as usual."

"Hello, Xavier."

"Have a seat," invited Karianna, now visibly intoxicated and loving it. "So... *'Junior Partner'*, huh? Are you pumped?" she investigated, tapping Charmaine's arm.

"Well, I won't say it's not overdue," he replied while pulling up a chair. "Oh, and speaking of 'overdue', could you please tell us what brought on your sabbatical?"

"Took her long enough," smirked Charmaine, graciously sipping her Merlot.

"At least my hair ain't got A.D.D.," Karianna fired back. "Now, Xavier, darlin', there comes a time when you have to set better priorities. I'm just not all anxious to have a man anymore like our girl over here. Besides, half the time, y'all men ain't shit, ain't got shit, talk shit, or smell like shit, so why should I be in such a rush to get one?"

Emil could not keep his eyes off of his former lover. Even when completely toasted, Karianna was luminous.

"But isn't almost a whole year just a bit drastic?" Xavier proposed.

"I know that I may be missing out," she said. "And I also know that I can't be as picky as I used to be… you know, ever since the accident…"

"What accident?" demanded Xavier. "You never told me… What happened?"

"I turned thirty."

"Aw, come on, now," said Emil before swigging his Evian.

"Face it. We all know it's true. In this culture, women just aren't hot after a certain age." She turned to Charmaine. "Ain't I right, honey?"

"Yep. Girl, in my early twenties I used to be able to just reel 'em in, didn't I?"

Karianna sloppily nodded back.

"I had it goin' on," Charmaine boasted.

"Yes, you did," inserted Xavier.

Temporarily blindsided by his comment, she then persevered, "And then, I don't know what happened. All of a sudden, my well just dried up. It really took me for a spin. Kari, you remember?"

"Yes, honey. I thought I was gonna have to check you into my clinic."

"Believe me, I haven't given up, but it's really difficult trying to find your so-called 'soulmate' out here these days."

"Especially here in Bible-Belt-Buckle Nashville," furthered Karianna. "The adultery and down-low capital of the U.S."

"The latter-day Babylon," assisted Charmaine.

"…Where you can get a blow-job while you check your mail."

"You know," said Emil, "Us guys have it bad too."

"Like when?" challenged Karianna. "The biggest dilemma you've ever had was trying to decide between pee-pee or punany."

Emil glared at her. That, sexy, vulgar little… "Perhaps some of us aren't just looking for sex."

Karianna responded with rolling eyes.

"E is right," said Xavier. "I'll admit that I love sex just as much as the next guy. But there comes a time…"

"When you start gettin' old…" Karianna contributed.

"When you realize that what you really want is to be part of a union comprised of respect, love, and uncompromising honesty."

As Emil raised his bottle, Charmaine sucked her teeth.

Having recently signed his final autograph of the evening, Andy had already been eavesdropping on his friends' conversation for a few minutes, and now felt it time to insert his own thoughts. "My problem is," he declared while snatching a chair from a neighboring table, "I just don't think I can be attracted to the same man physically, mentally, and emotionally. Because most of them, they're just... incomplete, you know?"

"Yes," agreed Charmaine, tapping Karianna on the shoulder. "How old did you say he was?"

"Twenty-four today. Give it one more drink."

"Heffah," Andy whizzed.

"Your mama." Karianna gulped down the remainder of her Dark and Stormy and rested her head upon the table to absorb its gifts. When she lifted it up a few seconds later, an extremely attractive six foot tall man was standing beside her.

"Excuse me, might I have this dance with you?" he asked.

A stunned Karianna wondered whether or not she should accept. She certainly did not feel like dancing. Then she felt a rap on her knee. It was Charmaine, urging her to join him.

Reluctantly Karianna got up and allowed the young gentleman to escort her to the dance floor.

Andy turned to his left. "See, Emil? That could've been you up there. Still a big loser, I see."

Emil squinted at him with pure rage. Andy hadn't seen that look since the night at the bar in Atlanta. It brimmed with shame, hurt, fear, and hate. And it scared him a little.

"...So, Andy," intercepted Charmaine, "We're all rooting for you up here. What's new in the works?"

"Well," he anxiously replied, "ABC wants to do a reality show with me..."

From the opposite side of the table, Xavier listened to Charmaine and Andy converse about his career. She definitely fed Andy's ego, he noticed. But Xavier knew this was part of her compassion. Charmaine, like everyone else, realized that Andy

starved for more than the occasional ego boost. She sympathized that he'd had rough times. And even if it meant being a little phony, she was determined to make him feel good whenever she could.

Xavier anchored his attention upon their every word, because if lucky, he could clamp onto the tail end of a phrase, upload himself into their discussion and get Charmaine to finally talk to him, or at least acknowledge him. Her flare for drama made it crystal clear that she was deliberately not paying him any attention tonight. But it also verified that his presence still affected her greatly.

Meanwhile, Emil had a mind that danced on the floor along with Karianna. He still wondered why she left him four years ago, with neither warning nor explanation? What had he done to cause such a strange and brutal severing of ties?

Xavier lost his patience. He would just shove his way into Charmaine's conversation, whether she liked it or not. But suddenly he heard someone calling his name.

"Xavier! Xavier! Pssst! Xavier? Over here!"

He turned around and saw a figure standing in a dark corner next to a door that swung slightly ajar. It was Alex.

Episode 12

Suddenly, that taste was back in his mouth. He hadn't spoken to her since that fateful night seven years ago, and had neglected to return her calls since then. Several times he dialed her number, but hung up before she picked up the phone. He wouldn't have known what to say.

She had taught him so much about himself and about life in general. For this he owed her many thanks. But he was still angry at the boyish belle for her part in messing up something so perfect. Yeah, Xavier was aware that it takes two to tango. He understood that he was ultimately the one to blame for hurting Charmaine. But the truth was, Xavier also had been hurt by Alex. He gave her his entirety – even losing his one true love as a result; she had taken advantage of his friendship and used him for her own sexual amusement.

And that stung.

Today Xavier would confront her and settle the whole thing for once and for all. Charmaine watched him walk to her. It was a painful sight: together once again, the two people who broke her heart that winter night.

On his way, Xavier passed by a whirling Karianna, who broke away from her dance partner long enough to offer a few words of encouragement:

"Good luck, luv. Let the bitch have it."

Xavier and Alex were now face to face.

"Hi."

"Hey!"

"Hi."

"Hey!" There was that beautiful gapped smile again.

As Xavier prepared to again say hi, Alex, much to his relief, interrupted him.

121

"So, can I get a hug?"

They did.

"Oh, still working out regularly, I see. Very nice, Xav."

"Listen, Alexia, I…" He noticed that, even after seven years, she still hung upon his every word. He'd missed that. But now, down to business: "Why'd you do it, Al?"

She appeared perplexed.

"I know this is very bad timing," he said, "With this being your wedding day and all, and I'm sorry. But I want you to know that it took me a long time to get over what you did. And I know that I did it too, but you knew at the time that I was very fragile sexually and emotionally but you did it anyway and it hurt because… well it was all so unexpected and you lied and it messed me up and I sound like a four-year old but so what."

The next wordless seconds felt like an eternity to Xavier, leaving him to wallow in the pure senselessness of his proclamation. It made him feel worse, and even more pissed off at Alex, who took a deep breath before finally speaking.

"Xavier, first of all, I have never lied to you, and I believe that you know that."

He hated it when she talked like this; it made him feel childish.

"I told you that I wasn't looking for anything long-term at the time, but that I did want to remain your friend. And I really meant that. I love you, man. But you wouldn't call me back and you made me feel unwanted. I'd really thought we were better than that. What happened was messy, and I fully accept my share of the blame. But it's been over seven years. And if Charmaine has forgiven me, why can't you? In fact," she said, "To be honest, I think you should actually be thanking me."

"What?" Xavier barked. "Why?"

"For doing you a really big favor. Face it: we had fun, and you are one big sexy mofo. But let's face it: it was *you* who were using *me*."

"How dare you!" tore Xavier, who somehow knew that her statement would grow truer every moment he thought about it.

"You were experimenting, and it's OK. I enjoyed being your guinea pig," she smiled. "But you were in love with someone else.

So no, I never wanted to take it any further than that. And neither did you. You were just being a kid."

Xavier could not speak. Everything Alex said was excruciatingly correct. Why hadn't he seen it before? "I..." he attempted.

"Xav, I'm really glad you're here. I wasn't sure you'd show up. You didn't even RSVP. But I'm honored that you were my best man today and I can't tell you how happy I am to have my buddy back in my life."

"I don't know what to say, Al. I feel really embarrassed right now. I apologize."

"No need, man. Let's just forget it and move on, OK? And by the way, thanks for getting Drew to come. I owe you one. Sherri almost shit herself, for real."

In her eyes Xavier discovered unconditional love and devotion to her new spouse.

"And I've seen the way you've been ogling Charmaine all night. What's going on there?"

"She still won't speak to me."

"You want me to talk to her?"

Just then, Sherri called for her new life partner to join her at their table. Something big was about to happen.

"OK, man, I gotta go, but you really should talk to Char. I'd bet hard cash that you're both on the same page. And stop by our table before you leave. I wanna give you our new number. We have something very important to discuss with you."

"Will do," said Xavier, still wildly mystified by the words of his newly rediscovered friend.

"Ladies and gentlemen," announced a voice from the speakers as the music faded. The spotlight unveiled that the voice belonged to Victor Love, one of Alex's Belmont colleagues. "We have in our presence tonight, yet another sparkling talent: 'Miss USA second runner-up 2000 and phenomenal vocalist, Miss Karianna Cojoure."

As the crowd buzzed, Karianna, still on the dance floor, realized that she had better sober up fast, because there was no way that she was going to escape what was coming next.

"She's now a very well known and highly respected social worker and human rights activist on the north side, and is

quite influential in local government there, as well. Who knows: perhaps a seat on the council is in the cards for the near future…?"

Karianna dove into her purse and yanked out her compact to make sure there was no lipstick on her teeth, and that her hair was in place: an emergency ritual that Charmaine taught her when they were younger.

"…But I digress," Victor said. "Tonight we want to take advantage of her amazing voice." He looked at Karianna. "You've been asked by Sherri to sing a song, darling. We've even got a band and some singers up here for you. Would you do us all the pleasure?"

The spotlight had now found her, and as she began to weave her path toward the stage, she teased, "I don't know… you got some money?"

The crowd capped their laughter with applause.

After entering the stage and briefly consulting with the band, Karianna sang the song Sherri requested: a soulful rendition of Alison Moyet's *"Midnight"* – the same song she performed at her Miss Tennessee audition. The lyrics flashed memories into Emil's head; memories of their last night together.

Midnight –
It's raining outside –
And I must be soaking wet –
Everyone is sleeping tight –
God knows I've really tried my best –

Xavier, next to feel the pang of resurfaced memories, glanced over at Charmaine, who, as usual, knew she was being watched.

Well honey you know it must look so bad –
Just lost the best thing that I ever had –
Still I don't know why I did him wrong –
But it's too late now, and yes he's goooooone –

The band was now in full swing as Karianna shook, shimmied, and rocked the standing audience into a frenzy with her electrifying stage presence, stunning physical beauty, and pipes of steel. Andy noticed that she frequently seemed to be singing in Emil's direction.

Baby, oh no –
Can't leave me now –
Just think about it, please –
'Cause I love you –
And I need you –
And I shoulda thought of that –
Before I did you wroooooong –

Andy next discovered a tear on Emil's face. No one else in the room was privy – for the brightness of the spotlight shining on her – but on her face as well, Karianna now possessed a few tears of her own.

The song ended with a bang, and the ecstatic crowd hollered as Karianna curtsied and walked back to the table.

Charmaine hugged her. "Oh, I love you!" she screamed. "You were wonderful. You guys planned it, didn't you?"

"Girl, I'm so drunk," muttered Karianna as she wobbled down into her chair. She looked up to find that her dance partner had joined them. "Oh, here! I want you guys to meet Christopher. His restaurant is hosting a private event on Monday night and he's invited all of us to be his guests."

Unable to fathom why she would want them to accompany her on her first date in almost a year, they all stared at her. But her eyes begged them to accept.

"Well," Charmaine said, "I think we can make it."

Andy agreed. "I guess I can stay in this wretched town a couple more days if you need me."

"Sure. Sounds fun," Xavier piped in. "I'll move some things around."

"Fine," Emil flatly acknowledged.

"Oh, wonderful," Christopher grinned. "It will be so great. I cannot wait for you to see the restaurant." He hugged Karianna.

"What's your restaurant called?" Emil inquired.

"Aisle C."

Charmaine's eyes widened. "Aisle C! Over in the Gulch? I've heard so many great things about that place! It's new and really popular. I hear everything is great: the food, the ambiance, the service – lots of big celebrities have been sited there. You must be very proud."

"Yes, I am."

"We'll be there," said Andy. "Thanks."

"Good. Until Monday, everyone." He kissed Karianna on her hand, then left.

Charmaine slammed her fists onto the table. "See? Now *that's* what I'm talking about: the man is fine, can move his ass, and has his own five-star restaurant. And girl, that cute accent! And you weren't even looking!" She held up a paper napkin containing her handwriting. "I'm working on my third personal ad today, and you're the one who ends up married. I'm not talking to you anymore. Where's he from?"

"Belgium."

Andy raised an eyebrow. "Oh, I've been there. Ain't that in Europe?" He took another swig of whiskey. Charmaine noticed that it was his fourth glass since sitting down.

"I think that's where he said he was from," Karianna admitted. "I told you I'm drunk."

"He seems suspect to me; perhaps on the down low," Emil coldly challenged.

She turned around. "Well, you'd be the expert on that."

Everyone knew what was about to follow: an all-out death match between the Drunk Diva and the Scorned Scholar, and no one wanted to risk being caught in the crossfire, so Charmaine did what she did best: diverted everyone's attention.

"Kari, you're showing."

"...Huh? Oh!" Karianna leapt up and shuffled to the restroom with Charmaine.

Xavier momentarily eyed Emil before speaking his mind: "What do you do, man – practice?"

Karianna turned on the nearest faucet. "Oh, girl, hand me some of those towels. Better yet, could you run out to the bar and get me some soda water ..."

Charmaine leaned on the countertop next to Karianna and folded her arms. Calmly she informed her friend, "Nothing's wrong. You're fine."

Karianna was confused. Why would Charmaine have lied to her? And about this, of all things? She viewed the mirror to discover the truth. "Then why did you..."

"Don't you think that maybe you could lighten up on Emil a little?"

Karianna stepped back. "Oh, so *that's* what this is about?"

"Look, E," said Xavier, "I know you guys have some bad blood between you, but that's no reason..."

127

"She dumped him," Andy honked while taking a swallow of his newest Vodka Rocks. "How *should* he be actin'? Start usin' your head for more than hairstyles."

"Shut up, boy."

Charmaine just couldn't take it anymore. There was a mirror right behind her. A big one. So she turned around and looked into it, instantly feeling better. While pulling a small container of lip stain from her purse, she continued, "You know, Kari, you really should watch what you say to people sometimes. Do you have any idea how you're sounding out there?" She dabbed her lips with color as Karianna prepared to respond.

"Andy's right. She dumped me, X. Hard. Tossed me aside like last week's TV Guide. And afterwards she showed absolutely no remorse. It was almost as if she had planned it."

"Maybe it's because you're bisexual," Xavier reasoned.

"Look, Emil started it," rebutted Karianna. "And none of this would even be happenin' if you hadn't insisted on draggin' me

here in the first place. What's your motive, darlin'? To appear as if you don't miss Xavier? To make him think everything's a hoot for you these days? *Please.* You still want him. And there's not enough concealer in even *your* purse that can cover that up."

Charmaine wasn't pleased. Was she really so transparent? Did Xavier know? Could he tell that she still had feelings for him after all these years? That every man she'd dated since him had been unforgivingly subjected to the "Xavier Jonson Measure-Up Test"? That indeed, no man had ever measured up? Why was Karianna always right? Wasn't this whole trip to the restroom supposed to be Charmaine's turn to be right about something for once? Darn her. Charmaine slung the stain back into her purse and marched to a stall. She was going to sulk.

"Uh-uhn," admonished Karianna, grabbing her friend's hand and pulling her to the door. "You are not gonna do this tonight, sweetie. Let's get back out there. They're probably talking about us, anyway."

"What was *that* supposed to mean?" demanded Emil.

"Maybe she just couldn't deal with your bisexuality, so she dumped you," Xavier nonchalantly declared while ferociously chewing a celery stick. "People get dumped, you know. All the time. It's an everyday thing."

Emil leaned toward him. "Who do you think you're talking to? When Char left your philandering ass, it tore you up. You were crazy for months. Hell, it's going on eight years and you still compare all of your little chickens to her. So don't throw that *'people get dumped'* crap into my face. Yes, I am bisexual, and proud of it. But I loved Kari so much that to this day, it hurts. So fuck you, and fuck her, because you're all going to hell after tonight." He slumped down in his chair and reached for his bottle of Evian.

Behind them, a few guests had begun tapping their glasses, chanting, *"Toast! Where's the best man? Toast!"* and prompting more to do the same.

After throwing back the last drop of his current glass, Andy announced, "I can see I need to stop dreamin' right now and just get me an old white man, 'cause y'all men of color – fine as you are – are all crazy. Can't decide what you want, always havin' to get high before we do it, wantin' me to be your bitch." He tossed a small ice chip into his mouth. "But I am a grown man. And I have the wants, needs, and desires of a man. I'll be so glad when somebody finally allows me to be the man that I am…"

Emil and Xavier snickered quietly.

"…Instead of some pathetic homophobic fantasy of a pussy with balls."

"How many drinks have you had?" Xavier interrogated.

"I'm alright."

"That's you're last. I'm taking you to your hotel."

"Toast! Toast!"

"Actually," Andy slurred, "I was hoping Emil could give me a ride – for old times' sake."

Suddenly Emil violently jumped from his chair, causing it to spin, fold, and fall to the floor with a mighty three-tiered clang. "OK, that's it!" He lunged across the table, grabbed Andy's collar, and began shaking him compulsively.

A crowd accumulated as Xavier attempted to convince Emil to unhand him.

"I ought to annihilate you right here, once and for all!" Emil yelled.

"'*Annihilate*'…" said a frightened, yet relentless Andy, "Hmm, care to spell that one for me, schoolboy?"

"Spell *'G.E.D.'*, punk!"

Karianna and Charmaine had now broken through the throng. "Guess I took the wrong child to potty," admonished Charmaine.

Emil looked up to find everyone in the room staring at him. Ashamed, he released Andy, grabbed his coat and stormed out of the building.

Andy, now face down on the floor, was quite shaken up; not because Emil attacked him (any physical contact at all with Emil was a good thing), but because he had inadvertently driven him away.

Xavier pulled him back to his feet.

"Well, we're gonna go," said a disoriented Karianna. "It's getting late, and I have to run budgets in the morning."

"Yeah, guys," added Charmaine, "And I've got an interview."

"On a Sunday?" Andy said.

"Are you sure you should drive?" Xavier asked. "I could drop both of you off."

"Oh, I'm fine now," Charmaine insisted. "So I can drive us both, thanks."

"I'm coming over tomorrow," Andy said.

"Good," Karianna replied. "You can take me out to brunch."

"Gee, thanks."

She smiled sarcastically. "OK, since today's your birthday, I'll pay the tip if you insist. Can't wait to catch up. I'll call you when I'm leaving work."

"Cool."

Karianna and Charmaine left the reception.

The sky sparkled with thousands of stars as Xavier drove a passed-out Andy to his hotel. But Andy's condition did not prevent Xavier from attempting to carry on a conversation with him.

"...But she was the bomb, though, man. I mean, she's fine – we all know that – but she's also sweet, kind... beautiful inside and out. She used to make me feel so good about myself, you know?" He looked at Andy, whose lower lip now sourced a train of saliva trailing to his lapel. Xavier chuckled. It was good to see the kid again after all this time, even if he did always seem to cause a ruckus wherever he went.

After carrying him up to his fifth floor suite at the Wyndham Union Station Hotel, a highly fatigued Xavier climbed back into his car and began the drive back over the bridge to his house in East Nashville.

It did not take long before Charmaine's image sultrily pranced into his mind. Xavier pontificated what he would have to do to make things right between them again. He was now on a mission, and turned on the radio to think. While singing along with Elton John to *"Lou Seein' Disguise Would Dine In"*, he turned the corner onto Bakman Street. Thankfully, he was almost home.

But something directly ahead caused him concern. Hot glaring red, yellow, blue, and white lights flooded his path, reflecting even stranger prisms of color from his hood as he inched forward. He began to hear the static generated by the muffled voices of city officials of varying ranks communicating with one another via walkie-talkies and radios. Then he noticed the fire trucks.

And the police cars.

On the front lawn of his house.

Half of which was burned to the ground.

Part Two: Take Off

Episode 13

Xavier couldn't believe it. His home, his refuge, was ruined. Wholly stunned, he almost stepped out of the car before shifting into 'park'. He walked around the front of the house, gazing up at its shambled remains in gross confoundedness, resembling the girl in "Carrie" who attempted to find the bucket of blood before being kicked out of the prom. Though the fire had now burned out, the blunt and pungent odor of burnt fabrics, charred paint, and moist smoke remained.

A small nervous grin materialized on Xavier's face. It was followed by a couple of faint chortles, then a borage of neurotic guffaws. Despite his wishes, he couldn't quell the laughter as he watched state workers shovel scraps of his life's dream off of the ground and deliver them to the dump truck on the curb next door. He felt as if he might hit the ground any minute. Then he heard a voice beside him.

"Sir, are you Xavier Jonson?"

He gathered composure for their conversation. "Yeah. This is my house, Officer…?"

"Twostones," she replied. "I'm Officer Belinda Twostones and this is my partner, Officer Toby Denelian. Mr. Jonson, I'm sorry about what happened to your home; it looks like you'd put a lot of work into it. But we'd like to ask you some questions, if that's alright?"

"Sure, go ahead." Xavier's steel facade was beginning to cave in to heartbreak.

"OK, Mr. Jonson, I'll make it brief. Your house caught fire at about 5:30 this evening. The heavy winds we've been having spread it like gangbusters. Do you have any idea how the fire could've started?"

"No, I don't."

"We've been trying to get a hold of you since we got the call."

"I've been at a wedding and a reception, just two miles away." He turned to Drexel, who, still in his pajamas, had recently sneaked closer to eavesdrop more precisely. "Drex, why didn't you tell them where I was?"

"I did."

"He told us, Mr. Jonson. We called the church but no one answered. So we went to the reception hall and you weren't there, either. Did you go straight there after the wedding?"

"Well, no," Xavier stuttered. "I left after the ceremony to do something first."

"Then where *did* you go right after the wedding, Mr. Jonson?" asked Officer Denelian.

Xavier did not like Denelian, but gosh, he sure looked awfully familiar. "Wait, are you guys suggesting that I started this fire? Who would do this to their own house? I love my house!" He grabbed Denelian's flashlight and ran into his living room. "Oh, my God!" he howled while touring the structural remains. "And you think *I* did this?"

"Mr. Jonson," said Twostones, "No one is accusing you of anything. We're just trying to gather the facts for an accurate report."

Xavier endeavored to calm down. "Fine."

A firefighter cadet invited Officer Twostones to pow-wow with a group of servicemen. There was a new finding in the rubble, perhaps sound evidence of the fire's origin.

Xavier walked up the hall to view the rest of the damage. He stared at the blackened soot-filled walls and the wet smoke-damaged garments that dripped from the rods inside his closets.

A satisfied voice contentedly declared, "Well, well, well. I believe we've found the culprit." Twostones was back. She lifted up the portable television Drexel had been watching that afternoon. "Looks like it exploded. This thing's really old. It should've been recycled ages ago."

Xavier turned to Drexel, who then scurried to the front of the house.

136

As Xavier and the officers collected on the front lawn, Denelian said something that would prompt Xavier to dislike him even more: "Well, look at the bright side, Mr. Jonson."

"Oh, and exactly which side would that be?" Xavier sniggered. "The one that no longer has a roof?"

"I meant that your insurance will probably give you more money than your stuff was really even worth."

Xavier wanted to escort Drexel and Denelian into a locked room and beat the shit out of both of them.

"Toby, go to the car," ordered Twostones. "I'll be there in a minute."

Officer Denelian swaggered away.

"I'm so sorry, Mr. Jonson. He's a little overzealous and can be an asshole, but he means well."

"It's OK. And my name is Xavier."

"Well, Xavier, where are you going to be staying tonight? Because if you need a place to crash, I have a bed in my spare room. My daughter sleeps in it when she's over. She's with her father now, so you're more than welcome."

"An officer and a lady," Xavier smiled, before probing, "...Your husband wouldn't mind?"

She blushed. "No hubby."

"Well, what about your..."

"No anything, Xavier. I'm quite the single girl."

"Oh."

"My intentions are innocent, though," she insisted. "I just believe that when someone's in need, you should try to help them out. You never know when it might come back to you."

"True," agreed Xavier. "Thank you for the offer. But I do have somewhere to stay."

"I see. Well, here's my card, and I'll write my cell number on the back. If you have any questions, or just need to talk to someone, don't hesitate to call. Believe me, I've been there."

"Thanks, Officer..."

"Belinda."

"Thanks, Belinda. I really appreciate it."

"You're welcome." She left to join Denelian.

Xavier felt a terrible weight exit his shoulders. People were still decent, and despite all the chaos in his life right now, everything was going to be OK. He slid Belinda's card into his rear pocket.

Suddenly, Drexel sprinted by, carrying the duffle bag he'd brought with him the day he knocked on Xavier's door.

"Hey!" Xavier called. "Wait! What are you doing?"

"My friend Maxine said I can sleep on her sofa."

"So where was Maxine when I had a sofa?"

"Huh?"

"Nothing," Xavier replied.

"You've always been good to me, man, and I really love you. But lately I've been a waste of space. I'm just no good anymore. So I'll go." He began walking up the street.

Xavier wanted to run after his childhood friend, but he couldn't move. Regretfully, Drexel was absolutely right. As his image succumbed to the distance, Xavier sadly watched it become one with the darkness that so peacefully surrounded them.

"I love you, too."

Xavier re-entered 1428 Bakman Street. It was dead.

He wandered into the living room, where the new eighty-two-inch flat screen television once showed old reruns of 'Sanford and Son', 'I Love Lucy', and 'The Jeffersons' after a long day in court.

Gone.

He walked to the dining room, where the cherry table and empty china cabinet once stood. They were gifts from a client whose mother had died. After Xavier wrapped up her case, they dated for a short while. But then she decided to move back to Virginia to be with the rest of her family. Xavier had cherished the dining set, for it reminded him of the good people in the world; ones like Katherine and her mom.

All were now gone.

He stared with agonizing melancholy at the site of the initial blaze: the warped and cracked tile floors, the island, the cabinets. This was no longer a gourmet kitchen.

He considered yielding to the tragedy by driving to the local bar for a few beers and then seeing where the night might lead him. Perhaps Officer Twostones's place, after all? Perhaps Charmaine's door? Maybe she would feel sorry for him and show a little kindness to a wounded soul?

"Bullshit," he reprimanded himself. If he was to get something new going with Charmaine, then it would happen without manipulation of any kind. What he needed right now was a bed. He walked out of the house, got into his car and drove back over the Cumberland River to Karianna's house in Germantown. On the way, he noticed how dark it had become. Dawn must be just around the corner. Hopefully, the same could be said about his life.

He pushed open the white wooden gate and traversed up the long narrow cement walkway that exhausted at Karianna's porch. The trees in her yard were routinely professionally coiffed, hedges trimmed, roses plucked. The yard looked like she: petite and sharp. He knocked on the door. A light popped on seconds later, followed by another one inside. The door then opened to reveal a yawning Karianna in a peach robe.

"My house burnt down," Xavier sighed. "Can I live here?"

"That was *you*?" Karianna asked, instantly waking up to model an expression that screamed, "Damn!" She pulled him inside.

Karianna's home was just that: a home. Every piece of furniture had a story, every picture a meaning, and each accent was fluffy and cozy. Melon and pear were the motif colors that

branched about the first floor. There were pillows everywhere that took the place of cats, which she loved, but to which she was allergic. Rag dolls of various sizes and cultural origins sat next to the magazine basket, under the coffee table, and on top of the entertainment center. Candles whispered vanilla and cherry scents throughout.

People always hated leaving her home. The Diva, however, had no problem putting anyone out. But to Xavier Jonson, her buddy since St. Elgin's, she would hand over an exceedingly heartfelt welcome. She took his coat as he plopped down on the sofa, the site of their semi-regular viewings of 'Jeopardy' where they would play along and eat popcorn popped by Xavier that contained, as Karianna proclaimed, "enough salt to cause a coronary".

"What happened?" she said.

"Drexel's TV caught fire in my kitchen."

"*He's* not coming here, is he?"

"Nope."

"Well, you made the news, darlin'," she informed while leaning on the arm of the sofa. "I didn't catch that it was you because I was so out of it. God, I must've looked like a complete fool last night."

"No bigger than the rest of us." He laughed. "We're all so ridiculous."

"Yes, honey. We should be on TV. Want some tea – I have caffeine-free?" she asked while heading to prepare a kettle.

"No, I think I'll pass. Thanks though, babe." He took off his shoes, propped a pillow beneath his head, and stretched out on the sofa. "I think I'm just gonna get some sleep…"

"You can have the extra bedroom upstairs."

"No, I'm good right here."

"Are you sure you're OK?" she asked while pulling two quilts and a comforter from the linen closet.

"Yeah, I am." His smile revealed anticipation of new beginnings to come. As he started drifting off, he recalled something at the reception that had caused him concern. "Hey, did you notice anything strange about Andy last night?"

"Strange, or strange for Andy? Because you know you have to clarify?" She tossed a plush quilt on him.

"Well, I don't know… It didn't seem to you like he was drinking a lot?"

While placing the comforter over his feet, Karianna replied, "Boy, you are asking the wrong person. But come to think of it, Char said the same thing on the way home. Maybe I'll bring it up to him today and see…"

"Just be careful: if you do, he'll think we're ganging up on him."

"You could be right, but…"

"Char was amazing, wasn't she?" Xavier smiled.

"Yeah. Congratulations – you two treated each other so civilly, unlike Emil and I. I swear, Xavier, that man can still turn me into a little child."

"At least you guys acknowledged each other. Char and I just sat there the whole night. We hardly said a word to one another."

Karianna jumped in response to the toot of the kettle and advised him, "You know what you need to do? Call her. She should be home from her interview by 1:00 at the latest." She poured hot water onto an Earl Grey tea bag in an oversized chartreuse ceramic mug that one of her clients made.

"What do I say to her? Dealing with me is still hard for her and I don't want to make her more uncomfortable."

"But you are interested," she appealed. "So just find out what she has planned today. Probably nothing, because despite all those personal ads she keeps throwing online, nothing good is popping up. And besides, let's not kid ourselves: she does miss you." She stirred the tea before taking a cautious first sip. "But she won't be single forever. She's seeing a doctor from her old hospital – good-looking, too."

Xavier was curious. "Oh?"

"Yes. To tell you the truth, I don't know how serious they are, but if I were you I wouldn't wait around. You know how anxious our girl is to tie the knot. She probably keeps a veil in her trunk, just in case."

"You're bad," Xavier laughed while closing his eyes.

"Look, I just don't want to see you two miss out because of some silliness. I think you should at least consider my advice. But you'll just do what you want to do anyway, so forget y'all. I got a date."

His eyes slightly opened. "Oh, thinking about finally loosening up that chastity belt?"

"Now, wait a minute, I didn't say all that… but he does seem OK, huh? What do you think?"

"He seems OK…" Xavier was fast asleep.

It was 6:45am: time for Karianna to get ready for work. After doing so, she kissed her faintly snoring friend on the forehead.

"Bye, boo. *Ya big doink."* She walked out the front door.

She pulled into the grocery store on the corner and emerged with a small bouquet of freshly-cut flowers. Then she drove to Mount Pleasant Cemetery and parked her silver Saab just inside the gate. After walking a few feet down an attractive brick path, she knelt and began praying at a grave site. Two tears escaped her eye as she placed the bouquet delicately upon the tombstone. She brushed away the pebbles that had accumulated since her last visit exactly one month ago. After a few more quiet minutes, she drove to the clinic.

Episode 14

Charmaine had arrived early for her appointment at Hilltop Medical Center: fifteen whole minutes. That ought to earn her some points; give the impression that she was always prompt. Today she was to complete her third and final interview for the position of Head Pediatric Surgical Nurse, and it was down to her and just one other woman.

She had, only an hour earlier, partaken of a power breakfast to get herself going: two egg whites, two slices of rye toast topped with cream cheese, and a cup of black coffee. She made sure to wear taupe - "*the interview color of choice*", says Essence magazine. And no cleavage. Instead, she wore a pastel yellow blouse that buttoned midway up her neck. Once before on an interview, she'd made the mistake of showing too much skin, and wasn't given a fair shot by the woman who interviewed her. That's when she realized that whereas a sleeveless blouse might go over well with a male interviewer, a female would most likely prefer her in a parka and snow boots. Today, though, Charmaine did not know whom she would be talking to because Hilltop's Assistant Head of Pediatric Surgery was new. Three days new, in fact.

"*If it's a woman, please just don't let her be overweight, plain, or my age,*" she prayed.

She was getting nervous. She wanted to cross her legs to conceal her shaking, but feared showing too much thigh. She thought of calling her mother for support, but decided against it. Besides, her parents' phone number was still, for some reason, disconnected. Maybe she would stop by their house after the interview, depending on how it goes.

143

She considered calling Evan – *"Dr. Evan-Patrik Torsche, Ob-Gyn"* – whom she was currently dating whenever she had nothing better to do. The two had enough in common: both were attractive and in search of a mate. But Evan was totally against Charmaine's interview today. He did not want her to remain a nurse. He felt that her time would be better spent by joining his M.D. program at University Hospital in Spring Hill, and getting back on the road to becoming a full-fledged physician.

"Truthfully, now, why schlep a Nissan when you could be pushing a Jag?" he would ask her.

Evan really cared about Charmaine and believed he had her best interests at heart. He had even asked her to marry him ("We can have the ceremony right after you make residency!"). She told him that she would think about it and get back to him. That was six months ago.

Dr. Evan-Patrik Torsche was smart, gorgeous, rich, and single. In other words, he was gold. Yet when with him, Charmaine experienced a sometimes-y passion; rarely any real sparks. And though she was grateful for his confidence in her academically, something special seemed to be missing.

Oh, well.

She wanted to pop open her compact and dab on a dollop of fresh lip tint, but worried that the lady behind the desk might spot her and pass word to the higher-ups that she was vain. And indeed she was. But she believed it shouldn't matter, because it had never interfered with her job performance. She was a great nurse, and had the credentials and the impeccable references to prove it.

Charmaine really needed this job. Her landlord would be knocking on the door at noon tomorrow to collect proof of her employment, or else hand her a twenty-four hour eviction mandate. So today's performance was crucial.

One more minute.

The door next to the front desk opened, and out stepped a matronly woman with homemade-blonde hair. "Dr. Randall can see you now."

The woman led Charmaine through a shallow hallway into a medium-sized conference room and offered her one of the larger leather swivel chairs in the bunch.

"Would you like some coffee or water?" she asked.

"Oh, no, thank you, I'm fine."

"The doctor will be right in," the woman said, then left.

Charmaine admired the office furniture while attempting not to fidget. She said a little prayer, attempting to suppress her nervous energy. Suddenly a peace poured into her. She knew that this job was going to be hers. She was calm. Then a loud voice made her jump.

"Charmaine Parker! I thought that it might be you! Remember me? I'm Connie Randall. From Perry High!"

Charmaine turned around. In front of her stood an overweight, plain woman, about her age. Charmaine did not remember her at all. "Umm… oh, yes, yes, Connie! How are you doing?" They hugged as Charmaine hastily struggled to figure out just who this woman was. "How long has it been? Eleven, almost twelve years?"

"It has!"

Charmaine, still unable to fully recall this woman, decided to take a chance anyway: "D-d-didn't you use to wear a bob and read Stephen King novels?"

"Yes! Oh, you remember!

No one would remember Connie. Least of all after eleven years. She was that girl whose face was halfway cut off in all the group yearbook pictures because she felt more comfortable standing on the end than in the middle amongst the other kids. And she appeared as if she worked at being hard to look at. Not ugly, just wrong.

Her long wavy dark brown hair looked as if it were trapped in a net. She wore a blue dress made of material that looked like it might have made a better t-shirt. It needed a pattern on it, or something. It was the same shade of blue that Charmaine's TV screen once became after she'd let two months go by without paying her cable bill; the day she pressed the power button on the remote and found "No Signal". The color clashed with Connie's pale skin and aqua-green eyes. Her beige pumps peeled and buckled in the front, exposing white feet adorned with partially chipped metallic grape toenail polish.

"If I could dress her just once," thought Charmaine.

Connie was likable, though. She had a wonderful sense of humor and quite an inviting personality which Charmaine found very charming. As Connie toured her through the hospital, Charmaine became angry at herself for not getting to know this fantastic person back in high school. People this cool don't just fall out of trees, she thought.

Only one floor beneath them, Stephen Drexel walked into the bustling urgent care waiting room and approached the receptionist to check in.

"Good to see you again, Mr. Drexel!"

"Yeah, thank you… you, too."

During the tour, Charmaine ventured to – in light of the high comfort level she shared with her new friend Connie – take the opportunity to reminisce about high school days:

"…And then after that, the principal finally went home. But we never did find that turtle, did we, girl!"

Connie was in tears from back-bending laughter, each giggle sounding like a raindrop falling into a fast-growing puddle. "Oh, Charmaine, I can't remember the last time I laughed this much! Whew! Those were the days, huh?"

"Yes, they were!"

"Stephen Drexel?" the admitting nurse announced from the door leading to the exam bay.

Drexel followed her to a vacant room, where she recorded his blood pressure and weight. The hard fluorescent lights above them gave the room a shiny, chrome-like haze that hurt his eyes.

"The doctor will be right in."

"OK."

After the tour, they walked into Connie's office and sat. Unopened boxes cluttered the floor.

"I'm sorry, please excuse this mess. I just got here, and the facilities department won't be helping me get settled until later this week."

"Oh, don't worry about it," Charmaine assured.

"So, I didn't see you at the reunion, but now I know that it's because you were in Botswana on your fellowship," noticed Connie. "You have quite a hefty resume: Chief Physician's Assistant in Cardiology at Veteran's Memorial Hospital under Dr. Selma Wade; you've served on the National Medical Research Board for the last two years, teaching associate at Trevecca School of Nursing, Baptist Hospital... Pardon me for asking, Charmaine, but why do you want to come to Hilltop? I mean, we're a stellar institution, but let's face it, we're overworked and understaffed here, big time. Honestly, what other hospital would ask someone to come in on a Sunday for an interview?"

"Connie, I'm just seeking a change, you know? A new road. And I can feel, from walking around and talking to your staff and patients, that this where I should be."

"Well, as long as you're aware that it's crazy here..."

The doctor entered the room. "Hello, Stephen. How are you feeling?"

"Fine, I guess."

"That's good." He peeped momentarily inside a folder, then closed it. "Well, I'm not going to beat around the bush. You've been waiting long enough. I regret to have to inform you that your test results have again come back..."

"Crazy is my middle name!" exclaimed Charmaine, now sure she was a shoe-in for the job.

"Well, you've got me convinced," smiled Connie. After talking to you, I am now...

positive...

...that you'll excel here at Hilltop!"

---

positive...

...and you are indeed very well past HIV detection and into the advanced stages of AIDS. We've also detected five more tumors on your temporal lobe since your last visit. Their rate of formation appears to be accelerating rapidly."

Drexel's frame suddenly weighed a ton, trembling with confusion, anger, and fear. It was real. He was going to die.

"I'm sorry," said the doctor. "I'd like to discuss some possible drug therapies with you..."

Drexel jumped out of the chair and ran out of the office.

"Mr. Drexel!"

But it did not bring him back. Drexel was gone.

"So does this mean that I've got it?" Charmaine prodded.

"Well, I have to talk to HR, but if everything turns out, you should be working here by the end of this week," smiled Connie.

"Oh, wonderful! I love new beginnings! And speaking of new beginnings, when are you due?"

"When am I due for what?"

"When is your baby due, silly!" Charmaine grinned, pointing at Connie's enlarged midsection and waiting for a response with a number in it.

The smile left Connie's face. "I'm not pregnant."

Charmaine felt her egg whites, rye toast, cream cheese, and black coffee resurrect and begin swimming around inside her. They churned impetuously as she drowned in the horror she had just concocted. She was sure that at any moment, they'd all be coming back up for a visit, but no matter how she tried, she could not move. Her humiliation and total embarrassment were like glue upon her soles. What had she done? How could she have, with only a few small words, completely sabotaged herself after such a promising hour of *"tee-hee's"* and *"yeah, girl's"*? Why could she not have just left well enough alone? Why did she have to frost the cake one last time?

Suddenly, her power breakfast added that much-needed pattern to Connie's blue dress.

No signal.

Episode 15

Karianna and Andy had just spent the last hour hunting for a lime green shawl to accessorize a dress she had recently purchased. They found nothing, so decided to eat.

As they entered the Canopy Grill, Andy bathed in the fulfillment that was moderate celebrity as some diners turned their heads and gushed, "Is it really him?" The host made sure, at the manager's request, to seat them in the center of the room, making Karianna self-conscious.

"Can't you put us over near that wall?" she pleaded.

"No! Right here is just fine," insisted Andy while he sat down, leaving her to follow suit.

"You haven't changed, Puppy." She took a sip of iced lemon water and began perusing the menu.

"So you've noticed," he replied while picking up his ringing cell phone. "Hello? Yeah, what's up? I'm in Cool Springs. Tell him I'll get with him tomorrow. He can just fax it to my hotel suite. I'm under 'Andy Peters.'" He looked up to find Karianna's unforgiving eyes scrutinizing him. "Look, I gotta go. Bye."

"You need to turn that thing off. We're about to eat."

"And I'm paying for it, so be quiet."

Once their orders were taken, Andy resumed conversation. "It's good to see you, though. I've really missed you since I moved to Miami."

"Apparently not enough to visit, but that's cool," she teased.

"Well, I'm sorry, but I still have issues with this place. Seeing everybody takes me back. I look at all of them and I'm fat and ugly again." He downed a glass of pinot noir.

151

"You've never been ugly, Puppy. You were always really cute. You couldn't see it, but we all did."

"Yeah, whatever. You didn't even meet me until after I lost all that…"

Karianna's phone rang. Upon noticing that it was Charmaine, she raised her index finger, urging Andy to park his thought while she took the call.

"Hello?"

"K! K!" a hysterical voice cried.

"Char? Charmaine, what's wrong?"

Andy became nosy. He could hear each of Charmaine's words.

"I messed it up! I messed it all up! God, what is wrong with me?"

"What happened?"

"I had it. I had that job in my lap, girl. And then, my mother came out."

"Oh, no."

"Yes. I asked the Assistant Head Pediatric Surgeon when her baby was due."

"Well what's so bad about that?" Karianna posed.

"There was no baby, Kari."

"Well," Andy offered, "The lady was probably just made funny. Like this dude who's trying to talk to me right now…"

"Shut up."

"What?" whimpered Charmaine.

"Not you, honey. I'm sorry. Go ahead."

"Kari, it was a fibroid. The woman had a damn tumor, and I called her pregnant. Jesus!"

"Look, calm down. You were only trying to be cordial. I'm sure she understands that. You're probably just worrying about nothing…"

"Well, at least she ain't fat," proclaimed Andy while stuffing a hunk of French bread into his mouth, followed by another couple of swallows of pinot. The bottle was almost empty.

"You're a great nurse, Char," said Karianna. That's all that matters to Hilltop."

"If I'm so great, why can't I tell the difference between a fetus and a tumor? I'm a joke! And now I'm homeless. I didn't get a job offer and my stank landlord is gonna evict me tomorrow!"

The waiter placed their salads on the table, providing Andy the opportunity to order a second bottle of wine.

"It'll be alright, luv. Really. You'll see."

"What am I gonna do now?"

"You're going to move in with me. I've got the extra bedroom, it's yours. But first, you're going to come out shopping with us. We'll pick you up at..." She suddenly remembered that Xavier was also currently staying with her. "Oh!"

"What?"

"Uh, nothing."

Andy giggled.

"Well, why don't I just skip shopping, rent a van, and move in tonight?"

"Yeah... sure, hon'. Just make sure you give me a call when you're on your way, OK?"

"OK. Thanks, Kari."

"See you soon."

"Bye."

Karianna hung up the phone to find Andy laughing.

"I swear," he said. "I love her, but that woman is more drama than an Orson Welles marathon."

"You better leave my girl alone."

"Ain't Xavier staying with you? Oooh, that's gon' be some good shit. You better hide all your cutlery." His phone rang again. "Hello? OK, well what did you tell him? Look, this is stupid. Why can't you just handle it? I already told you, that's not good enough! Ash, you're not doing what I pay you to do. Get them to listen, or I'll find somebody who will. Bye." He slammed the phone shut.

"Puppy, for goodness sake, I thought this was supposed to be a vacation for you?"

"It is. Now eat," he instructed, as his phone rang again. After imbibing his first taste from the new bottle, he picked it up. "So did you fix it...? Oh. It's you." His tone deflated. "How many times do I have to say this? It's over. Now quit being a dumb jock and get it through your big head. I don't wanna see you. You shouldn't have followed me here. Go back to Miami. I just might be staying up here a while, anyway." Then worry suddenly began to invade

153

Andy's freckled face. "Listen, asshole, if you come anywhere near me this time, I'll have the cops and the media on you so quick… *Just leave me alone!*" He threw the phone at the table, prompting diners to take even more notice.

"Puppy, is everything alright?"

"Everything's fine. Just drop it, OK?" He ignited a cigarette and inhaled it long and hard.

The host appeared at their table. "I'm sorry, sir," he announced, "But no smoking is allowed inside the restaurant."

"What? But we're in back-ass Tennessee! Third-graders smoke here!" He yanked the cigarette from his mouth and dangled it before the host. "Well, do you want me to put it out on my bread? Here!"

The humiliated host plucked the cigarette from between Andy's fingers and walked away as Andy poured another glass of wine and drank.

"You know," Karianna said, "I'm just gonna come out and say this because I love you, so…"

"…*Don't you think you're drinking a little too much, Puppy?* That's what you were gonna say, right?" Andy accused. "Damn. And here I thought we'd be able to sit, enjoy a nice meal and catch up. But I should've known better. See? And you wonder why I don't visit. Alright, so tell me: which one of them put you up to this? Prince Charming or Snow White?"

"We're all just concerned about you, Pup-…"

"And screw the 'Puppy' shit, OK? My name is Drew Niles, and I'm not a kid anymore. I've had a hit HBO special, a gold CD, two major film roles, and liposuction. Sorry if not even all *that* qualifies me to be in the same league as Aniah."

Karianna was struck cold by that name.

"That's right, I said it. She's dead now, Kari, so let's finally talk about her, shall we? Say what we *really* feel. Wasn't she just divine, with her three degrees in one hand and her Coach bag in the other? She was fiyah, huh?" He then slyly whispered, "You can say it: you were jealous of her, right? Just a little?"

"I didn't even know her, Andy. You were the jealous one. The things you've said about her sometimes, I could've sworn that you might've even hated her."

"I did not hate my sister."

"So tell me, did you love her?"

He became sullen. "How could anybody not love her; she was…"

"Did *you* love her, Andy?"

He stared at his plate, then swallowed more wine.

Sensing his reticence, Karianna grabbed his hand. "It's OK, baby. I know it hurt. But this is what I do for a living, remember? So please tell me, did you love your sister?"

"Yes," he muttered.

"Did she know? Did you ever tell her?"

"I got tired of standing in line, I guess."

"Is that why you hurt Emil? To get back at her?"

"I wasn't trying to hurt anybody, Kari. I know nobody believes me, but I really did like him. But just like everybody else I've ever cared about, he didn't take me seriously, either." He fell back into his chair and flushed a sigh of regret. "I've tried to apologize to him over the phone a few times. He accepted, but it didn't seem genuine."

"Andy, you laced his Kool-Aid with GHB to get him to have sex with you, right after he'd finished nearly thirty weeks of drug addiction therapy. Your little deed forced him to start recovery all over again from day one, while you just skipped town without telling anyone after your sister died. I don't know; if it were me, I might not have accepted your apology at all. I might've even thrown your ass in jail. But he may come around eventually. Emil does have a huge heart…"

"First of all, Pippi Longstocking, it wasn't Kool-Aid. It was Tang."

"*Whatever.*"

"Secondly, if anybody would know about Emil's *'huge heart'*, it would be you. You guys are still such big hypocrites. You were his therapist, my dear. And you boinked him regularly, even though you knew he had a fiancée."

Karianna was at an outright loss for words. Only Andy Niles could do that to her, and it pissed her off. "Well, at least *I* didn't need to get him high to fuck him!"

They sat silent for about four seconds, engulfed in the desperate echo of her claim before finally bursting into hysterical laughter.

"Well! Honey!" Andy roared, "What's that on top of your salad? Croutons or Meow Mix?" After more laughter, he admitted, "Geez, if I've been jealous of anybody, it's you."

"Me?"

"You were the one he really loved, Kari. Nobody else could even compete." He leaned back again. "Man, how could one dude have three folks all feenin' for his ass at the same time?"

"Well," smiled Karianna while biting into a bread stick, "As we both know, Emil's heart isn't the only part of his anatomy that's huge."

They howled and slapped hands.

"*OK!*" toasted Andy. "I had to get three stitches! …But seriously: why did you break up with him? It wasn't because he's bi, was it?"

Karianna became visibly tense. "No. It just… wasn't the right time for me to settle down. Him, either. I mean, with his recovery and then your sister's death… It just wasn't the right time…"

Andy was skeptical, but just as he prepared to delve a bit deeper, his phone rang again. "Drew here. Yeah… yeah, yeah… uh-huh… Well, what did they say?" His excitement launched into orbit. "Really? Are you serious? You're not shitting me, are you? 'Cause if you are, I'll fire you and sue your ass so fast… yes! See? This is what I pay you for! Fax me the proposal, and I'll call when I get it. Alright." He hung up the phone. "*Yes!*"

Karianna ignored Andy's elation and raised her hand. "Check, please!" Then, beginning to feel guilty for popping Andy's bubble of victory, she submitted, "Congratulations."

Right then, Andy's phone announced its limited remaining battery power.

Thank goodness," she gasped. "Now maybe I can have you to myself for a few minutes. Wanna go to the Frist Museum? If you're good, I'll buy you a falafel."

He grinned. "Yeah." He emptied his wine glass, placed a credit card on the table, then headed to the rear of the restaurant.

"Wait," she asked, "Are you going to the restroom again? Didn't you just go twice before we walked in here?"

"Oh, um… well, you know… it must be all the wine. Just go wait in the car. I'll only be a couple minutes… I promise."

Episode 16

Xavier didn't want to know what time it was. Finding out might make him feel as if he had cheated himself out of a few more hours of well-deserved sleep. But feeling incredibly refreshed, he sat up on the sofa. The first thing his eyes captured was the grandfather clock standing guard in the southeast corner of the room with two ragdolls atop it.

He was right. He had cheated himself.

"I'll sleep long and well tonight for sure."

He walked into the kitchen to fix a bowl of Frosted Mini-Wheats, then brought it to the living room. Xavier was the only person Karianna ever allowed to eat there, and he was rather proud of that fact. After slurping the last drop of milk from the bowl, he sat on the floor and stared at the telephone sitting on the end table. One extended sigh later, he picked up the receiver and began dialing.

"Hello?"

"Hi."

"Hi, Xavier. I'm glad you called. I was afraid that after last night…"

"No, no, it's OK." He hesitated before asking, "Would you like to get together tonight for dinner? Just the two of us?"

"Love to. What time?"

"Say, around 9:30?"

"OK. Where?"

"How about Midtown?" he suggested.

"That'd be good. Exactly where would you like to meet?"

Xavier wanted someplace well-known but not too out in the open. "How about at the corner of Church and 17th in front of the

159

laundromat? There's a new Belizean restaurant over there I'd like to try out."

"9:30?"

"You got it."

"Great. I'm so glad you called me, Xavier. There's a lot for us to catch up on. I can't wait to see you again."

"Yeah," replied Xavier, before hanging up.

He then pondered the potential circumstances of his actions. He was unsure if he was doing the smart thing, especially when so much of his life was now ablaze. But he was curious, and really excited about tonight. Something else excited him, too: Karianna's words from earlier that morning echoed so loudly in his head, that the only thing that could overpower them was the sound of the new numeric tones he now found himself dialing.

"Yes?"

"Char?"

"May I ask who's calling?" She knew who it was.

"Hey, it's Xavier."

Nothing.

He cleared his throat. "I was wondering what you're up to this afternoon?"

Charmaine, leaning against her kitchen counter and holding a pint-sized box of Haagen-Dazs vanilla ice cream in her left hand, and a mixing spoon in her right, spoke: *"Honestly? Nothing."* She swallowed a spoonful and added, *"...Although I'm already beginning to wonder if I should've lied about that."*

Xavier laughed nervously. He was encouraged that she had not yet hung up on him or asked if she could call him back later. It was now or never. "How about we go go-cart racing? And then maybe a movie, if that's cool? It'll be fun. I mean, hey, we're both adults here, right?"

"I guess we've got to stop avoiding each other someday," she surrendered.

"Yeah," replied an increasingly heartened Xavier. "...Hey, how did your interview go?"

"It went," she replied while inspecting her apartment, now filled with moving boxes, clothes, and never-unboxed gadgets

from the Home Shopping Network: all the ghastly consequence of her gross lack of tact earlier that morning. She threw away the half-eaten box of ice cream. *"...Straight to hell."*

"Aww..."

"Don't bother. I've already cried enough for both of us. So, when are you picking me up?"

"Well, I have to run over to Macy's, then take a shower... How's 2:00?"

"I'll be here."

"Great. See you then."

"...Oh, and Xavier?"

"Yeah?"

"Thanks for helping me reclaim some of my maturity."

"I'll see you soon, Char." He hung up and smiled. He was extremely anxious to see if Charmaine still knew him, still felt him after all these years. Was there hope for them yet?

February 15th, 2010: 12:02pm

Professor Emil Hubbard sat in his Vanderbilt University office sipping green tea and grading the exams he had recently administered to his intermediate-level French classes. Normally his teaching assistants performed this task. But every now and then, Emil liked to personally catch a peek of his students' progress.

As Delibes' *"Flower Duet"* pulsed from the Bose stereo system, Emil's red pen suddenly ran out of ink. He scoured his desk drawers for another, then deduced that he must have taken the last one home. "OK, so green ink it is." He was talking to himself a lot today, as he always did when he was upset about something. He hoped his utterances would drown out his unrelenting thoughts of the previous evening. He reached into the top drawer and pulled out

a green felt pen that had attached itself to a letter he'd stuffed there nearly two weeks ago. He held the letter up in front of him. *"American Embassy Paris,"* he quoted in a thespian tone. He began to spin around in his chair. *"Embassy. Embassy..."* he repeated more and more loudly, desperately trying to erase last night from his head. But it wasn't working. Karianna Cojoure might as well have been standing naked on his desk, carrying Andrew Niles on her back. He stopped spinning. "Shit."

"...Did I come at a bad time?" asked the voice from the doorway.

The letter fell to the floor. Emil looked up. It was Ramon.

Backstory: *emil and ramon*

On a hot Friday afternoon that May, Emil drove over to the offices of Page, Seavers, and Markowitz to take Xavier out to lunch as retribution for losing a friendly bet to him earlier that week. Emil walked in to find him amidst discussion with a man in his late twenties who seemed rather irritated about something. Xavier appeared to be trying to calm him down. Emil thought it best to just wait for Xavier in the foyer. As he reached for a magazine to peruse, someone walked up to him.

"Hi."

Emil raised his eyes. In front of him stood a tall lean caramel-skinned man with impossibly thick curly black hair, razor-sharp cheekbones, gothic jaw line, flawless skin, stunning smile, and a body arguably more well-sculpted than Emil's. He wore a crisp white linen shirt, dark blue jeans and black Adidas shell-toe sneakers, and carried a sloppy stack of books and pamphlets from various attorneys' offices, soon to be recycled.

Emil swallowed. "Good afternoon."

"Are you here to see Xavier?" the man smiled.

"Yes."

"You must be Emil, then. I'm Ramon, his intern. I'm just going to drop this stuff at my cubicle, and then I'll let him know you're here."

"Thanks, Ramon." *(...with your beautiful ass.)*

Emil chuckled at his attraction to the intern, then brushed it quickly from his mind when the irritated man from Xavier's office scooted out.

"Well, Xavier, all I know is that I can't be held responsible for what happens when I'm backed against a wall. I'm trying to be nice, but..."

"Theo, Theo," Xavier said, "I'm sure that no one is following you. I think you're just under a lot of stress lately, with the retrial coming up. But I've kept you out of prison before and I'll do it again, so don't worry. You should take some time and spend it with your new girlfriend. What's her name? 'Ho'-something?"

"Oh, no – the Hawaiian girl? She's old news. I've got a real keeper now. Classy. She owns her own business and everything. Antiques."

"Wow, I'd love to meet her someday. But right now, I've really gotta get some lunch and I suggest you do the same. Lay off the caffeine for me and try to enjoy life a little, OK? No one is following you. Let me deal with the case. The worst is behind you."

"Fine," Theodorio reluctantly agreed.

"All right, then. See ya."

"Bye." Theodorio boarded the elevator.

Xavier strode to Emil. "Now you see why I get paid the big bucks. I tell you, ninety percent of this job is playing therapist. Bet I could give Kari a run for her money. What's up, man?"

"Not much," said Emil. "So you finally broke down and got an intern?"

Ramon appeared again. "Hey, guys!"

"Oh, hi, Ramon. This is my good friend Dr. Emil Hubbard. He teaches over at your campus. And Emil, this is Ramon Del Peral."

"Yes, we've met."

Xavier observed their interaction, then paused before exclaiming, "You really don't know who he is, do you, E?"

"I'm sorry, should I?"

"Man, we all knew you were a big nerd, but he only plays for your school, for God's sake."

"It's OK," said Ramon as he shook Emil's hand. "It's a pleasure to meet you, Dr. Hubbard."

Emil was unsure whether he was just imagining that Ramon was holding onto his hand a bit longer than the norm.

"Ramon is an eighteen-year-old sophomore," Xavier explained, "But he's already going to be starting quarterback for the 'Dores this fall. Can you believe it?"

"Oh…" Emil looked up at Ramon. "Well, good for you."

*(Eighteen? He looks at least twenty-four.
What are they feeding athletes nowadays?)*

"Don't you also teach French, Dr. Hubbard?"

"Among other things… I mean, yes I do. And call me Emil. Please."

"I'm going to be in your '214' class this summer."

"Oh, well then… good."

(Ramon Del Peral is SUPER HOT)

"So, see you then?"

"Absolutely."

Ramon smiled and gave Emil a pat on the shoulder that subtly became a firm rub as he exited the foyer, leaving behind the faint sweet smell of Egyptian musk.

Emil's eyes followed him out, then peered back over to a suspicious Xavier. "Well, he seems nice."

"Yeah, he is," agreed Xavier. "He helps out my team three days a week. You ready? E? Emil!"

"Huh…? Yes! Where would you like to eat?"

Xavier simpered at his smitten friend and teased, "How about Mickey D's? That way you could bring the toddler back a happy meal."

"Oh, be quiet," admonished Emil. "He's way too young! I'm a minister, for crying out loud. And you heard him yourself: he's going to be my pupil soon. Get your mind out of the gutter."

Episode 16

"You first," laughed Xavier as they walked down the stairs and across the street to lunch at Watermark Café.

On a warm rainy evening one week later, Emil departed his office after a Y.L.C. meeting ran late due to a voting miscount that warranted investigation. He was excited to get out of his clothes, into his pajamas, and curl up with his latest new book find. But while driving along James Robertson Parkway, his car began to emit several loud banging noises. He wasn't sure if they were coming from his engine, because his "check engine" light was always on. But seconds later, all the other dashboard warning lights joined it, and his 1998 Buick Regal coupe stopped running. Emil was stranded. Alone. On the bridge. At night. In the rain.

"Great." He reached for his phone and looked up the number to his insurance company's roadside assistance hotline. While dialing, he noticed two headlights slow down and pull up behind him. A tall male figure exited the car. Cautiously, Emil rolled down his window to find...

"Ramon?"

"Emil? Hey! What happened here?"

"I guess she's just tired. I'm calling a tow truck now."

"Well, after it comes, I'd be glad to take you home."

Emil thought about it. Should he accept Ramon's offer, or should he just pay the extra sixty bucks and let the tow truck guy bring him home?

Wait. Money doesn't grow on trees. And besides, surely nothing was going to happen. Despite his trivial attraction to Ramon, the young man carried no reciprocal interest, whatsoever. It was all in Emil's mind. Plus, the boy was only eighteen. So...

"Thanks, Ramon. I would appreciate that."

165

On the ride to Emil's apartment, the two laughed and joked about the crazy life of a college football jock. They even ventured upon more serious topics such as U.S. foreign trade policy toward China and female genital mutilation in Sudan. Emil was quite impressed by how aware Ramon was of the world around him. It was refreshing, even at Vanderbilt, to talk to an undergraduate who could actually argue an opinion of something substantial.

By the time they arrived at Emil's building, he definitely wished to continue their conversation, but decided it best not to invite Ramon up.

"Well, thank you. It's been a pleasure. How much do I owe you?"

"What? Nah, man, you don't owe me anything. But do you have some clothes I could borrow? Mine are soaked all the way through."

"Oh… *(thank God)* of course. You can park anywhere on this side of the street."

———————————

"My bathroom is tiny. You can use my bedroom to change." He handed Ramon an old sweat suit from his own undergrad days. "These aren't the best threads, but they are warm and dry."

"Thanks."

"Would you like a glass of something?"

"O.J. would be cool."

While Ramon walked down the hall into the bedroom, Emil pulled a carton of orange juice and a natural cherry soda from his refrigerator and brought them into the living room. He couldn't wait to revisit their hot topics. Plus, he had come up with even more thought-provoking questions to ask his new friend. This was going to be a good night. Then…

166

"Yo, Emil!" hollered Ramon from the bedroom in a firm timbre that somewhat titillated Emil.

"Yes?"

"Could you come here a minute, please?"

"Sure." What could be wrong? Was there a hole in the sweat suit? How embarrassing. He knocked on the door.

"Come in."

Emil opened his bedroom door to find Ramon Del Peral, eighteen year old Ramon del Peral – Vanderbilt Commodores starting quarterback Ramon Del Peral – six-foot-one-dark-handsome-gorgeous-perfectly-assed-wonderfully-made-Lord-have-mercy-Ramon Del Peral – standing on the bed.

Naked.

"Uh... yes?" Emil asked.

"O-o-over th-there," Ramon stuttered while pointing underneath the window sill, where stood a small white mouse, chewing on an old piece of bacon.

"Damn! How did he avoid the trap again?"

"I d-don't know, but c-could you get rid of it, please?"

"Oh, sorry." Emil chased the mouse into a hole next to his chest of drawers. "There we go – all gone. I apologize. I'll just be waiting out front..."

Ramon jumped off of the bed, leaving nothing of his anatomy to the imagination. He wrapped his hands around both of Emil's triceps. "Thank you. But now can you do me a small favor?"

Emil cleared his throat. "What?"

"Don't tell anybody. If word gets out on campus that I was afraid of a mouse, I'm a goner. It's hard enough that I'm so much younger than the rest of them."

"Your secret's safe with me, kid."

"What? Hey," Ramon teased. "Who are you calling a kid?"

Emil dared not allow his eyes to focus on the Latin Adonis again.

"I said, who are you calling a kid, dude?" he smiled while circling Emil to prevent him from exiting the bedroom.

"OK, OK, you're not a kid. But put some clothes on. Your juice is getting warm."

"I'm not embarrassing you, am I?" interviewed Ramon. "Being in the buff? Try playing on a team. Guys walking around with their packages in your face all the time. Gets pretty routine." He knew that he was getting to Emil, and he enjoyed it.

"Ramon, please put on the pants."

("Ramon, please unfasten my pants.")

Ramon smiled. He pulled on the sweat suit and swaggered into the living room. "I'm sorry. I can see I freaked you out a little back there."

"Oh, you didn't. I just…"

"How long have you and Xavier known each other?"

"Just about nine years now, I think," Emil answered.

"So, have you guys ever… you know?"

"I'm sorry, I'm afraid that I do not."

Ramon's voice smoothly transformed into a whisper that was somehow even brawnier than its normal pitch. "Have you ever… messed around?"

"Not that that's any of your business, but no. Xavier is straight."

Ramon's grin contained a knowing that exceeded his years. "Where I come from, every man has his price."

"Why don't we get back to our previous conversation, please?"

Ramon swallowed some juice, then stared silently at Emil. It was working. He forfeited the couch and walked over to the loveseat to sit right next to the rigid professor. Then he ran his fingertips firmly down Emil's eight-pack, leaving his body to react – favorably.

At once stymied and aroused, Emil said nothing. Ramon then unbuttoned Emil's fly and pulled him all the way out into the open. He began to stroke him.

Emil's eyes closed. His body, losing its tenseness, sank down into the loveseat. He pushed his fingers through Ramon's thick mane.

Suddenly the thought of Karianna invaded his brain.

He jumped up. "Ramon, please leave."

"What? Why? You don't want this? Are you for real?"

168

"I'm just… I can't."

"Oh, you have somebody else?"

"Yes. I mean, no. I mean… I'm not sure if it's prudence or compunction driving me to say this, but I would appreciate it if you left right now."

"I can't believe you're just gonna pass this up," Ramon huffed while begrudgingly retrieving his wet clothing from down the hall.

"Look," contracted Emil, "I'm going to be your teacher in a few weeks, and face it: I am way too old for you. It's just not going to happen. But no hard feelings, OK? This'll be our little secret."

"OK. I'm sorry. Well, thanks for the clothes. Catch you later."

The door closed behind Ramon. As he advanced outside toward his car, his apologetic gait viscously morphed into a muscular, confident strut. He paused momentarily before cranking the ignition, his perfect smile now exposing a demonic crust. *"Not going to happen',* huh? That's what you think, pa."

Episode 17

Ramon passed French 214 with flying colors and elected another of Emil's classes for winter semester. Now in French 226, Ramon sporadically visited Emil's office to discuss his academic progress. Emil wanted to help insure that he would not lose his place as starting quarterback for a second victorious season.

Neither party ever mentioned that hot rainy night eight months ago at Emil's apartment. And Emil never let on that as a result of that night, he was still, to this day, having explicit dreams of

Ramon.
Cuban-Puerto Rican Ramon.
Tall, dark, hot, gorgeous, Cuban-Puerto Rican Ramon.

Eighteen-year-old Ramon.

February 15th, 2010: 12:03 p.m.

"Oh!" replied a startled Emil. "Of course it's not a bad time, Ramon. Please come right in." He removed his glasses to search the floor for the letter.

"Good. May I have a seat?"

"Of course you can."

"I didn't think you'd still be here, seeing as how it's almost 7:00."

"I'm always here. I'm old and have no life."

171

"You're funny," said Ramon while closing the door. He noticed that his test was currently being graded. "So how did I do?"

"Well… you *passed*."

Ramon's face whitened.

"…With an eighty-seven percent," Emil concluded. "You didn't cheat did you?"

Ramon's laugh was wonderful. And sexy. So much so that Emil tried to avoid much eye contact.

(Eighteen-year-old Ramon)

"So, why did you come to my office this evening?"

"Well, mon conseiller, Madame George, est malade, si maintenant, je n'ai pas un conseiller, et je voudrais pour vous etre mon conseiller temporalement, jusqu'elle retourne."

Emil was impressed. "Alors, comment peux-moi resiste un requeste comme ca? Of course, I'd be honored to become your new adviser. Actually, it just so happens that my own advisee suddenly had to drop out this semester, so…"

"I know."

"Oh?" Emil began playing with a button on his cuff.

"So you said you're old," recalled Ramon. "But you don't look it to me. Exactly how old are you?" He lifted his muscular honey-cast legs upward to plant them on Emil's desk.

"Thirty-six."

"That's not old."

"It is when you become it."

"Well, both my parents are in their sixties and they're still doing their thing."

"You're still a baby," Emil judged. "See if you feel the same when you're my age."

Ramon pulled his chair to the desk. "Are you really gonna make me wait that long?"

He was close enough for Emil to feel his breath moistening his neck. He brushed his hand onto Emil's, cueing his instant arousal. Then Ramon pressed his soft lips gently, repeatedly along Emil's neck, causing his successive breaths to deepen, widen.

Suddenly, Emil seized Ramon's athletic waist, picked him up and slid him onto the desk. The cup of tea fell to the floor.

Emil jumped.

"Oh, I guess I'd better get going," Ramon maundered.

"Ramon, if you need to talk to a counselor about your feelings…" Emil knew he sounded silly.

"No, I'm good… See you next class." Ramon picked up his backpack and bolted out of the office.

Emil stared at the door. "What just happened?"

He called Charmaine.

"Well, just goes to prove you still got it, boy." She was getting ready for her date with Xavier and experiencing the usual hair trauma.

"Will you come on?" Emil chided. "I'm serious. He made a pass at me again, Char! I don't know what to do about this kid. Don't you realize how delicate this situation is? He's eighteen. He's our star quarterback, for Christ's sake! And I almost just gave him what he wanted."

"So, why didn't you?"

"…Whuh?"

"Why didn't you have him?" she asked while struggling to pull her brush from her hair.

"Because he is my student, Charmaine. Have you been listening to me, or has solipsism once again taken you hostage?"

"Maybe he's looking for a daddy. Like Andy."

Emil gawked at the receiver.

"Just kidding. Oh, my God, that really wasn't nice. I'm so sorry. OK, go ahead."

"I can't help it if toddlers find me beguiling."

173

Charmaine put down the brush. *"I guess I'm just trying to live vicariously through everyone else these days, Emmy. I'm happy there are people in your life who still find you attractive, because God knows on my end…"*

"Charmaine Parker, be quiet. I don't feel like hearing this nonsense. You should just call…"

Charmaine's doorbell rang.

"Who's that?" he interrogated.

"You'll never guess." She turned to her front door. *"Coming!"*

Emil smiled. "OK, I'll leave you and your roommate alone."

"I'm sorry?"

"He's staying at Karianna's for a few days. She didn't tell you?"

"No."

"Well, have a good time. You deserve it."

"Thanks! Bye."

Charmaine hung up the phone and opened her front door to find the man she once so deeply and fearlessly loved, smiling back at her.

After go-cart racing, they went inside and played a game of pool – she won – then had lunch at Marie's Bistro in Belle Meade, where afterwards, they made the decision to catch the new Chiwetel Ejiofor film. On the way to the theater, Xavier began frantically searching through his car.

"What's wrong? Did you lose something?"

"Yeah. Could you do me a favor and look beneath your seat?"

Charmaine began her search. "By the way, what am I looking for?" She then felt a soft mushy plastic object and declared, "Oh, this must be it." She pulled out a one-pound bag of strawberry Twizzlers, her favorite guilty pleasure food. "Oh, Xavier! You still remember!"

"How could I forget? All those times you made me drive to Walgreen's at 1:00 in the morning to buy you a bag of those things," he laughed.

"OK, so, I'm just gonna ask... are you seeing anyone these days?"

Xavier held up his right hand and said, "Does this count? Because if it does, I'm married with three kids, a dog, and a mistress named Su-Ying."

Charmaine laughed. This man still made her feel complete.

"And how about you?" he inquired. I hear there may be someone serious in your life?"

"Leave it to my big-mouthed girlfriend to just put all my business into the street," she blushed. "Well, OK, yeah, there is someone, but to be honest with you, I'm not sure exactly how serious we really are. I mean, he's a great guy. But something just feels strange."

"Well, I gotta tell you, Char, this right here feels mighty great to me."

("You've got that right.")

Inside the theater, Xavier waited until after the movie's opening credits disappeared from the screen, then leaned back into his seat and brushed his leg securely up to Charmaine's. She made no attempt to stop him, and furthermore placed her hand upon his thigh, coaxing a peaceful exhale from his person. It all felt so good, like old times.

After the movie ended, they engaged in fast-moving, exhilarating conversation about their present lives, and reminisced about prior days as he drove her back to her apartment. Once they arrived, he walked her to her door.

"What a great afternoon. Thanks, Xavier." She searched for something else to say. "...So it was nice of you to get Andy to do the reception."

"Thank you." He gazed into her chestnut eyes. "I had a really good time today, Char."

"Hey, me too. I can't tell you how long it's been since I've been able to just chill with a normal guy, you know?" She found herself struggling for words again. "It should be fun being roommates, huh? I really am so sorry about your house..."

Xavier slightly bent his knees to level his face with hers, and with capable grip, cupped her hips into his large strong hands. He kissed her, slowly lifting her off of her feet to join him at his own height. Charmaine wrapped her arms and legs around his body and squeezed with formidable selfishness, kissing him as they leaned ambitiously against her front door. Her custom-made lover had returned. She had once again found complete bliss.

"May I come inside?" he whispered.

"Yes..." she panted. Then her eyes opened. "Wait a minute. No."

He placed her upon the stoop and stepped back. "I'm sorry."

"For what?" she challenged. "You didn't do anything I didn't want you to. Hell, if I had any sense, I'd be naked by now. But how about we exercise some restraint, at least 'til later? I'll see you at Kari's, OK?"

Xavier nodded his concurrence. "It's great to have you back in my life again, Char. I've missed you so much."

"See you tonight."

Charmaine entered her apartment, closed the door and leaned back up against it, wearing a satisfied grin. That is, until she looked around at the disaster area that was her soon-to-be-vacated apartment. She checked the messages on her machine. The first had been left by Evan the night before, begging her one last time to reconsider her decision to interview at Hilltop *("Let me teach you how to really save lives, Charmaine. And make real money.")*. The second message was Karianna wanting to know how the date went *("Did you guys elope?"),* and asking exactly what time she would be moving in that evening.

Charmaine erased both and dialed the phone. "Hey, Andy, is Kari there? Well, could you ask her if it'd be cool for me to just come on over in about half an hour, then move the rest of my stuff in tomorrow? Oh, great! See you soon, then – I've got another call coming through." She clicked over to the other line. "Hello?"

"It's your mother."

"Hi! Where have you been lately? And what's up with your phone line? Is it being worked on? I keep getting a busy signal when I call."

"*Nobody answered the phone because I have a new number,*" Mrs. Parker said.

"Well, I hope it's easy to remember because you know how long it took Dad to memorize the last one you guys had…"

"*No, Charmaine. I have a new number. I've left your father.*"

February 15ᵗʰ, 2010: 9:29 p.m.

A freshened Xavier walked up to a very handsome man on the corner of Church and 17ᵗʰ streets in the heart of Midtown, Nashville's up and coming trendy new gay-forward district.

"Hi, Miguel."

"Hello, Xavier."

They walked two blocks south on Church to Blue Café. Miguel held the door as they walked inside. The restaurant reminded Xavier of one where he and Charmaine used to meet for lunch between classes. That restaurant was gone now.

A bubbly red-haired singer-slash-waitress jaunted over to their table and took their drink and appetizer orders. Xavier stared out the window, losing himself in the vehicular activity of the busy intersection just feet away. Suddenly he noticed that he hadn't said much. He looked up to find the attractive man gazing at him and smiling eagerly.

"What is it, Miguel?"

"Oh, nothing. You're just so good-looking. You know I'd love nothing more than for you to stay with me as long as you need to." Miguel was an olive-complexioned gentleman with slightly salt and pepper hair, about two inches shorter than Xavier.

"It's OK," Xavier replied. "I've got a place to stay. But I do appreciate your generosity. I know that it's sincere."

"Perhaps I'm trying a little too hard, huh?" Miguel smiled and caressed Xavier's hand.

Xavier looked into Miguel's dark brown eyes. "No worries. Listen, I'm sorry about cutting it short yesterday. I had the reception to go to…"

"You don't have to explain. You're a grown man. You don't have to answer to anyone but yourself and God."

The statement annoyed Xavier. "God, huh? You still worship that guy?"

"You don't?"

"Well, I must admit that over the years, I have had my doubts," Xavier answered. "But all in all, my faith is still pretty strong. It's just hard to believe that someone who's done the things you have, actually has the courage to worship somebody who can make you pay for all of it. I suppose I'm impressed by your cajones."

Miguel pressed up to the table between them. "Xavier, I know that what I did to you was wrong. And I'm also aware that you've been hurt more than your share in life. I just want to try to make it up to you. Please don't be upset."

It was too late. "You'll just have to pardon my behavior. I get a little bitchy when I've been abandoned, ignored, and neglected for thirty-two years."

"What can I say, son? I'm sorry…"

"Well for starters, don't say that," Xavier snapped. "I'm definitely not ready to hear *'son'* come out of your mouth. He then stood up, reached into his pants pocket, and placed a twenty dollar bill onto the table. "I realize now that this whole thing was a mistake. I apologize for wasting your time. Good bye." He barged for the door.

"You really hate me, don't you?" called out Miguel, causing Xavier's trudge to slacken. "To tell you the truth, I think I'm actually relieved."

Xavier stood facing the exit sign.

"Shows you've got conviction," Miguel expounded. "I didn't even think you'd return my first phone call. But – and this is not an

excuse – I was very young when you were born. And your mother just dropped you off on my buddy's doorstep before disappearing for good. I had no clue how to be a dad. I was fourteen, for God's sake. And on top of that, I was running from the law. When I finally got out, I was afraid that after all that time, you wouldn't want to know me."

Xavier wiped his eye and turned back around to face his father.

"Look, Xavier, maybe one day you'll understand, maybe not. I don't exactly have the highest of hopes at this point. I'm just thankful for the moments that I have with you now. Did you know that you have a brother?"

Xavier walked over to the table as Miguel pulled out his billfold and unveiled a picture of a boy. "You both have my forehead, unfortunately. His name's 'Xander'. He's thirteen."

"He's very handsome," Xavier marveled, staring avidly at the picture of his brother. His little brother. Two weeks ago, Xavier had no one, was nobody's child. And today, he now had a father and a brother: people whom he could call, 'Family'. "Guess we'd better order, huh?"

Miguel smiled.

"You've done what?" Charmaine blurted, nearly dropping the phone.

"You heard me. I left him, finally," Mrs. Parker said. *"Best thing I ever did. I just couldn't take it anymore."*

Charmaine was stupefied. "Take what? What could he have ever done to make you do something like this?"

"Girl, I'm still your Mama, so don't be talking to me like I'm Karianna."

Charmaine sighed. "You're right, Mother. And I apologize. But you have to understand… I mean, I knew you had your problems,

but every married couple does. Heck, I even knew that he's been sleeping in another bedroom…"

"Another bedroom in another house, Charmaine."

"Huh? What are you saying?"

"Exactly what you think. Your father is cheating on me, and I'm not playing Bubu the Fool no more. I'm sick of it. So I packed up all my things, and I moved myself the hell up outta that house."

Charmaine was astounded. Her parents had split up after thirty-one years of marriage. The news sent numerous chills of confusion spearing throughout her body. She felt sick. What was happening to her life? In less than twelve hours, she'd lost a job offer, gotten evicted from her home, reunited with an ex-lover, found out that her father was cheating, and learned that her mother had moved out of the house she grew up in.

"Are you still there?"

"Yes, Mother, I am."

"I realize that this may be a lot for you to take in right now. I thought about coming over and telling you face-to-face, but the cable man is on his way and I'm still unpacking."

"It's OK."

"Write this down: '615-555-1517'. That's my new number. I don't know what your father's is yet, but I'm sure he'll call you once he gets it. I'm about to call Karianna next."

"I'm sorry Mother," Charmaine posed, "But I have to ask you this: are you *sure* you aren't just dreaming up this whole 'cheating' thing? I mean, you do sometimes have a tendency to draw conclusions before all the facts have been gathered…"

"…Oh, so now I'm stupid?"

"No, Mother, that's not what I'm saying…"

"I tell you, you push her through your cooch, rippin' yourself to smithereens in the process…"

Charmaine knew what was coming next. It was a speech she'd already heard many times, and would likely hear at least as many in the future.

180

"...Then, you feed her, raise her, give her the best home trainin', send her off to college, and one day, she just up and decides that you're an old nut."

"Mom..."

"I can't believe you would even think of doubtin' me while that low-life is probably somewhere out in the streets right now with his ho."

"I don't doubt you. But what gave you the impression that Dad was cheating in the first place?"

"What else? I saw 'em walkin' into some restaurant out in Hermitage, just a-kissin' and carryin' on. It made me straight ill. Took all I had not to run 'em both over."

"When did all this happen?"

"A few years back right after my second cataract surgery."

"Are you positively sure you saw what you think you saw? With the eye patch and all the medication?"

"I saw that she was puttin' her mouth all over my husband's face. That's what I saw."

"So have you approached Dad?"

"No."

"Why not?"

Mrs. Parker paused. "Because it's embarrassing, Charmaine. I just couldn't bring myself to do it. He chose somebody else. I'm not good enough for him anymore."

Tears welled in Charmaine's eyes. "Don't say that, Mom. Are you sure he's even still seeing her?"

"No, but he doesn't love me, so it don't matter. What am I gonna do Baby?"

Charmaine was completely numb. "I don't know, Mother. I just don't know. Would you like some company?"

"Naw. I've got lots to keep me busy over here. But I live about six miles from the house. Maybe you can come over sometime this week... if you don't have other plans?"

For the first time in her life, Charmaine heard vulnerability tremble from her mother's lips. It both touched and scared her. "Yeah, Mom, sure."

"So have you found yourself a job yet?"

"I'm still working on it."

"*Well, you need to start workin' a little harder, else they're gonna throw you right up out of that apartment. And I won't be able to board you, 'cause soon I'll be living my own life, if you know what I mean.*"

Charmaine knew. The mere thought tickled her.

"*Don't laugh. There are plenty of men who want me. I've just been trying to be the good and faithful wife. But forget that now. I'm 'bout to get buck wild. Make up for lost time.*"

"You work it, honey!"

"*Well, I have to make some more calls. I'll check back with you tomorrow.*"

"OK."

"*All right. I love you, baby.*"

"I love you, too, Mom."

After finishing their meal, Miguel and Xavier, father and son, walked outside toward the spot where they'd begun their evening. Xavier had enjoyed listening to Miguel's story of his road from being a homeless boy, to a convicted felon, to becoming the president of his own successful carpet cleaning company. Xavier was impressed, proud and inspired by his father's unwillingness to give in to adversity.

Charmaine fumed behind the wheel of her Maxima as she sped down Interstate 40 toward Karianna's house. Her head still

in a fog, she was absolutely furious. "I can't believe that dog! How could he do that to his own wife?" Charmaine was quite familiar with her mother's ability to test anyone's nerves, but why couldn't he have just divorced her? Oh, the things she was going to tell him whenever he decided to call. She looked up at her low-floating gas gauge and thought it prudent to stop and refuel. So she exited the freeway at Church Street and pulled into the Mapco Station across the street from the laundromat. It was late, and they knew her there.

While waiting for her gas tank to fill, Charmaine took in the scenery to try to take her mind off things. Just across the street, she caught view of a man who looked amazingly similar to the man with whom she had spent her afternoon. Determined to find out if it was indeed Xavier, she raised her hand in preparation to flag him down. Then, she saw someone else with him. Quietly, she watched.

"Well, Miguel, it's been... something," Xavier smiled.

"For me, a genuine pleasure. I know it's quite early for this, but here's my address."

Charmaine looked on, inching toward the curb as the other man wrote something on a piece of paper and handed it to Xavier. She began feeling queasy again.

"If you ever want to come out to the house," Miguel continued, "We would really love to have you. Xander would pee his pants to meet his big brother. But it's up to you. Regardless of what you decide, thank you for tonight."

Charmaine watched the man's lips say:

"I love you, Xavier."

"Good-bye." They hugged.

Charmaine continued to watch with the concentration of a tigress on hunt. She did not hear the gas pump stop.

Then the man kissed Xavier. On his lips.

Hurt, shock, and fury exploded like boiling radiator coolant beneath Charmaine's skin.

The two men hugged once more, then parted ways.

Just steps away from his car, Xavier looked up to find Charmaine standing in front of him. She wasn't happy. She catapulted the

bag of leftover Twizzlers at his face, leaving him speechless and disconcerted as each of the bright red rods fell to the ground.

"I don't even know what to say," she said, "And I *know* you don't, so don't even bother!"

"Hey, Char, what's wrong…?"

"I can't believe it. I just can't motherfuckin' believe you, Xavier! You're actually doing this to me *again*!"

He began to realize what was happening. "Oh, no, let me explain…"

"I already know: Alexia wasn't quite man enough for you, so you had to go and get yourself some real dick? Why would you lead me on like this? You sadistic piece of cat shit! I'll be damned if I ever so much as look at you again!"

A crowd began to gather around them.

"Baby, please…"

"Fuck *'baby'*. Save that for the bastard you just kissed."

"You tell him, girl!" shouted a bystander.

"Listen to me, Char…"

"Xavier," she screamed, "I would rather slurp radioactive maggots from a dead cow's rectum than listen to your lyin' ass!" Then, with all of her venom-fueled might, she socked him in his jaw, causing blood to splash from his bottom lip. "I *hate* you!" she yelled, so hard that it burned her throat. "*Bitch!*" She rambled ferociously back to her car. "*Wait* 'til I tell Kari…"

"All right, now! Woo, woo!" yelled the crowd, as Xavier watched Charmaine walk out of his life.

Again.

Episode 18

Since Xavier and Charmaine would now be staying with Karianna, Andy elected not to do the same. There just wasn't enough room in that house to accommodate all four of them to any pleasant degree, he concluded. Besides, he had a plush suite awaiting him at the Union Station Hotel. So after hugging Karianna good-bye, he jumped into his taxi and instructed the driver to take him to it. As the cabby pulled off with fee and tip in hand, Andy walked into the lobby, noticing that the number of guests seemed to have greatly increased since that morning. He ambled to the front desk.

"'Peters'. Any messages?"

"Oh, there you are, sir," greeted the clerk. "We're so sorry for the inconvenience. I'll go get your bag. We have it right back here."

"Wait a minute, what are you talking about?"

"Your toiletry bag. Your manager left it here by mistake when he checked you out of your suite this afternoon."

As Andy's right eyebrow slowly elevated, his pulse followed. "Excuse me? My 'manager'?"

"Yes. The rather tall gentleman."

"My manager is in L.A. inkin' my next deal," insisted Andy. "So, what you're telling me is, you people gave all my shit to a total stranger?"

The clerk shuttered. "Mr. Niles, the gentleman was privy to all of your personal information, including your secret PIN code, as well as both of your aliases. He told our manager-on-duty that you'd suddenly been called away to New York for an important meeting, so you would no longer be requiring your suite."

185

"Well, somebody lied! And your hotel is in big trouble. I'm calling my attorney, as well as the Metro Nashville Police Department!" Suddenly, a sharp pain jolted from the base of Andy's skull to his right eyebrow. "*Ahhhgghhh!*"

"Mr. Niles, oh my God, are you all right?"

"Gimme my bag."

The clerk placed the bag on the counter. From it, Andy extracted three bottles of prescription pills. After shimmying the contents of each bottle into his hand, he swallowed three tablets and four capsules. He then looked around to find nearly everyone in the lobby monitoring his moves. "Wutch'yall gawkin' at?"

"Would you like a glass of water, sir?"

"I would *like* my *suite*. Complimentary, of course. Then maybe I'll forget about legal action."

"I'm so sorry, sir…we've given that suite to your manag- …I mean, the man who claimed he was your manager."

"*What?*" Andy, now shaking, lurched.

The clerk typed a few codes into his computer, then looked back up. "A *'Mr. Ishmael Caimbridge'*. Surely you must know him? He's out right now, but perhaps we could contact him and ask if he'll allow you into his suite. He left a number for you to call…"

Andy tried to relax via deep breathing exercises he'd learned while guesting on a talk show. "OK, look, I understand that things happen. So I have an idea. Just relocate him to a different hotel, and we'll call it a night, cool?"

The clerk nodded his willingness. But after typing a few more keys he looked up. "Sir, because the suite is in his name, he would have to approve the move himself. And every other hotel within a thirty mile radius is booked solid due to the gaming convention this week. Perhaps you could share the suite with Mr. Caimbridge, just for tonight. We'll be glad to pick up the tab for the inconvenience we've caused you."

The news rush-delivered additional concern to Andy's face. His eyes now moistening over, he gestured for the clerk to step closer so that he could speak more privately. "Please… please," he begged. "I cannot stay with that man. I really need somebody to just get him out of my suite. I'll even pay you double. Triple. Cash if you want."

The clerk could see the immense fear in Andy's eyes. "OK, sir, if you'd like, I'd be more than happy to check an area further out to see if a hotel has a vacancy. Perhaps up near the Kentucky border…"

"You know what? Fuck it. Just fuck it!" He knew exactly who had swiped his suite and his luggage. He knew why. And he dreaded the thought of what he might have to go through tonight to get them both back. Briefly, he considered just chalking it all up as a loss in order to avoid a potentially fearsome confrontation. But he knew that if that happened, the same scenario would only reoccur in some other city. Apprehensively, he picked up his phone and dialed it.

"I see you found your bag."

"Ishmael, please let me have my suite back."

"Gladly. I'm pulling in right now. Meet me up there."

Ishmael walked into the suite. Cautiously, Andy followed.

"So you decided to cancel our plans without telling me? That wasn't cool."

"We didn't have plans," replied Andy. "And I don't appreciate being stalked all the way to Nashville. Where is all my stuff?"

"In our bedroom where it belongs."

"It belongs to me. I'll just go get it…"

"You'll *just* sit down." With a firm sweep of his muscular arm, Ishmael flung Andy down onto the large white sofa, then sat next to him. His massive six-foot-eleven frame scared the young comedian.

"Please, Ishmael, I don't want to fight."

"Me, either. So, let me just take your coat so we can both get a little more comfortable."

"No. I need to go. I'm staying somewhere else tonight."

"With who? Emil?"

Andy looked up. "How do you know that name?"

"He left a message for you here. So, who the hell is he? Your other piece?"

"So what if he is? You and I are over. You have a girlfriend, and I told you that I don't play that game no more. If you're that desperate for some dick, find somebody on your team. Now please just give me my clothes and let me go!"

"Motherfucker..." Ishmael Caimbridge, point guard for the Miami Heat, seized Andy's throat with a grip that extracted liquid from his eye sockets and made him gag. "You do know I'll kill you, right?" he informed a flailing Andy, lifting him off the couch. "And nobody will ever find your little faggot ass, trust me. So basically it's like this, Drew: either you take off your fuckin' coat right now and act right, or I swear I'll just keep right on here squeezin.'"

Andy could not breathe.

Ishmael dropped him back onto the sofa.

"O-O- OK, I'm s-sorry," Andy gasped. "Can you... just take my coat then?"

"That's better, baby. See? You make me act so bad sometimes. I love you, Drew. I've never told anybody that. Not even my kids' mamas. Not even my bitch. Fuck that ho. You'll never be away from me. Ever."

"I know," said Andy, calmly. "Hey, could you fix me a drink? You know what I like, boo."

"Yeah, I do." Ishmael filled up a glass with Grey Goose vodka, brought it to him, and sat down.

Andy took a small sip. Then, with more swiftness than even he knew he could muster, he chucked the remaining liquid directly into Ishmael's eyes, smashed the glass onto the coffee table, then dug its jagged edges across Ishmael's scalp, causing thick rivers of blood to gush from the gashes.

"Aaaagghh! Bitch! You're dead!"

Andy grabbed his coat and bag and ran out of the suite and into the elevator. The immediate strenuousness of his actions was quickly wearing him out. He dove into another taxi. "Just drive,"

he begged, praying that Ishmael would not catch up to him. He pulled out his cell phone and pressed two buttons.

"Hello?"

"Can I still stay with you?"

"Sure, but you'll have to sleep in my room. We're going to bed, so try not to make a lot of noise when you come in. I'll leave the door open for you."

"OK. Thank you."

"You're welcome, Pup- – I mean Drew." She listened carefully for a moment. *"Are you alright? You sound out of breath."*

"I'm fine. Be there in a few minutes."

———————————

February 16th, 2010: 12:26 a.m.

Xavier arrived at Karianna's porch. Thoroughly exhausted, he had now run out of energy to do anything else that would delay his having to face Charmaine. Twice that evening he had tried to leave her a voicemail message, but she would only pick up, then immediately hang right back up. He could only assume that she ignored his three texts, as well. But now he was beat, and that sofa was calling his name. He opened the front door.

But she was waiting.

Xavier looked up to find a boot flying directly toward his head. He quickly ducked, then leapt back outside.

Charmaine watched as he drove off into the night. Then she climbed the stairs and cried herself to sleep.

———————————

February 16th, 2010: 7:38 a.m.

At the firm, Xavier dove right into his work to relieve his mind of the overwhelming events of the last two days. He decided to avoid contact with his friends for a few hours until he could get his head back in good order. He went to retrieve a glass of orange-pineapple juice from the kitchen. On his way back into his office, Ramon stopped him.

"Hey."

"Hi, Ramon. Thanks for coming in so early today to help me with this retrial. I know it's time-consuming, but we all appreciate you. You're on your way to being a great lawyer. Hope I never have to go up against you."

"Thanks, Xavier. I learn from the best," he replied. "Just a couple of things: first, I'm a little concerned about my performance in Emil's class right now. I'm doing OK, but I feel like I could do better, you know? I just don't know what to do to make it happen."

"Have you asked him?"

"Yeah, but he seems a little preoccupied. So I was wondering if maybe you could let me invite him to dinner here at the office one evening while we're working late. Maybe he'll be more receptive with his best friend around."

"You know, perhaps you're right. E can be a bit cagey when he's not around familiars. Look in my calendar and find a day for us to meet, the sooner the better. Then call him and set up the whole thing. He's always ready for Thai food. We'll just order in, and while you guys talk, I'll work."

"Thanks," smiled Ramon. "Oh, and if you don't mind, please don't tell him that it was my idea, OK? I don't want him to think that I'm trying to take advantage of either of you."

"No problem," said Xavier. "Now what's the other thing you had to tell me?"

"You have a visitor. A police officer. She's in your office."

"Thanks." Xavier walked in to find Officer Belinda Twostones sitting in front of his desk, her long wavy raven black hair now flowing over her left shoulder. Without it pinned up in a bun, he noticed that she was, in fact, downright fetching.

190

"Hello, Xavier Jonson."

"Hi," said a pleasantly startled Xavier. "To what do I owe this surprise?"

"I should've called first, but I was in the neighborhood and saw your car, so I decided to drop in." She placed his gold-plated Slinky back on his desk. "Is this a bad time?"

"No, not really. I was just about to call my friend Drexel. You remember him?"

"Yeah," she said. "OK, then, I'll be brief. You have a client: a Mr. Theodorio Beals? Goes by 'Theo'?"

"Yes, I do. May I ask why?"

"The Nashville Police Department has reason to believe that he's been responsible for three separate building fires in the Metro Nashville area in the past six weeks."

Xavier raised his chin slightly. "Wait a minute, Officer..."

"Belinda."

"Belinda, would I be correct to infer that you came into my office today to pump me for information on one of my active clients?"

"Well, yes."

"You've sure got balls. Oh – I apologize."

"No need for that," assured Twostones. I take it as a compliment. Look, Xavier, my partner and I have been on his trail ever since you got him that hung jury a while back."

"Oh, man," deduced Xavier. "*That's* where I knew Denelian's face from. You've had him planted outside this building for weeks, trying to get at Theo. And I suppose it was no coincidence that the two of you just happened to end up at my house the night it caught fire?"

"Considering the circumstances, we thought initially that Mr. Beals might have played some role in it."

"So, trying to lure me back to your house that night was just a rouse to get me to talk?"

"No, Xavier. Really, my intentions were pure when we met. I just wanted to help you." She crossed her legs and smoothed out her pants. "But if you really want the truth, quite frankly, I do find you extremely attractive. Believe me."

191

"I don't know if I can believe you. In just two minutes, you've shown me that you don't mind breaking the rules to achieve an advantage. I could report you, you know."

"Yes, I suppose you could." She revealed a vague smile. "But the bottom line is, whether you want to admit it or not, your boy Theo is a pyromaniac. And now, on top of that – and you didn't hear this from me, but – these days, some very valuable stuff is coming up missing from the crime scenes. We have reason to believe that he may now be working with a coconspirator. And with his mafia ties…"

"*Alleged* ties, Officer – Belinda. Nothing has been proven."

Twostones then stood up, causing her long shiny locks to now discover both shoulders. "Xavier, you can defend Theo all you want. He looks like a nice guy, but you and I both know the truth. And I don't care how good of a hotshot lawyer you are, my friend. I am going to bring him to justice, with or without your cooperation."

"You seem a tad confident, Officer," a kindled Xavier coaxed.

"I've handled harder."

("You sure about that?")

"We'll see. You sure do think like a criminal, I'll give you that. You don't seem to care about playing fair."

"Fair is overrated. I play to win."

Her confidence, and her scent, were intoxicating.

"I trust that you still have my number, counselor," she continued. "If you decide to use it, just know that whatever we end up discussing, or doing, is entirely up to you. You know where I stand." She picked up her hat. "Got me?"

There was a knock on the door. It was Ramon.

"I'll get out of your hair now," Twostones said. "I'm sure you have lots of hot-shotting to get to."

("I do now.")

Xavier smiled as he watched Officer Belinda Twostones walk out of his office. Somehow she managed to be both sexy and

menacing at the same time. Had he finally met his professional match? Life was continuing to become more complicated by the minute. He looked at Ramon. "Yes?"

"Sorry to bother you again, but this letter just came for you by courier. It's marked *'Urgent And Confidential'.*"

"Oh?"

"Here you go. And by the way, I've set up our dinner meeting for this evening. Emil has accepted your invitation."

"Uh-huh..." mumbled Xavier, staring at the peculiar envelope. "That's fine. Thanks, Ramon."

"You're welcome," Ramon responded with a savvy grin. "I'll just be heading off to class now."

Xavier opened the envelope, then sat down to read its contents:

> *Dear Xavier,*
>
> *I am writing you this letter because you are the greatest friend that I have ever had, and I want you to know how much I have appreciated it. Ever since the orphanage, you have been good to me even when I wasn't good to you, or even to myself, for that matter. Me always messing up, and you always cleaning it up.*
>
> *I won't beat around the bush. I have tested positive for AIDS. Not HIV. AIDS. It has already started killing me. The cancer I have has been eating away at my brain for some time now. I got the final results yesterday.*
>
> *I am dying, Xavier.*
>
> *But not from cancer. It is from my own hand. Twenty minutes before writing this letter, I injected a good amount of Nembutal into my blood stream. I should be dead within thirty minutes of completing this letter.*
>
> *I did a lot of crazy and unsafe things with a lot of people, X. And drugs, you know I did those. Shared needles sometimes. I could've gotten this virus anywhere, from anyone, so locating the source does not concern me.*
>
> *But I want you to know that I love you. And I always have. You have been a great friend, and I know that you will achieve everything you desire. You deserve it.*

Live well.

Drexel

P.S.: My closed-casket wake will be this afternoon at 4pm at Wills Funeral Home near Fisk University. I'm sorry I wasn't able to give you more advanced notice. But my insurance won't cover everything if I wait too long. I hope that you can come.

You are my hero, man. Take care.

Please destroy this letter immediately after reading it.

Xavier felt as if his chair would engulf him. Struggling for air, he heard each of his tears thud down onto the letter, blotching its ink to near illegibility.

"I love you, too, Stephen."

Xavier sat inanimate for five minutes. Then he picked up his phone and called his home phone for messages. There was one from his insurance company, and one more from Karianna:

"Xavier? Where are you? Baby, are alright? I missed you this morning. Did you check into a hotel last night without telling me? Call me. Bye."

He wiped his eyes, blew his nose, then called her direct line at the clinic.

"This is Karianna."

"Hey."

"Where were you? I was worried."

"I spent the night in my home office."

"Doesn't your home have a big ol' hole in it?"

"Yes, but the damaged areas are sealed off now. They start the repairs in three days."

"Good."

"So... I suppose you've heard."

"Heard what?"

"Charmaine didn't tell you about last night?"

"I haven't seen her yet. She was already gone when I woke up. She's probably taking the job hunt into overdrive. What happened? You get her pregnant?"

"She caught me with someone else."

"*Again? Xavier Nathaniel Jonson, do you just get off on this sort of thing? What's wrong with you?*"

"It was my father."

"*Don't blame him for your evil ways,*" she admonished. "*You need a good whoopin'. And some therapy. I am simply amazed that you...*"

"No, baby, that's who she caught me with. My father. She just doesn't know it yet. She wouldn't give me the chance to tell her."

"*Really? Sugar, you didn't tell me you finally found him. You didn't hit him, did you?*"

"No, Kari."

"*Well, come to think of it, I'm kinda glad you made her mad, 'cause I just sanitized all my sheets.*"

"You're crazy," laughed Xavier.

"*And you love me for it. Anything else?*"

"Yeah. I need a favor. It looks like I've got a wake to attend later today. I was wondering if you'd come with me."

"*Depends on who died.*"

"Drexel."

"*Oh, my God. Of course I'll come. What happened? How... Xavier? You still there?*"

Xavier was beginning to feel very uneasy. He didn't know the exact source, and chose not to bother her with it. "I'll tell you once we're there. It's at 4:00 at Wills. I'll see you?"

"*You know it. Bye, luv.*"

They hung up.

The uneasy feeling gave way to shortness of breath. His chest began to tighten as sweat poured down his forehead, completely drenching his collar, chest, and back. He pulled off his tie and unbuttoned the top two clasps of his shirt in an attempt to push more air into his lungs. He unfastened his cufflinks and rolled up his sleeves. Suddenly, the burning house, the newfound father, the big retrial, the scornful ex-girlfriend, the tempting policewoman, and the dead childhood friend were all there in the room with him.

Xavier was having a panic attack.

———————————————————

February 16th, 2010: 9:57 a.m.

It was time for Professor Hubbard's French 226 class. The large room quickly filled with throngs of students anxious to find out their exam grades. Emil walked in and pulled the tests from his leather bag. "Bonjour, classe!" he piped.

"Bonjour," replied the class in monotone drone.

"Allaient comment vos week-ends?" he inquired as he passed out the tests. Though he tried soliciting individual responses from several students, most were obviously only interested in finding out what grade they'd received, so Emil just shut up and handed them out.

As a song of "Yays", "Cools", "Sweets" and "Damns" leapt from the crowd, Ramon sauntered into the room and right up to Emil.

"Gimme."

Barely retaining his poker face, Emil searched through the pile of leftover exams and placed Ramon's in his hand.

Ramon walked to the back of the room and sat in the far corner, positioning himself to be visible only to the professor. He then slowly scrunched down into the chair.

Emil was determined not to submit to Ramon's raw oozing sexual power today. He struggled to organize his thoughts and retain his composure...

Ignore   Ramon.

Ramon.   Fine-ass

Forget

…while discussing the correct exam answers with the class. "Alors, commencons avec numere un: '*Patrick will have been late for school when his mother arrives home*'. Natasha, what did you have?"

As Natasha read the correct response, Emil noticed that Ramon seemed to be sliding one of his hands beneath the waistband of his pants.

Aloud, the students continued reviewing the exam, some of them asking Emil questions along the way. Emil obliged them with his knowledge, attempting not to stutter. But stupendous Ramon was sitting right there, licking those soft thick pink lips and stroking that big beautiful brown dick, enjoying Emil's disoriented reactions.

French was the last thing on Emil's mind now. He could no longer hear any of the students' questions. And though he refused to even look in Ramon's direction, he still saw only the young quarterback. After a few moments of baffling silence, the students began to wonder what had suddenly happened to their…

"Professor? Professor? *Professor Hubbard?*"

Emil exited his stupor to find ninety-three students staring up at him. "Huh? Oh! Yes. Remember, it's the past participle."

They continued to stare.

"Excusez-moi; I will be right back." Hiding the crotch of his wool slacks with his Franklin Planner, Emil rapidly hobbled out of the room.

The classroom buzzed with amazement.

"Oh, my God. Did you *see* his hard-on?"

"Honey, you could see that big ol' thing from Mars, OK?"

Minutes later, a slightly less-disoriented Emil reemerged. "Are there any more questions?"

Though his inquiry received no response, quite a few impressed giggles welcomed him back.

"Alright. I will let you go early today. Read pages 89 to 115 in your blue books for Wednesday and complete all of the exercises for your TA's," he hurriedly instructed. "And remember, your papers are due next Monday by 3:00 in my office. I haven't heard from too many of you, so I'm assuming they're going well. Au revoir."

197

"Au revoir!"

Ramon walked out the door amongst the others. At last, he had permanently cracked Emil's hard and determined shell.

"Tonight, it's on."

Episode 19

Xavier and Karianna walked into Wills Funeral Home. The Jones Suite was packed with Drexel's friends and acquaintances, some in tears, and others sitting calmly while reading the eulogy.

"My goodness," she whispered. "How many people did he know?"

"For some reason, I'd always gotten the feeling that Drexel had many lives."

Karianna searched the room for two empty seats. Instead, she found Emil Hubbard standing outside the Jones Suite's south entrance, almost appearing to be hiding. "Emil?" she mustered.

Emil had no choice. He had been caught. So he walked up to them.

"I thought you didn't care for Drexel," said Xavier.

"Well, people apparently experience sudden changes of heart, right?" Emil responded, peering at Karianna.

Xavier and Karianna were flabbergasted to find Emil Hubbard at Stephen Drexel's wake; Emil: the guy who once publicly referred to Drexel as, "a virus with eyes". Why was he *really* here today? That was the question of the hour.

Until Charmaine walked in.

"Hello, everyone," she blushed. "Beautiful day, huh?" She sat down in the empty back row. "Get out of the aisle, you guys. You're being rude."

Emil, Karianna, and Xavier were now drenched in complete befuddlement. How did Charmaine Parker even know who Stephen Drexel was?

To avoid having to acknowledge her astounded friends, Charmaine and Emil faked an involved interest in the memorial service. But truthfully, all four were now too preoccupied to notice what was going on in front of the room.

"And now, let us pray," urged the speaker.

"Thank God," mumbled Charmaine.

———————————————

Moments after the wake, Xavier and Karianna found themselves completely abandoned of the others.

"I doubt that I could get any more confused than I am at this very moment," Xavier announced, swallowing two tablets he'd pulled from his pocket.

"What are those?" Karianna inquired.

"Just something my doctor prescribed me today for tension. Nothing serious."

"Uh-huh… So do you wanna go bully Char for information?"

"I think I should stay away from her for a while. She doesn't wanna see me right now. And I've gotta get back to the office."

"So, how about I talk to her?"

"No, Kari," Xavier instructed. "Do not say a word. I got myself into this and I need to explain the whole thing to her myself. I'll do it when we're at dinner tomorrow night."

"Xavier, our dinner is tonight. 'Monday', remember?"

"Oh, geez – right! I'm a wreck. I completely got the days mixed up."

"Well, don't try to use that as an excuse to bail. You are still coming, right?"

"Do you think I should? Because Char-…"

"Be there, Xavier. It'll work out. Please, I need you guys."

"Don't worry, gorgeous. I'll show up."

"Thank you. And if you ask me, you and she are just being silly as always."

200

"Since when do we ever ask you?" he heckled. "By the way, thanks for coming to this thing. I'm sure you got more than you bargained for, and then with Emil showing up…"

"Yeah, well I'd better get home and get ready. See you soon. I love you, boy."

"Love you too."

February 16th, 2010: 6:05pm

Xavier was stumped. How could he have been so absent-minded as to schedule dinner at the office with Emil and Ramon on the same night as dinner with Karianna and her new beau? Moreover, why didn't Emil mention it when Ramon called him to confirm?

"Because I forgot about Aisle C," said Emil. "I'd already decided that I wasn't going to attend."

Xavier was disappointed. "But Kari invited you. You know she wouldn't have done that if she didn't really want you there."

"Why? So she can rub her new boyfriend in my face? I think not. I'll just take home all of this wonderful take-out you ordered and have my own little private pig-out party."

"Well, actually…"

"Actually, what?" asked Emil.

"You won't have to party alone."

"What do you mean?"

"Hey, guys! Something smells good." It was Ramon, freshly showered and wearing Emil's sweat suit. "And I'm starving."

"I invited Ramon."

"What?!"

"Is something wrong?"

"Uh, no…"

"Good. Emil, there's way too much food here even for your greedy ass, so both of you can just dig in. I've got to get showered and changed for the restaurant."

"Wait, Xavier – you're not staying with us?" said Ramon.

"No, man. I'm sorry. I completely forgot about my other plans tonight, and they're kind of important. I could've sworn I'd put it in my calendar myself…"

"No, I never saw anything like that in there. But if you'd like, I could double-check…"

"No, that's OK. I've just been a little crazy these past few days. I've gotta go. You two enjoy yourselves. And don't worry, Emil. Our cleaning person is fantastic. She'll take care of any mess you guys make. Ramon, could you lock up when you guys are done?"

"Sure thing. Thanks."

"See you later, E. I'll tell everyone you couldn't make it. And don't forget you owe me an explanation about this afternoon… E?"

"Yes, uh, thank you. And give my love to Char, would you?"

"Sure, if she lets me within speaking distance," thought Xavier.

———————————

Ramon closed the door behind Xavier and locked it. He next inched slowly across the office to Emil.

Keeping his eyes aimed downward, Emil began to gather up the containers of food. He could feel Ramon's body percolating next to his own. "You knew Xavier had other plans," he snarled.

"Yeah, so what?" snickered Ramon. "He'll still get to his precious little dinner in plenty of time. I didn't jeopardize anything important."

"I wouldn't be so sure. You know I could get you fired," he weakly threatened.

"On what grounds, professor?"

Emil finally looked up at Ramon, who was well-aware that his sparkling white teeth were every bit as perfect as his awesomely-crafted body.

"…Forgetting a silly little dinner date?"

Focusing on the carpet again, Emil huffed, "All right. I'm going home now."

"No. You can't go." He stepped solidly into his teacher's path. "I need to talk to you about my upcoming paper."

Emil slammed the bags onto the conference table and sighed, "What about it? Do you have a topic yet?"

"It's not the topic I need help with," Ramon explained. "It's the research."

"What are you researching?"

"Sex."

Emil almost looked up, but didn't.

"My paper is called, '*The Sexual History and Practices of the Francophone Colonies*'. I hope that's OK. You've actually travelled to a few of those countries, right?" He swept his fingers up Emil's right bicep, pausing selectively at his collarbone. "So you could like… share your first-hand knowledge with me, right? Why don't you take a look at what I've got… then give me some pointers?"

Emil tried painstakingly hard to maintain his cool. "Look, Ra – mon *(hot Ramon)*, I don't…"

"I'm over here," Ramon teased, seating himself on the table.

"Why are you doing this?" Emil bled. "What do you want from me? I am your teacher!"

"True… so teach me something." He grasped Emil's right hand and balled it into a fist. He then unwound Emil's index finger and slowly inserted it between his lips. The manipulated moisture of Ramon's playful tongue was the stuff of Emil's deepest fantasies. Then, one by one, Ramon siphoned in each of Emil's remaining fingers, sucking

sucking.

Ramon would not allow Emil's gaze to depart his own again. He was eerily comfortable with his formidable power over Emil, and he was quickly convincing Emil to be, as well.

Emil's fingers were now glistening with Ramon's warm saliva. Ramon grabbed Emil's hand and coerced it downward into his

sweatpants, directly to his penis. He then manipulated Emil's fingers to massage him while he tilted his head back and enjoyed each subtle motion.

Emil enjoyed it too.

"It's not wrong to like me," coaxed Ramon. "I'm a big boy. Besides, who am I gonna tell?" He removed his shirt to reveal the chest, abdomen, back, and arms of a starting quarterback. He then pulled Emil's hand back up to his lips and began repeating his previous actions. Next, he guided Emil's middle finger directly to the threshold of his eager pulsating cavity.

"Um…" Emil stuttered.

Ramon kicked his sneakers off and gently tugged on the drawstring of his sweatpants to loosen the knot. He pulled them off – no underwear today. Once again, that honey-dipped body Emil had so many nights dreamt about stood completely naked in front of him, wanting to be handled.

Ramon kissed Emil's face and neck. Emil's aroused nature began to rear itself more prominently, enticing Ramon even more. He unbuttoned Emil's shirt and licked his entire chest, slowing down to worship his large nipples as a bliss-ridden Emil moaned heavily. Ramon then knelt down to the floor, unbuttoned Emil's slacks, reached into his boxers, and pulled out Emil's big, throbbing cock.

He licked it.

Emil dared not watch. He had only recently reestablished full credibility with his peers. If anyone were to find out about this, he would be ruined, this time for good. But Ramon's precious lips felt so marvelous wrapped around his pulsating branch. He did not want him to stop, and now wondered what Ramon's asshole might feel like.

"When's the last time you had some real fun?" Ramon exhaled, his Cuban accent becoming more pronounced as his excitement increased. He then grabbed the back of Emil's neck and pulled their lips to passionately adjoin.

Emil could remain passive no more. He pushed Ramon down onto the table, disarraying the bags of food in the process.

Then Emil ravished the beautiful athlete, grabbing his hard shaft and sucking it, rapidly, rabidly, worshipping it industriously, forcing him to shriek his untamable lust as he lay gyrating turbulently upon the table.

"Suck my toes," cried Ramon as he lifted his left leg and placed his size thirteen foot upon Emil's chest.

"Huh…?"

"Do it, man, now!"

Emil took hold of Ramon's left foot, admiring how delicate it was. He placed Ramon's big toe into his mouth and slowly began to suck on it, watching the incredible young man's body heave upward in absolute gratification. Emil was also now stroking his own jock as he dipped his limber tongue between Ramon's delicious cinnamon digits, devouring each one with the anxiety of a newborn on a fresh breast. Then Emil then grabbed his right foot. Ramon had now entered ecstasy, and Emil wasn't too far behind.

As Emil licked and kissed his right sole, Ramon stretched his left leg towards the ceiling and guided Emil's index finger to his tight hole.

Emil pressed inside of Ramon.

"Oh, yeah, yeaaaah – just like that, pa," cooed the grateful student.

Emil teased Ramon's orifice, moistening his middle finger and squeezing it inside as well. He relished the writhing hot Ramon's appreciative reactions. Then, Ramon reached down to his duffle bag and pulled out a condom and a small tube of lubricant. "Fuck me, papi," he begged.

Emil froze.

"Man, why are you stopping? I said fuck me!"

Emil, hesitant and unsure of whether he should actually execute his desires, pulled on the condom anyway.

"Don't worry, I can take big dick. Go!"

Then Emil entered Ramon. Eight months of fantasy fulfilled itself as he advanced inward, deeper with each moment, being careful, despite his excitement, not to injure the youthful god in the process.

"Ohh, papi… yeah! Tap that ass, pa!"

Emil was smiling. Widely. He had in his very hands a fine, glorious young masculine dude who loved dick. Even Emil's eleven-inch pipe wasn't too much for Ramon to accommodate. He thrust in and out of Ramon's grateful ass, monitoring the athlete's face for any evidence of discomfort, but only finding maximal pleasure.

"Yeah, yeah?" Emil taunted. "You like all my shit, don't you?"

"Yeah, daddy!"

"Then say it."

"I like it! *Amo su bicho gordo!* Déme mas! *Mas!*" His eyes remained focused steely upon Emil's. "Siente tan bueno!" he screamed, his spine still raised inches above the table, showcasing his spectacular chest. He used his muscular arms and quarterback hands to grab Emil's thighs and pull him even further inside him. He was sweating and wearing a smile almost as large as Emil's – but Ramon's was a tad more sinister. He liked being bad.

And that turned on Emil even more. He'd always known Ramon was hot, but not this hot. This guy was a stupendous lay – the kind that men have been known to leave their wives and families for. If more women could fuck like Ramon, more women would have men.

Ramon pulled both of his legs completely above his head and grabbed his ankles so that Emil could gain maximum entry. Ramon's feet now protruded over the edge of the table, and his wet pink impatient hole was fully exposed. Emil enjoyed the sound of each consecutive pop of Ramon's curled toes as his crevice greedily and repeatedly swallowed up Emil's colossal heat.

Unexpectedly, Emil began to wonder why he had not yet felt even a minimal urge to nut – he could probably literally ball with Ramon all night long without coming.

In one powerful fluid motion, he pulled out of the quarterback, flipped him onto his stomach, grasped his abdomen and lifted his body into the doggy position. Then he momentarily rested his monstrous piece upon Ramon's lower back, causing him to moan his endorsement of its gross poundage. Emil then grabbed Ramon's neck, swayed him into a headlock, and pushed back in.

"Ohhh, yesssss, babyyyy! Yeeeessss!" Ramon yelled in submissive gratitude, his accent now in full exhibition as his back aimed his firm muscular butt toward the ceiling.

But then...

Out of nowhere, Emil's thoughts shifted completely away from Ramon. And directly to Karianna.

Karianna. Who was at the Aisle C Restaurant. With some other guy. And Emil wasn't doing a damn thing to fight it. He was going to just let it happen. He was about to allow the only person he ever loved to just leave him. Probably for good this time.

Emil began to decrease. He stared at Ramon's back for a few seconds before admitting, "I'm sorry. I can't continue."

"What?" Ramon turned over. "What's the matter? Don't you like it?"

"Yes, Ramon, I really do." It's just... If you must know, I'm in love with someone else, and I have to pursue that."

"Love? What's that got to do with this?"

Emil was amused by – even somewhat jealous of – the freedom that Ramon's total lack of inhibition gifted him. "This? Nothing. That's why you and I are done here. Listen, I know you're young, and you wanna have fun. But I'm just not right for you. I'm sorry."

Ramon was baffled. But more than that, he was angry. He stepped off of the table. "Is this about that little white chick you like? I don't give a shit about her. She can have you, I don't care. I have a girlfriend, too. It doesn't matter." He stepped closer and planted Emil's hand upon his left butt cheek. "Don't you wanna do the stuff with me that you can't do with her?" He licked Emil's neck, up to his earlobe, causing Emil's heartbeat to again accelerate. "You can't seriously tell me you don't wanna keep on taggin' this, man." Then he stepped back somewhat, acquiring a devilish sneer. "...Or do you want me to fuck you? 'Cause that's wassup!"

"No, Ramon," Emil insisted. "I've made up my mind. Please put your clothes back on."

Ramon was now livid. "You know what – I'm so sick of your on-again, off-again shit! You are gonna regret this, *professor*," he vowed, while grabbing his clothes and yanking his bag from the floor. "Yeah, you can bet on it. You just wait 'til tomorrow." He

walked back over and stood directly in front of Emil. "Man, you are really sad. We could've gotten a good thing going. But you're nothing but a stupid pathetic loser. And guess what? You're about to lose a whole lot more."

"What are you talking about?"

"I'm talking about '*the Baptist minister and Vanderbilt professor sexually assaulting one of his students*', asshole!"

The comment caused a searing fear to asphyxiate Emil. "Ramon, i-if you spread a mendacious rumor like that, I'd instantly be ruined. I would lose both my jobs, my reputation, everything! I'd never be able to recover – I'd be completely washed up!"

"Yeah, bitch – I know," Ramon unyieldingly proclaimed while pulling on Emil's sweatshirt. "Shoulda thought about that before you fucked with me."

"Well, then… I'll just tell everyone the truth. See where your football career goes then."

"Like anybody's going to believe a fucking heroin addict."

Emil was shocked. How did he know? "That was years ago."

"Tell that to Human Resources, asshole."

"Ramon..."

"Bye, big guy. Oh, and remember to lock the door."

Ramon was gone.

And Emil was scared. Checkmated by the popular quarterback now hellbent on destroying him by morning, his entire life dangled before his eyes. What would he do now?

He left to find Ramon.

Episode 20

February 16ᵗʰ, 2010: 7:20 p.m.

Karianna was nervous. She had not been on a date since last March, and was beginning to reconsider whether accepting Christopher's invitation was a mistake. Sure, he was a good dancer, and not at all hard to look at, but did she feel anything for him?

"It's just the first date. I'll know more after tonight," she concluded.

The doorbell rang. It was Christopher, holding a beautiful floral arrangement. He kissed her on the cheek before escorting her to his car.

Andy and Charmaine had driven to Aisle C together, and arrived fifteen minutes early. Though the two old friends loved each other, they were thankful to have a greater selection of conversation partners when Karianna walked through the door.

"Well, hello there," sang Andy, admiring Karianna's new black dress and handsome date.

Upon Christopher's instructions, the hostess seated them and brought over a bottle of chilled 1996 Dom Perignon. Charmaine and Karianna were impressed.

"Oh, this is so nice," cooed Charmaine. "Marry this, honey."

"Now, I can order anything I want, right?" Andy established. "You ain't gon' be gettin' cheap on me?" His cell phone rang. "Excuse me," he said while walking to the restroom, as ever fancying the attention he gathered.

"Oh, honey," announced Charmaine, "Wait 'til I tell you what your friend Xavier did *last night*."

"C, I need to talk to you about that…"

"Ladies, would you like to sample the hor d'oerves?" offered the waiter.

"Ohhh…"

Chat would have to wait a bit longer.

―――――――――――

Andy ended his phone call. All of a sudden lightheaded and exhausted, he ran to the nearest sink and splashed water on his face.

"Sir, all you all right?" asked the attendant.

"I'm fine. Go away, please." He entered a stall, sat down, and reached into his shirt pocket for five small white pills, two red capsules, and a blue tablet. He swallowed them all.

―――――――――――

Moments later, Xavier pulled up to the valet station. After slipping his ticket into his jacket, he headed for the restaurant entrance.

As Andy rejoined his friends, Christopher inquired:

"So, Andy…"

"Drew."

"Drew, Karianna tells me you are a stand-up comic? That is very nice. Tell me a joke."

Andy looked to the door. "Xavier's here."

"Shoot," said Charmaine. "I can't believe that bastard actually had the nerve to come here after last night."

"Char..." said Karianna.

"What happened?" popped Andy. "Tell me!"

Just then, the head waiter approached the table and requested Christopher's assistance in the kitchen.

"Excuse me, please," he apologized while accompanying him. "I won't be a second."

As the hostess escorted Xavier to the table, she observed Karianna, Charmaine, and Andy gabbing tempestuously. "Well, your dinner mates appear to be rather preoccupied. Wonder what they're discussing?"

"Probably whose turn it is now to hold the eye."

Just as he reached the table. the band began to play "*Afro Blue*".

"Good evening."

"Fuck you." Charmaine leapt up to make her way to the dance floor.

Xavier followed her.

Andy, now on another call, snuggled his finger over the receiver. "What is she wiggin' about *now*?"

Karianna lunged for his phone, but missed.

On the dance floor, a joust was taking place. Charmaine's dance partner, a man whom she'd ripped out of his chair and away from his business colleagues to prevent Xavier from cutting in, was an awful lead. She ignored him and created her own fancy moves. She also ignored Xavier, who stood right next to them, attempting to talk to her.

"Leave me alone, Xavier."

Xavier then extracted a fifty dollar bill from his clip and held it in the man's face. Within three seconds, Xavier was Charmaine's new dance partner.

They were hot together, and since she relished the attention their snazzy salsa steps were beginning to accumulate from other diners, she did not try very hard to stop him.

"Hey, remember when we first started dating?" he asked. "In that dance class? We were pretty good, huh?"

"Yeah. I should've known right then your dumb ass was just a big ol' faggot."

He twirled her three times then dipped her so flawlessly that many onlookers applauded.

Disheveled and slightly out of breath, Emil was the next to enter the restaurant and walk to the table.

Karianna noticed that he seemed rather irritated and preoccupied, but declined to exhibit concern. "Hi, Emil. We were wondering if you were ever gonna show up. By the way, those shoes are hideous."

"Perhaps the left one would look more appealing protruding from your rear."

Andy hung up the phone and laughed, "Y'all are too much. Emil, you should just move into her house with all the rest of us. She might still have some room available on her right titty."

"Shut up, boy," they slammed.

––––––––––––––––––

"Char," Xavier urged, "You have to let me explain. What you saw, wasn't real."

"Wasn't real?" she repeated as their dance took on an increasingly sensual tone.

"Well, yes it was…"

Charmaine halted her steps. "Xavier, you're talking in circles again. You're a partnered attorney, for Pete's sake. Use the skills Vandy taught you."

"The man you saw me with last night was my father."

Charmaine took two uncalculated steps backward. "Your father? But you're an…"

Xavier pulled her back to him and led her directly into a spectacular cumbia. "For some reason I still can't figure out, he looked me up out of nowhere and called me last week." He twirled her again, four times. "We had dinner last night."

Charmaine hadn't felt so exceptionally exhilarated in months. They were now dancing up a storm. It was slightly affecting her ability to navigate his story. "So that man – was your long lost dad? He's cute. Is he married? I'm kidding. Have you told anyone? Emil hasn't mentioned…"

"I haven't told him yet. I'm still trying to process all of this myself. I never thought I'd actually meet my father. But now he lives practically ten minutes away from me. With his kid – my brother. And yes, he's single."

She gleamed.

"I've hated him for so long. But I can't anymore. I think I actually really like him."

"Well, from the looks of it, he's a great kisser," she teased.

"So…" He dipped her, this time very slowly. "You ask Emil about me, huh?"

"Look at them out there tearing it up," said Emil. "They really belong together."

"Yes, they do," Karianna sighed.

As Charmaine and Xavier weaved through the applause and back to the table newly refreshed, they noticed Christopher in the kitchen wearing an apron and stirring a batter of some kind.

"Isn't that…" Xavier squinted.

Karianna brushed a couple of stray hairs from her eye. "Um-hmm."

"Wow, even though he owns the place, he still helps out in the kitchen?" Charmaine chimed. "That's the mark of a real pro. He's so amazing."

"Hey, Emil – you're here!" acclaimed Xavier. "Changed your mind, huh?"

"Yes."

"Is something wrong?"

"No," he replied, struggling to relax.

"So, Xavier, I take it you finally told Char," said Karianna.

"Told her what?" Emil asked.

"Xavier's dad looked him up."

"Really? How long has this been the news?"

"About a week," Xavier confessed.

"A week? Xavier!"

"You know I was going to tell you, E. You're my best friend. It's just been a crazy few days. Now, can we just order? I'm starving after that romp."

Christopher rejoined them, and after everyone submitted their orders, he offered an apology. "We're short one cook tonight. Someone did not show up. Typical. *'Good help'*, you know?"

Emil twisted his lips at the dazzled, nodding Charmaine.

"So, Chris," began Andy, "...May I call you Chris?"

"Pher", he replied while dipping a slice of bread into olive oil.

"Whaa?"

"'Pher', as in "Chris-to-'PHER'. That's what everybody calls me. *'Pher'.*"

Karianna, Charmaine, Emil, and Xavier knew that it was imperative to not make eye contact now, or someone would surely laugh out loud.

But Andy resumed. "Well, 'Pher'..."

Emil directed his chuckles toward his lap. Karianna scowled at him while beginning to wonder about her date.

"...Do you always help out in the kitchen?" Andy asked after gulping his wine.

"Yes, yes. I must do that."

"That's wonderful," said Charmaine while grabbing his arm. "I just love this man."

A curious Andy delved even further. "So, why can't you just hire more people?"

"Andy!" Emil reprimanded.

"...Eh? Oh, no! Ha, ha! I see, you people think that I own this place. Oh, how humorous! Ha, ha, ha!"

Charmaine's smile faded. "Wait... you don't own this restaurant?"

"No!"

Emil's goal was clarification. "Oh, so you manage it?"

"Nope."

215

Confused and now somewhat annoyed, Karianna wanted answers. "OK. OKOKOK. What *do* you do here?"

"Is it not obvious? I am a cook. Right now I specialize in salad, but they are training me for dairy."

Another waiter requested Christopher's assistance.

"Excuse me," he grinned, turning to Karianna. "Duty calls. I'll be back tout suite, ma cherie." He returned to the kitchen.

"OK, let's go," she said.

Charmaine disagreed. "Aw, come on, guys, it's not that bad. It was just a little misunderstanding. At least he has a job, girl. But wait, does this mean we're going to have to pay for our meals? Ask him what his discount is. Girl, I hope they take ATM, 'cause…"

Andy freaked. "*Pay?* Oh, no, no, no! He said we wouldn't have to pay fa shit."

"Andy, you made more money last year than all of us combined," Xavier recollected. "What's your problem?"

"Yeah," agreed Emil. "You should be paying for all of us."

Andy air-kissed him. "I'll pay for you. How much for a hand-job?"

"Given your resumé, shouldn't we be asking you that?"

"Y'all, don't start," Karianna requested.

———————————

Dinner was now served and Christopher was back. "OK, no mo' botherins. Y'all gots me to ya'selves fo de ressa da nite."

Emil noticed his odd switching of accents. The others quickly caught on.

"Dey got somebody ta cuvva fo Jerome."

Karianna grew more alarmed. "Christopher, um, sweetie… are you talking differently?"

"…Huh? Oh, yeah, my axcint is gon.'"

"But, when I asked where you were from, you said Belgium."

"Naw, boo," he insisted while picking a stray piece of asparagus-seared lamb from between his teeth. "You axt where my *axcint* is from. Dey make us all speak wit a forn axcint here. I guess dey think it look mo wurlly or sumthin. So I chose South Belgian. Erry now an din, when I go out to pawties an' funerals an' shit – I brush up on it to..."

"Impress da bitches?" Xavier assisted.

"Right, *ya feel me?*" Christopher winked. "I ain't from no damn Belgium. I don't even hardly know where dat is. I'm from Waco."

A caught off-guard Charmaine began to choke on a small chunk of filet mignon. She was coughing violently. Karianna slapped her back twice to help clear the debris from her esophagus.

"*Lord, Jesus,*" Andy honked.

Charmaine then rose from the table and grabbed Karianna's hand. "Please excuse us." They ran toward the ladies room, but on the way, Charmaine lost her ability to hold it in:

> "*Ha-haaaa!!! Haaaa!!!!* Ha, ha, ha! Oh, Karianna Cojoure, you are forbidden to ever date in this town again, girl!"

After dessert, as the friends waited for their vehicles, Xavier surrendered, "Well, it turned out to be quite an enjoyable evening. I really needed that. And hey, Christopher is cool."

"Yeah," agreed Andy. "Too bad he had to stay behind to vacuum."

A valet attendant approached Emil. "I'm sorry, sir, but we can't seem to get your car to start."

"Emmy!" Charmaine admonished, "When are you going to finally buy a new one? You make enough money, boy."

"So..." concluded Karianna, "My place, anyone?"

Episode 21

They climbed Karianna's porch stairs.

While unlocking her door, she urged, "Drew, help me with their coats, please. The rest of you, just make yourselves at home, as always."

Her guests siphoned in behind her and settled in the living room. Its awaiting coziness provided welcome respite from issues of late. Karianna powered on the radio and pulled the mini-bar from behind the kitchen door. Meanwhile, Andy would bravely battle the heft of Emil's tweed overcoat, then wince dejectedly at the sight of the six marijuana joints that tumbled out of its left pocket, onto the floor.

"Damn, dude. *Again*?"

"Emil! What is this about?" Karianna pressured, waving them above her head for all to see.

Charmaine prayed that he would have a solid explanation.

"It's not what it looks like. I confiscated them from two students last month and just forgot to dispose of them afterwards. Go ahead and flush them down the toilet, would you?"

Xavier swiftly sprung to his feet. "Unh-uhn! No! Give me one of those," he commanded, snatching a joint from Karianna's fingers. "You guys do not know the last few days I've had. I deserve this. Andy, throw me your lighter." Upon catching the handmade antique gold lighter, Xavier sat down, ignited the cigarette, then voraciously inhaled. "Thank you, *Jesus*!"

Tickled, the others filed to the mini-bar to concoct their own mood-tranquilizing elixirs. Within the next half-hour, Xavier, Charmaine, Karianna, and Andy would lie sprawling across the sofa

219

and living room floor, puffing and passing. The air grew foggier and more opaque with each minute, thickened by the smoke of recreation. By the hour's end, the entire room had absorbed the bouquet of dried herb. Vanilla and cherry were now a thing of the past.

The friends laughed, gossiped, and appreciated the pacifying effect of the marijuana on their bodies and minds. Emil, the lone nonsmoker, nevertheless felt his body finally begin to unwind while stretched on the recliner in the corner. There, he sipped tea and sang along in his clear bass-baritone to Aretha Franklin's '*I Sing My Song*'.

"Wow, you guys…" Charmaine slurred. "I just can't believe it. No wonder Drexel was so friggin' O.C.D. about condoms. Most men I've slept with tried to invent reasons not to use one, but not him…"

"*What?*" they collectively rattled.

Charmaine flung her tendrils over her right shoulder and submitted her best pose of self-assurance. "*Yes, we did.* One year ago, back when he was still managing my building."

Karianna slowly sprouted a mischievous smile. She was impressed. Charmaine had actually managed to shock her tonight.

She'd shocked Xavier, too: "Drexel managed your apartment building? I thought he'd fallen off the planet before moving in with me."

"I think he wanted it that way." Charmaine took another hit. "He promised that as long as I didn't tell anyone where he was, he wouldn't raise my rent. I had no idea why, but I didn't think anyone would care. Why else would I have stayed in that apartment for so long?"

Andy snickered. "Hussy."

"And here we all thought Kari was the ho," laughed Emil.

"Don't judge me, you guys."

Andy chuckled while getting up to refill his glass.

"Look," Charmaine continued, struggling valiantly to execute proper annunciation despite the effects of the alcohol. "Drexel might've been a little different, but he was fine as hell. And, might I add: very talented. Besides, I hadn't met Evan yet, and I was horny. It'd been nearly nine months since I…"

220

"Stop tellin' all your bizness," scolded Karianna.

Charmaine giggled. "OK, let's change the subject. I can see some of us are getting a little uncomfortable with this one."

"You tell 'em, slut!" Andy shouted.

"I have an idea," she suggested. "We used to play this game back in college. We'll start by everyone answering this question: 'Name the card game that best represents your love life.' I'll go first... um, probably 'Solitaire.'"

"I'd say it's more like 'Old Maid'", said Andy.

"Boo, hiss!" smiled Emil.

"Shut up, Andy. What about you, Xavier?"

"Hmm... These days? 'War.'"

"Ooh!" they blared.

"Well, mine's easy," volunteered Emil. "Hangman."

"Uh, that's not a card game, bruh," argued Xavier.

"Oh, yeah, you're right."

Andy faintly chortled, "He must've meant 'Hung-man'. Kari, your turn."

"Let me see..."

"Connect Four," blurted Emil.

"No, Neanderthal, that would be your friend, Alexia. And don't they have card games in Afghanistan, 'cause you ain't mentioned one yet."

"Ouch," agreed Xavier and Charmaine.

"OK, I've got it," Karianna piped. "I say... 'Uno.'"

"Good answer!" congratulated Charmaine.

"...Andy?" interrogated Xavier.

Andy sat still. He gazed off beyond his friends temporarily to reflect on his life as of late. He had not expected to come across so many things that disturbed him. Even amid all of his success, not very much had changed since the days of Richard M., Dream Maker. He was still barely escaping dangerous tricks with his life. And he was still scared. It briefly rendered him unable to speak.

"...Well?" Emil poked.

Andy raised his glass skyward, and with a hint of melancholy that would momentarily darken the room's mood, announced: "Gin." He then swallowed more liquor.

"So, E," Xavier coughed in an attempt to reclaim a more jovial atmosphere, "You never did tell us why you were at Drexel's wake?"

Andy spit up a tiny puddle into his glass. "Wait! Don't nobody say nothin' yet. Let me go pee first!"

Karianna glanced at him. "No spills on my new carpet. Don't make me send you back to Miami with a limp."

Emil took a large breath. "Stephen Drexel was my drug dealer."

The silence that immediately attacked the room threatened to deaden even the tones emitting from the radio. Andy, Charmaine, and Karianna apprehensively awaited Xavier's reaction: he was the only one Emil had never told about his heroin addiction.

"Drug dealer?"

"Yes. That's why Andy introduced me to Kari. I was a heroin addict, and I was losing my grip." He looked at Karianna. "She saved me, X."

Xavier had now risen to his feet, his mind already piecing together historical breadcrumbs that coincided with Emil's confession. "I remember that time… back when you looked really bad… and I wanted to ask you about it, but I was afraid you might get angry. I'd just broken up with Char and I couldn't risk losing… *mother fuck, E!*"

Emil walked to him. "Xavier, please calm down. I know that it was wrong not to tell you. You don't know how much I regret that."

Xavier ignored him. "I'm your best friend, man! I could've helped you! Why didn't you come to me?"

"Because in your eyes, I was still a hero. Please understand: I hated myself back then, and I needed to still feel like a hero to *someone.*"

Xavier surveyed the room harshly. "So I take it everyone knew about this but me? Some friends you all are," he frowned. "What else are you hiding?"

"You're one to talk," Charmaine shot while attempting to pull herself from the floor. "Oh…" she exclaimed upon realizing that at first effort, she could not.

"X, forgive them. I made them swear not to tell you. And none of them were privy to my dealings with Stephen."

"You can say that again," admitted Charmaine, now racing to the bathroom, beating Andy by only a few steps.

Xavier considered his friend's testimony while weighing the severity of his deed. All in all, he was just glad that Emil was OK. Deciding that no major harm had been done, he gave in. "Y'all lucky I'm high," he informed them while taking a seat next to Karianna. "Otherwise, I'd storm right out of here and take all the kush with me."

As the festive climate continued, Andy began to feel ill again. His right shoulder started twitching as his rapidly increasing body temperature dampened his forehead and neck. While patting himself down with a couple of napkins he moistened with the sweat beads from his glass, he slowly slid down the wall to the floor, being careful to eschew any jarring movements that might supplement the growing thud in his head. Unwilling to allow the others to discover his discomfort, he retained the smile on his face.

Xavier looked at his best friend. "I'm really proud of you, E. Here we were, smoking up a storm, and you didn't tweak once."

"It didn't bother me. Marijuana was never really my drug of choice anyway." He sighed introspectively. "I'm just happy to be here. I'd really missed this house."

"So, Emil," Karianna cordially inquired, "How's life these days? I hear you're still turning it out at Vandy. One of my colleague's nieces was in your class last semester."

"Everything's fine."

"And, how's what's-her-name – Haley?"

"Haley's gone," Emil replied. "She cheated on me nearly two years ago."

"Well, I'm sorry to hear that you two didn't work out."

"Please say you don't mean that."

Long ago, Karianna promised herself that she would never again look into Emil's eyes. They possessed too much power. Instead, when speaking to him, she would focus on his nostrils. Or his lips; maybe even one of his ears. That would still give the impression of direct eye contact. The plan had worked perfectly for two solid days. But *"Please say you don't mean that"* completely stole her grounding, causing her to stumble. She needed something to hold onto while she deciphered what he meant. Without thinking, she chose his eyes.

And fell right in.

It had been four years. And Emil had been waiting for her, quietly. But now he'd come for her; welcomed her back to him; beckoned her into his mysterious dark pools of cathartic freedom. He held her soul dangling midair.

Then he let go.

"I'll be back." He jumped up and headed into the kitchen.

"OK, what was *that* about?" Charmaine pressed.

Less than a minute later, Emil skipped back into the living room, holding Karianna's camera. "Everyone?"

They all turned around.

"Say cheese!"

"Oh, no, Emil!" Karianna laughed. "Stop! No, I look a mess!" She bolted for the dining room as Emil chased after her, pointing and compulsively clicking and flashing the camera in her direction. Like schoolchildren at recess, they raced around the table, laughing more enthusiastically upon each lap.

"I'm going to tell everyone, 'This is what she looks like when she's high!'"

"Give me that! Come on, Emil!" They playfully tussled, falling to the floor. "Emmy! Emmy, give it to me! Give it to me now!"

Charmaine turned to Xavier. "So much for that sabbatical."

Episode 21

Later, Xavier, Charmaine, Karianna, Emil and Andy sat quietly appreciating how composed their environment had become. They reviewed their lives of the present, interspersed with memories of the past, and some hopes for the future.

"Hey, what happened to us?" Charmaine said.

Karianna looked up. "What do you mean?"

"When did we get so... 'grown'? I mean, when we were younger, everything was so much simpler – at least it seems that way now... I wanna go back and start all over. Do you know Mom left my father?"

"What?"

"Yep. He's been with someone else. I know my mother is no catch of the day, but how could he just go and do that? And what kind of woman would allow herself to be a whore?"

"Charmaine, please don't call me a whore."

Episode 22

karianna cojoure and howard parker

"Hi, there! What brings you over here! It's great to see you! Come on in!"

"Hey, Kari," he said, walking up the stairs to her office.

Howard Parker had aged well, with the exception of the eternal "*Yes*" weighing down his brow. The tiny wrinkles in the corners of his eyes were very attractive whenever he smiled. Though dispirited, he was resiliently peppy tonight, as if his goal was to somehow not become depressed. He was examining his life.

"I was just straightening up," Karianna mentioned. "We ran early tonight. Can I get you something?"

"No, I know you're working. I just left Charmaine's, and just wanted to stop by and say hello. It's been a while. And since some people don't visit…" he joked.

"I am so sorry. Come here," she smiled as they hugged. "I'm just really busy, is all. I know that's a lousy excuse."

"Oh, come on now, you can tell the truth: you just don't wanna run into Ernyleene," he laughed. "She'll squawk your ear clean off about nothin.'"

"No, really that's not it. In fact, Char and I are trying to schedule a day to take Mrs. Parker shopping. But with her second cataract operation coming up, we may have to wait – which is fine, because this place needs all my attention."

Howard scanned the clinic. "Everything looks good to me. Seems like you're doing a great job. Are you sure it's not something else? You havin' man trouble again?"

"I don't have anyone." The impact of her statement shook her. She closed her eyes to recover.

227

"Are you OK?"

"Oh, I've just been running lately nonstop. I probably just need to eat something."

"Then let's go. My treat. It's still early. We can catch up. Besides, there's something I want you to see."

Ever since the night Emil left her to be with his fiancée, Karianna had prayed diligently for a diversion.

81 days

Seeking just a moment of peace from his clamant memory, she took on more projects around the clinic, baffling volunteers who would now sometimes arrive to find nothing to do to keep them there.

She enrolled in a 'Basket Weaving for Babes' class at the Y.

She bought and installed a cookware caddy above Xavier's stove.

Emil Hubbard

She took up doodling.

She organized a neighborhood task force. For another neighborhood. Her own already had one – she was president. Oh, and mental note: it was time to start working on her re-election campaign - elections were a short seven months away.

Karianna no longer enjoyed being home. Home hurt now.

Emil's voice used to bounce triumphantly off of each wall, even when he wasn't there. Now, the house seemed to have coldly forgotten him. If only she could do the same, just for an hour. One hour.

please

She was unable to silence his emotional renderings of a suburban Waterloo, Iowa childhood; his realization of a life-long dream to attain a PhD; his first day of teaching at Vanderbilt University.

She missed him listening. She missed him quietly absorbing her over tea after a long day at work; asking how she was feeling and clasping devotedly to her reply. She missed his eyes – Emil's laughing, consoling eyes – seeing her, protecting her from everything. His arms, *(oh)* she yearned to feel the faint stroke of the sweetly-scented hair upon those powerful, gentle arms, tickling her path to a delicious dream.

She prayed for a bad recollection of him. How she wished he stunk, or had acne. She tried to reduce him. But he was far too beautiful.

Would someone please erase Emil's fingertips from upon her shoulders? His lips from upon her back? His body from upon her body, making charged love to her...

Karianna had prayed for a diversion.

"Let me get my coat."

As they walked out of the clinic, Karianna searched for Mr. Parker's Ford Ranger pickup. He was always working on it, and she wondered what new gadget he couldn't wait to show her. But there was no pickup. She began to worry.

"Where did you park?"

"Right here," he replied, pointing at a brand new black Cadillac Escalade.

"Wow! When did you get this?"

"Last week, for my fiftieth birthday," he proudly answered, escorting her inside. "I figured I deserve it. I'm semi-retired now, and I can use it for my fishing trips."

"It's great," she said, admiring the heated power leather seats, tinted windows, moon roof, dash-mounted voice-activated television-navigation system, and room to comfortably seat eight. "It seems to have everything."

"Yeah, it's loaded." He pushed the 'start engine' button.

"You know, I must say I never figured you for the 'rims type', but yours are bangin'!"

"Thanks." He pulled away from the curb. "I didn't even know that half these options existed. But I wanted to try some new things. And I got a great deal, so..."

"What do Char and Mrs. Parker think?"

"Charmaine loves it. Already wants to know when she can borrow it."

"That's our girl," Karianna giggled.

"Erny told me to return it."

"Oh... well, maybe after you take her for a drive..."

"Thing is, I started to do exactly what she said, just to keep the peace as usual, you know? I was actually behind the wheel, driving back to the dealership, and then something happened. I just pulled over to the side of the road. I couldn't do it, Kari. Not again. I've already sacrificed so much to keep her satisfied."

Karianna listened.

"All I wanted," he continued, "Was something of my own for once. And I was expected to give it up – just like that. But I couldn't. That may sound selfish, but..."

"No. That doesn't sound selfish to me at all."

"So I made a u-turn and drove right back up into my driveway. Erny hasn't said a word to me since. She just gets on the phone with who-knows-who and blesses me out for hours. I tell ya, if I'd known that was all it would take to get her to stop pestering me, I'd have done it years ago," he joked sorrowfully.

"Well, I'm sure that things'll work out."

"I don't know, Kari. It's gotten real bad. I'm sure Char's told you we're in separate rooms now?" He looked across the street while stopped at a light. "Italian sound good?"

"Yes."

After ordering her meal, Karianna advised, "You know, maybe you two should try counseling? I could hook you up with a really good professional..."

"I've already tried that. Frankly, I think she's been convinced for a long time that we were a mistake. The only thing I've ever done right in her eyes was give her Charmaine. Sometimes I think she may be right."

"Hey, you should never talk like that. Don't make me have to give you one of my infamous lectures."

"You know what?" Howard shifted, "I wanna talk about what's going on with you?"

"Well, I'm just living... trying to stay on point. I recently had a little bump in the road with a guy, but I'll be fine."

"All those years of breaking hearts finally came back to bite you in the bottom, huh?"

"Yeah," she replied. "Took out a big ol' chunk. None of my panties even fit me right anymore. Oh – I'm sorry! My mouth!" It felt so good to laugh.

"No need to apologize to me. You're funny."

"Two '*Leonardo's Specials*,'" announced the waiter, placing their entrees on the table. "Can I get you guys anything else?"

"No," they smiled. "Thank you."

"You're welcome. Enjoy!"

As they ate, Howard looked up to see the smile on Karianna's face had faded.

"Kari, what's wrong?"

"I can't find my key again, Emil. This new purse is just too big. I need to switch out."

"I'll just use my key. Here, let me... Ta-da! After you, baby... If you want, head on up and I'll get the bath started.

"Yes, Professor."

"Karianna!"

231

"Oh – hey. I'm sorry. It's been a long day I guess. I'm still processing some things."

Howard grabbed her hand. "You know, you shouldn't lie. Particularly not to old folks."

"Don't say that. Fifty is the new thirty. And you look great. I've always seen where Char gets her looks. I just might have to call Mrs. Parker myself and try to talk some sense into her head before some new woman tries to snatch you up."

"Do that at your own risk."

"Well, I had a crush on you growing up," she grinned, "So I'm sure that someone else potentially could."

"Wait, you had a crush on me?"

"Well, it was more like, 'on your photograph'. The one you guys kept on the end table, with you in uniform. You look so great in that. Since you weren't in the States much, to me that picture basically *was* you."

Howard became pensive as he monitored a family birthday celebration across the room before admitting, "Yeah, I was away more often than not. I'm sorry."

"For what?" she queried. "You haven't done anything."

"I wasn't there enough for you, Char and Erny. I just sent money home and left Erny to raise you both by herself. Seems like I went overseas and when I got back, you were all grown up." His vocal began to crumble. "Funny, it felt like I was doing the right thing at the time."

"You were. You took care of us, as well as your country. Char and I understood, and we were proud.

"At least I got to catch up with her after my final tour. But by then, you were heavy into your pageants, and with all the traveling you were doing…"

"It's like we never really even got a chance to know each other."

"Yeah." He lightened up. "But Erny did fill me in over the phone. Trust me, I still knew what was goin' on."

"I bet you did," she laughed.

"That is, of course, everything but the 'crush' part."

They enjoyed their entrees.

"So, ya wanna drive it?"

"Hmm...? Me drive this big ol' thing? No, it's wet out here. I don't wanna kill us."

"Please," he insisted. "It has traction and stability control, plus all-wheel drive. You couldn't wreck if you tried. Come on, take the wheel." He jingled the fob in her face. "You know you want to."

An increasingly interested Karianna considered his proposal. Finally, she broke. "Give me that." As she landed in the driver seat, it adjusted her position perfectly via a few quiet whizzes from the controls. After tinkering with the rearview mirror, she shifted the transmission and slowly pulled off.

Within minutes, she was totally comfortable behind the wheel. Driving through Nashville, she was awestricken by how well the behemoth handled. "I thought it would be hard to adjust to," she admired. "But this feels almost just like what I'm used to."

"I know. Isn't it great?" He was now, per her validation, even prouder of his purchase.

"I can't believe she told you to take this back. I mean, no disrespect to Mrs. Parker, but I probably couldn't have returned it either."

"Maybe you should get yourself one. Then we could race."

"Oh please, you'd definitely win. Char is the one who drives like a bat outta hell. Oh, and this system is nice. May I?"

"Go ahead."

Karianna flipped through the satellite radio channels, thoroughly enjoying the sounds enveloping her from sixteen separate tweeters and woofers. She stopped at a classic jazz station. It did not take long for the song to pull her into a melancholic trance.

"Oh, this is my one of my favorite composers," Howard cited.

"Me, too. Thanks for bringing me here. You always seem to know exactly what I like."

"You're welcome. Happy birthday, Kari. I love you."

"Emil... Please don't ever leave me. I mean it. Ever."

"Don't worry. I'm yours forever."

"Kari slow down, there's a stoplight here!"

Karianna jumped out of her trance and slammed on the brakes. Recognizing her negligence, she pulled over to the curb and parked, causing the lamp above them to illuminate. Staring blankly out the window, she sat as still and quiet as that day inside Bu. Howard watched carefully, now knowing that something was definitely wrong. He didn't say anything, but instead stood guard in case of an emergency.

"I'm sorry. I guess I got a little carried away," she laughed. Then, deciphering Howard's concern, she realized that suddenly she could no longer mask her despair. Her vehement smile collapsed into two unstable lines that felt like they would encircle her entire head. She lost it. She could not stop her tears from flushing down.

"Oh, noooo, come here," he insisted, gently pulling her quaking body over to his, causing her legs to sweep up onto the seat she once occupied. "It's OK. It's OK, baby. See? We're all right. There wasn't anybody at that intersection anyway." Unsure as to her condition, he waited before asking, "What's really the matter, Kari? Please tell me."

"I… Th-there's s-someone," she sobbed. "The guy I told you about. We used to be to-geh-eh-ther, but he left… We… I loved him so much. But he went back to his fiancée and I don't know if he's ever coming back. I thought I could just get over him. But I can't. It's been almost three months and I still can't stop thinking about him. I don't know what to do. Nobody else knows this, not even Char. But I'm about to crack wide open, I can feel it. I miss him so much! He was perfect."

"I'm so sorry," Howard spoke, silently recounting his own turmoil.

"I know he's just a person, and I shouldn't be getting this crazy over a man. I know that, really… but, *God*! I can't even think straight… I'm making stupid mistakes at work… I've never been this way about anybody!"

"Aww, come on, that's alright," he coached, now rocking her to a significantly faster rhythm than the one coming from the speakers. "I know it hurts now… but believe me, it'll get better."

She looked at him with the hopeful eyes of a repentant child. "How do you know?"

He was no longer able to tell the difference between her suffering and his own. The rocking ended. "It'll just have to."

"He's a g-good man, really," she hiccupped while wiping her face with her coat. "He actually reminds me of you, now that I think of it. But he has someone else."

The shiny gold knobs and buttons on the amazing new SUV had originally been intended to upstage the ache of a marriage gone bad. The dark windows were supposed to veil the mental and emotional chaos bred by the sudden knowledge of domestic nonsuccess. But tonight, something had gone terribly wrong. The glowing white lights on the dashboard now only served to highlight the halo of ache and doubt loitering in his eyes. The noiseless engine only reminded Howard of how alone he really was. The car had turned on him. Tricked him. Trapped him.

"Like… me," he whispered.

Karianna wished she were stupid. But she wasn't. She understood exactly what he said, and moreover, what it could mean if she allowed it to. Within his grip, a grip she'd never felt until tonight, she had now been given license to choose both their fates.

They searched each other's eyes for a condensed eternity, seeking thoughts. Hoping to discover a way out. A way in. A way. But all they found was pain. Familiar pain. She recognized that all he desired was to have again what he deserved, what he had worked so hard for so many years to achieve. He understood her justified yearning for what had been so mercilessly ripped from her routine, leaving her to suffer with no one.

The light above them was fading.

Their faces were now so close that they could taste each other's breath. Howard could feel himself beginning to thicken. He was extremely ashamed, for she had to have felt it, too.

But she said nothing.

"...Kari. I love you..."

Karianna's body was numb, except for where the warmth of his own seeped through her clothing. She prayed that he not let go.

"...exactly what I like..."

Why was he here? Why couldn't this have been Ernyleene? When was the last time she'd allowed him to hold her like this? Why couldn't she feel this good in his arms? He was fully aroused.

"...just too big..."

Her eyes closed. She could feel her body caving into his.

He squeezed her comprehendingly, wringing every last decaying eighty-one-day-old emotion from her bruised armor. Finally. Miraculously.

"Don't worry."

When their lips first touched, it felt weird. Amazingly enough, however, the feeling quickly and forgivingly conceded to a peculiar comfort that was slowly disentombing their cold souls.

So they followed its lead. The line had now been crossed, so they sprinted covetously toward the next, feeding each other tasty delusions of reclaimed power. With each kiss, they grew stronger, and more detached. Validated by their common need, safe inside a bottomless pocket of incoherent thought, they held a single goal. Now teammates versus the universe and all of its foul plays, they would accomplish the unspeakable, proving that bliss could indeed be theirs again, even if it were with each other.

Desperately they held onto one another, for if one were now to let go, the other would certainly shatter, plaguing both infinitely. They must not fail at failure. It was up to them to make this sweet.

Or at least sweet enough to convince them once it ended *(but please don't ever let it end),* that it needed to happen; that they had been necessary.

They were excited yet haunted by their endeavor. It was scary with a slight chance of perfection, like all things in life worth striving for. This was to be no accident. This was defiance in all of its strange pleasantness.

His next tear fell onto her.

Episode 23

Charmaine's nostrils seized enough air for three breaths. The sheer force pushed her entire upper body forward. She felt like her lungs were kissing her uvula. She was self-conscious. And she was growing fists. "Excuse me, what did you just say?"

Xavier, Andy, and a saddened Emil, now dumb with amazement, were unable even to blink.

"Char, I'm sorry. It was all my fault, not his. I just lost my mind. But I am not his mistress. I promise you we were only together that one time."

Fearing for both women's safety, Xavier adopted a stance that made it easier to get to them in case any sudden moves were made.

With each thump in her chest, Charmaine felt her rage magnify. Still, she could not cry. All she could do was wonder: "Why? How? What...?" She briefly wondered whether she was hallucinating – she didn't smoke weed often. But everyone's faces assured her that her mind was sound. Her best friend in the whole world, her confidant, her sister, her guardian had betrayed her in the worst-ever imaginable way.

As the fever in her chest traveled up through her shoulders and neck, Charmaine grimaced at her inability to imagine an excuse that would make Karianna's act the least bit acceptable. It was cruel, vulgar, and vile. And Charmaine was on fire.

"He's my father, you sick bitch!"

"Char...!" Xavier yelled, running to her.

"He raised us! How could you?"

239

"Charmaine, we didn't mean it to happen. You know neither of us would ever hurt you."

"Don't you dare say that to me. I will never forgive you! You'll fuck anybody: your clients, your best friends' daddies… Emil's right: you're nothing but a filthy-ass whore!"

Though Andy was enraptured by the exchange, a suffocating fatigue again began to attack his body.

"Charmaine, please, that's enough," Emil begged.

"Oh, no, it's not enough, but I'm about to make it enough." She threw off her left earring. "After all we've done for you, this is what my family gets in return? You went and seduced…"

"I did not seduce him, Char!" wailed Karianna. "I know it was wrong, but we were really in pain! Both of us needed somebody and we were there for each other. Maybe you don't know the whole story of your parents' marriage, but it hasn't been in good shape for some time…"

"Don't even talk about them!" screamed Charmaine, jettisoning her right earring onto the end table. "You don't know the first thing about what makes a relationship work. You let go of the only man who ever really gave a damn about you …"

"Char, there's more to it than that. Emil and I…"

"We took in your trashy ass when nobody else would – not even your stank alcoholic mama! You ate our food, wore the clothes my mother bought you, and finally learned how to carry yourself with some class and style. We even paid for all your stupid-ass pageant training…"

"It wasn't so stupid when you wanted it."

Charmaine froze. How dare she? Now she was really going to whip this bitch's ass.

"You know I never wanted that pageant life," continued Karianna. "I '*didn't have enough class*', remember? I was just a backwoods piece of trash, right? That's why you couldn't stand it when *I* was the one who started pullin' all the trophies, and not you!"

"That is *so not true*, bitch!"

"Yes, it is. You hated the fact that your own mother decided that I was the winning ticket, and started entering me into all the pageants instead of you! Being pretty had become your whole

identity. And if you couldn't even succeed at that, then what good were you? But you know why you never won?"

"I'm about to beat the shit outta you in your own muthafuckin' house, heffah!"

"Because you have no talent!"

"Bitch! *Aaaaggghhh!"* Charmaine leapt for Karianna's head, only to be intercepted by Emil's massive chest.

He grabbed her arms before she fell to the floor. "Charmaine, please," he negotiated.

"Let go of me! She's about to see I'm talented enough to beat her ho ass!"

"Let her through," encouraged Karianna. "I can still take her. She's top-heavy. That's always been her weakness.

"No, Kari," said Xavier, pulling her to the other side of the room. "Both of you, stop this now! You're acting like children."

A dizzy and disoriented Andy now struggled to remain centered on the entertainment.

Emil escorted Charmaine toward the dining room. "You're both under the influence. Don't do anything you'll regret."

"Too late, Emil," panted a contrite Karianna. "I agree that I deserve a good beat-down for what I've put everyone through. But believe me… since then, I have suffered more than any of you know."

Emil at once sympathized with and pitied her.

She freed herself from Xavier's grip. "Char, believe it or not, I love you more than I love myself. So I won't stand by anymore and watch you ignore your demons. I know what that can lead to."

A shaken Charmaine still kept guard as to how she might get past Emil.

No one noticed Andy staggering off to the bathroom.

"Ever since I made Miss Tennessee, you've felt that maybe you fall short on substance," Karianna theorized. "That's the real reason you stopped going for your M.D., isn't it? Because you were afraid that – just like with the pageants – when the pressure's on, you might not be able to handle it?"

Charmaine shuddered, but quickly regained her might. "I cannot believe that the woman who claimed to be my best

friend, then fucked my father and ruined my parents' marriage, is standing here trying to psychoanalyze me."

Xavier had an idea. He gently pecked Charmaine's shoulder. "Hey, kiddo, why don't we go for a walk? Get rid of some of this haze? It's a beautiful night."

"Get away from me." Still monitoring Emil's impenetrable guard, she grabbed her coat and ran to the door. "Why do the people I love the most in this world always hurt me the fucking worst?" She walked out.

Karianna's eyes were nearly swollen shut. Emil grabbed her hand, then, sensing that she needed more than just that, pulled her into a heavy embrace.

Xavier had witnessed this scene before. And the last time it occurred, he let Charmaine just walk out. But this time he couldn't do it. This time, he had to at least attempt to bring her back to him. He loved her. And watching her walk away was no longer an option. He headed for the door.

But in walked Charmaine. "Forgot my purse."

Suddenly Karianna felt that something else was very wrong. "Where's Drew?"

"Don't try to change the subject."

Just then, a thunderous crash detonated from the bathroom. Karianna bolted in, followed by the others. At their destination lay Andy's limp unconscious body face down in the bathtub, his left arm hanging over the side. The faucet pounded ice cold water onto his head, where a large open gash gushed his blood down into the drain. His lips were blue. He wasn't breathing.

"Puppy! Oh, my God!"

The Baptist Hospital emergency room brimmed with desperation. Xavier could not help but be stricken by all of the

pain in his wake. To his left was Charmaine, her brain no doubt whirring with thoughts – some coherent, some not – of her mother, her father, her best friend, and now Andy. To his right sat Karianna, who hated hospitals. Now she was sitting in one on the worst day of her life. Off to the center of the room was Emil. The love of his life and one of his closest friends may end up hating each other forever.

Suddenly, Charmaine got up. Dr. Evan-Patrik Torsche, an exotically dark and attractive man of European descent, was walking over to her. The others huddled around them.

"Well? How is he?" Charmaine asked.

"I'm sorry, Char. He lost a lot of blood. And he suffered a stroke.

"*What?*" Karianna was nearly hysterical. "At his age? Oh, God!"

"Alright, Evan, please tell us everything."

"We also found alcohol, speed, marijuana, and antidepressants in his system. His blood alcohol level is .29, which as you know is dangerously high. Oh, and the lining of his esophagus is ruptured. That's a sign of bulimia."

Charmaine and Xavier were shocked speechless as Emil held a delicate weeping Karianna.

"One last thing: I don't know if you're aware that he's also a type two diabetic."

Xavier hurled his eyes heavenward in disbelief.

"This isn't my hospital, but I can assure all of you that these doctors are making sure that he receives the best treatment possible. They're moving him to intensive care. I won't lie to you, though: no one can promise that he'll make it through the night in his condition. His body is functioning at less than fifty percent. If that continues for the next twenty-four hours, then I would prepare for his death. Does he have any family?"

"They're not normally in touch," replied Charmaine, "But I'm making phone calls."

"Ohmygod," said Karianna. "The press. We have to keep this out of…"

"Don't worry about that," Charmaine said. We'll do what we can to hold them at bay." She pulled Torsche into a corner about

twenty feet away from the others. "Thank you for coming all the way over here in the middle of the night, Evan."

"Thanks aren't necessary. You know that I care about you very much. I love you. I do wish that you would reconsider my offer."

"So be honest with me. What are his chances?"

Torsche removed his designer frames to reveal a face marked by wisdom and beauty. "I'm sorry."

"I know."

February 17th, 2010: 2:51 a.m.

Karianna sat on the emergency room sofa contemplating the potential outcome of her confession. She was broken by the notion that she may have destroyed the best friendship she could ever hope to have.

Charmaine walked over to the group.

Karianna stood up. "Char, please let me try to…"

"Step off, bitch. I used to work here. I really don't want them to see me act a fool right now."

"But…"

"Kari," Charmaine snapped, "He's my father. Maybe you can't see the significance of that since your own parents were such fuck-ups, but… tell me: how is what you did *ever* gonna go away?" She walked out of the emergency room and out of the hospital.

Karianna fell limp on the sofa. Emil knelt down before her and snuggled his head into her lap. Emil, the love of her life, was caring for her again, attentive to her needs again. But because of her own foolish actions, she could not enjoy it.

"She'll come around," he said. "Don't worry. You will work through this, and everything will be fine. I promise."

Attempting to muster a smile, she glared down at him. He was incredible. And she enormously appreciated what he was trying to do. But his efforts, no matter how grand and selfless, were powerless against the fortitude of tonight's happenings. She could not believe him this time. Things would never be the same again.

They waited.

Episode 24

"...and coming up at 10:00, another fire ravages through an upscale jewelry boutique in Green Hills. $400,000 worth of diamonds, rubies, and one very rare antique sapphire necklace are now believed to be missing in what is now the third Metro Nashville arson-robbery in less than two months. Police officials believe the incidents to be related.

But first, police are still gathering clues in last night's deadly bludgeoning of Vanderbilt Commodores quarterback Ramon Del Peral. Eighteen year old Del Peral was found around 9pm in a vacant East Nashville lot, having suffered several broken ribs, four broken fingers, crushed legs, a snapped spine, and extensive internal bleeding. He appeared to have been beaten with a blunt metal object. Del Peral, who was rushed to Centennial Medical Center, died on the operating table early this morning. His family is asking for your prayers. Police officials say the vicious attack appears to have taken place between 7:00 and 8:00 last night. The future of the team is now uncertain. If you or anyone you know has any clues as to the whereabouts of Del Peral's assailant, please call the number on your screen, or your local police precinct.

And now, in entertainment, more sad news: notorious gay actor-comedian and Brentwood native Drew Niles suffered a stroke last night while having dinner at a local restaurant. Sources say that Niles overdosed on a potentially lethal dose of drugs and alcohol, and that he is also anorexic."

February 17th, 2010: 9:45 a.m.

"Shit! They're already lyin' their asses off," Karianna barked. "I can't believe this." She turned off the television. "Emil! Xavier!"

The two buddies walked through the I.C.U. waiting room doors carrying three fresh cups of coffee.

"Could one of you get me out of here for a few minutes?"

"Sure, let's go," offered Emil. "Xavier, would you…"

"No worries. If anything happens, I'll call you."

"Thanks, man."

While walking in the courtyard, Karianna spoke. "Emil, you are an extraordinary man for supporting Andy like this. And where did you learn CPR?"

He smiled. "At church. But Andy's a good kid. He's made mistakes, but he defied a lot of odds when most people didn't think he could. My only regret is that I never fully reconciled with him."

Karianna stopped walking. "OK – about us."

"Kari, before you begin, there are some things I have to say to you. Regarding our break up: I still don't understand it. I mean, the thing with Mr. Parker, I must take some of the blame for that…"

"No. No, Emil. It was my fault…"

"But you'd have to concur that the way I handled our situation was quite deleterious. I left you alone, and I was too engulfed in my own calamities to see that I was letting you down. I'm so sorry and embarrassed of my ignominy," he sighed. "But when you dumped me, none of it made any sense. You just cut me off completely." He pulled her to him. "I love you. You're everything to me, Kari. No one else comes close. You had to have known that."

"Got about an hour? There's someone I want you to meet."

karianna, howard parker, and...

"Thank you for meeting me on such short notice." She kissed him on the cheek.

"No problem," Howard said. "Back when I was on full duty, I never really got the chance to enjoy this part of town as much as I should've. I love the restaurants in Hermitage."

"So how is Mrs. Parker?"

"Just takin' it easy since Monday's surgery. I think we'd better ease up on the phone therapy sessions, though. Now that she's got more downtime on her hands, she's startin' to get paranoid."

"So maybe I shouldn't have kissed you on the way in here?"

"Oh, come on, now," he laughed. "I'd hardly think a peck on the cheek qualifies as suspect behavior to anybody with good sense. Charmaine gives me bigger kisses than that." He enthusiastically continued, "You've been so good for me these past few weeks, Kari. You're a great counselor. Our conversations have really encouraged me since that night.

"You're so welcome! It's the least I can do. You're a good man and you're important to a lot of people. You deserve to feel good about yourself. Don't ever forget that." She was happy that he was in a good mood.

"Thanks. Well, how are you? You look great. What have you been do-...?"

"I'm pregnant."

"Welcome to the Red Dragon Restaurant! We're glad to have you today. May I start you guys off with something to drink and maybe an appetizer?"

Howard was absolutely mortified. He did not know what to say. But he didn't want to appear unable to handle the new information. He adjusted his posture. "Not to sound callous, Kari, but are you sure the child is ours?"

She nodded. "You're the only one I've been with since that night, and the last man before you was Emil. When I didn't get my

period, I waited around for a while because I didn't want to cry wolf. After six more weeks, I went to the doctor. She gave me the news."

"I'm fifty."

"I'm unmarried."

"I'm married."

"I'm screwed."

"Do you want to keep it?"

"Yes, I do."

"Good. I couldn't live with any child of mine being aborted. Even if my life will change drastically once he's born."

Karianna was relieved to hear that. It meant she had an ally. And she really needed one, because soon, she was destined to be attacked from every imaginable angle. "Thank you. I really appreciate that."

"Kari, whatever you need me to do, I'll take my responsibilities seriously, regardless of the consequence." He began to work on a game plan. "We'll have to figure out what to do about Erny. I guess I should tell you: I'm considering leaving her."

Karianna was surprised, and wondered how that news, on top of her own, would affect Charmaine.

"I wanna be happy," he went on, "And who knows? Maybe this is my cue to start over. I'm not gettin' any younger. And I want to start meeting new people, maybe get back into the dating scene. And, I want to raise my kid the right way this time."

Karianna smiled. Her worries were beginning to relinquish strength. Could there be a silver lining somewhere in this?

"I'm not sure about what's going to happen," he stated. "But I do know that you've helped me to heal, and I'm grateful. I actually feel good again."

"Me, too."

Episode 24

Emil Oliver Cojoure
2006-2006

"Twenty-two days later, on my way home from work, I got an awful burning cramp in my abdomen. It felt like something was jumping around inside of me. Of course, I was really scared. I drove straight to the hospital. Emil, I was miscarrying. My doctor made sure that everything was clear and that I was OK. I took the next week off work, screened all my calls, and did nothing but cry. My life was just a big mess. I would've told you, but it's one thing to stray; it's a whole other ball game to carry another man's child."

February 17th, 2010: 11:13 a.m.

"So you broke it off between us?"

"I wanted to be free of that whole episode of my life. Breaking up with you was the only way I could figure out how to start making that happen," she explained. "I know that I was so cruel to you, but I was going nuts. Maybe I thought that making you hate me would make everything easier."

"I could never hate you, Kari." He pulled her to him and hugged her.

"I may lose my two best friends today, Emil."

"You really have to think positively. You're not a bad person. What you did is in the past. Please have faith. Remember that God is infinitely powerful, and can right all wrongs."

"You say that almost as if you're trying to convince yourself."

Emil's eyes reflected a wealth of simultaneous elation and anguish.

"I don't deserve you, do I?" Karianna declared. "I can honestly say that I don't know anyone who does."

"Well, maybe someone in Paris will."

Her face brightened. "You finally accepted their offer?"

"They wouldn't stop hounding me about it. You know the French: so rude. But it pays a lot more than what I make now, and it is a great opportunity."

"When are you leaving?"

"Tomorrow. I'm giving my notice at work this afternoon."

"Tomorrow! Emil, this is great news, but why so soon?"

"I- I've just got to get on with my life. And I believe this would be a great start. I've been dangling the carrot long enough and now it's time to just do it. They're anxious to have me. They've purchased my ticket, and they're arranging my move and my housing. All I have to do is get on the plane."

"Well, as always, I am so proud of you," she smiled.

They kissed.

"I love you, Kari."

"I love you, too. Come on, luv. We'd better get back. I just wanna scoot by my place first to freshen up a little."

Karianna couldn't dilly-dally. She had to shower and change clothes quickly, for it was imperative that she get back to that hospital fast. But boy, was she looking forward to getting clean. "I'll be right back – it won't take me fifteen minutes."

"I'll be here," Emil assured.

She closed the car door and scurried up her front walkway. While ascending the porch stairs, she noticed that her front door was slightly ajar. She began to worry, then rationalized the fair probability that someone neglected to shut it when they rushed to the hospital the previous night.

Still cautious, though, she walked inside and grabbed the baseball bat from behind the grandfather clock. That's when she saw the little white unmarked envelope on the mini-bar.

"The maid doesn't come til tomorrow," she remembered. "So who's this from?" She ripped open the envelope and read:

"Bonjour, Petite.
Fifteen years is a long time, huh?
Well, they just let me out.
You shouldn't have said all those bad things about me in court.
It was very hard for me behind bars because of you.
So I think you and I have some unfinished business.
And I've waited long enough to give you your due.
See you soon.
-Papa"

Episode 25

Karianna fell onto the back of the couch. Extremely frightened, she peered over her shoulders and about the first floor for any evidence of a foreigner's stain. Or even worse – signs that he was still there. She began hearing creaks in the foundation that she had never heard before. She was sweating. She felt as if he were breathing down her neck. The next few seconds seemed like forever as she shot for the door, flew down the porch stairs and jumped back into the car.

Emil immediately sensed her horror. "Baby, what's wrong?"

"He's out," she gasped. "My father's out of jail, and he's been in my house." She handed him the note then peeled off the curb, blazing back to the hospital to convene with the entire group. She desperately hoped that someone would know what exactly to do next.

February 17th, 2010: 12:09 p.m.

They walked into the waiting room, where Charmaine stood. Dr. Torsche was next to her. This was not a good sign.

"Oh my God," Karianna screamed. "What happened? Where's Xavier?"

"I'm right here," he chimed, returning from the cafeteria. "Oh, hey, Char, I'm so happy you came back!" He kissed her on the cheek, but could tell that something was wrong – she did not kiss him back. He then advanced over to the others. "Kari, you look hysterical. What's wrong?"

255

"That doesn't matter right now. How's Andy?"

Dr. Torsche stepped forward to speak to the group. Charmaine then grabbed his arm to alert him that she should be the one to inform them. He agreed.

"Everyone... unfortunately..."

"Oh, God, no!"

Emil, himself scared, grabbed the immensely fragile Karianna.

"Unfortunately, Andy's condition has not changed," Charmaine stated. "Things do not look very good. I'm so sorry."

Xavier briefly closed his eyes. "But at least he's still alive."

"Thank you, God," Emil whispered.

Karianna dashed to Charmaine. "I'm glad you're here. We can't stay at my house for a while, because..."

"Oh, I won't be staying at your house at all. In fact, my things will be out by tonight."

"What? Please, let's not let this get even worse..."

Xavier butted in. "Char, please think this through. This has been a lot for all of us to swallow, but you know that Kari loves you. Besides, where would you stay?"

"With my husband."

"Your *what*?" Emil yelled.

"Everyone, say hello to the new 'Dr. and Mrs. Evan and Charmaine Torsche'. We just tied the knot downtown and couldn't wait to tell you!"

Xavier felt sick. "But, I don't understand..."

Charmaine walked over to him. "Xavier, you're wonderful. And I love you. But you're not what I need. Evan is. I'm sorry. I hope that we can still be friends."

Xavier sat down and stored his head between his thighs.

Emil and Karianna looked at Charmaine. Between the three of them, no one had any idea what should come next. Charmaine tossed her hair a couple of times, hoping it would bring something to mind. But it didn't. She had nothing to say.

"Uh, um..." said Evan, clearing his throat, "I realize that this must be a great shock to each of you, especially considering the current circumstances. But Charmaine and I really love each other..."

Xavier looked up.

"...And felt that now especially would be a great time to celebrate that. Mr. Niles has made us see the necessity to cherish life without fail. We just couldn't wait another moment to declare our undying love to each other. We hope that you will be able to celebrate with us once everything is taken care of here, don't we, baby?"

"Yes, absolutely..." Charmaine was now able to look anywhere in the room but into her friends' eyes.

"Excuse me, but I have something to say," Emil adamantly broadcast.

"Emil, no," Karianna begged. "Please."

"I'm sorry. Something is on my mind, and as a Christian man I simply cannot remain silent..."

Suddenly, a team of seven police officers, led by Officer Belinda Twostones, stormed into the Baptist Hospital intensive care waiting room, their hands clutched readily upon their weapons.

"Hi, Xavier," she said. "Which one of you is Dr. Emil Hubbard?"

"I am."

"Dr. Hubbard, you are under arrest for the murder of Ramon Del Peral. You have the right to remain silent."

Karianna was perplexed. "What? What is this! Emil..."

"Anything you say can and will be used against you in a court of law..."

"Wait a minute!" Xavier asserted. "I'm his lawyer! Hey, Belinda, may I just speak to him for a quick second?"

"Belinda? Who's 'Belinda'?" Charmaine secretly questioned.

"Sure, down at the precinct. Let's go."

Twostones handcuffed Emil, then signaled for a subordinate officer to escort him to her car. Xavier kissed Karianna, glanced once more at Charmaine, then led the throng of officers out of the building.

February 17ᵗʰ, 2010: 12:35 p.m.

Emil sat in a metal chair with a torn orange cushion that erupted mounds of dirty foam. Needing something to expend the increasingly chaotic energy racing through his body, he leaned the chair against the wall and rocked back and forth on its two rear legs. He was afraid.

"Your counsel is here."

Xavier walked in more slowly than Emil had anticipated he would. On the ride over, Emil had daydreamed that his friend would swoop in like a peregrine falcon, ready to kick ass, take names and unhinge him from his impending dilemma. Reality was different. Xavier took his time. He studied Emil's body language. He made Emil more nervous.

"How are they treating you, E?"

"Fine. Thank you for coming."

Xavier sat, then looked down at the table. Suddenly, he broke. "So, did you do it, bud?"

"What? Did I... no, of course not! How could you ask such a thing? You know me better than that..."

"Wait, now," Xavier said, "Let's stop and think about that statement. Because in the last few hours, I've found out that I really don't know any of my friends."

"Xavier!"

"So how long had you and Ramon been seeing each other?"

"We weren't seeing each other. That was the problem."

"Oh, you beat him to death because he wouldn't date you?"

"No! No, Xavier. He had been chasing after me for nearly a year. Ever since the day you introduced us. I'm convinced that he even rigged my car."

"What?"

"Ramon was a borderline sociopath," Emil professed. "I know it may be hard for you to believe because he's the star quarterback and everyone loves him. But he was not a stable person. Some might even categorize him as a predator. Last night – the whole take-out thing... don't you find it rather odd that you'd just totally *forgotten* about dinner with Kari? Well, you

didn't forget. Ramon planned it. He had been trying to bed me for months."

Still unconvinced, Xavier wanted to hear more. "Had you ever given him a reason?"

"We... petted a couple of times."

"Is that all?"

"We've kissed..."

Fed up with Emil's evasive wordplay, Xavier demanded, "Have you and Ramon had sex, E?"

"Yes. Last night."

"Oh, shit!"

"I wasn't thinking straight..."

"He was seventeen!"

"Huh?"

"Ramon Del Peral wasn't eighteen years old, Emil. We just got word from downtown that he was actually a seventeen year old minor who falsified his records to leave Cuba and come to school in Tennessee – a state where the legal age of consent is eighteen years old! If they find so much as your fuckin' snot anywhere near his body... *Oh my God!*"

Emil placed his cuffed hands upon the table. "Xavier, I realize that Charmaine's news may be affecting you negatively, but..."

Xavier convulsively grabbed a chair and thrashed it at the south wall, eliciting a crash that sent hundreds of tiny bunches of dingy foam bits flying about the room. "Leave Charmaine outta this, fucker!"

Two armed guards ran in.

"We're fine here," he assured them. He extracted four pills from his pocket and swallowed them.

Emil was very worried. Things did not look good for him, and without Xavier on his side, he was surely a goner. "I am your friend, X," he tugged. "Do you really think that I..."

"Emil! Do you understand the seriously deep shit you're in? If they find any motive for you to have harmed him in any way, you're looking at a minimum of thirty years." Completely exasperated, he sat down and looked into Emil's eyes. "Look, I want to help you. But you have to tell me the truth. They've found the assault weapon

259

in some bushes behind your building, and your apartment looks like a fucking tornado hit it. His fingerprints and his blood are splattered all over your living room floor and walls. I've seen the photos, E!"

"I… I don't know what you're talking about."

"What time did you leave my office last night?"

"Around 7:00."

"But you didn't arrive at Aisle C until almost half past eight. Where did you go?"

"I drove around town for a while," Emil stammered. "To clear my head. There was a lot to think about. I was agitated."

"I remember. Did you have any additional contact with Ramon before the restaurant?"

"Yes. I went to ask him one last time not to turn me in to HR, because when I told him I'd no longer have sex with him he said he was going to…" He stopped right there.

"Motive. Son of a bitch."

"But Xavier, I didn't…!"

"So have you had sex with Andy, too?"

Emil was aghast. "It wasn't… why are you asking me that? Why would you…?"

"I've seen the way you act around him," Xavier pounded. "As if you're uncomfortable. Like the other night at the reception. What exactly happened between you two?"

"Uh…"

Xavier had no more patience left. "Emil, this shit will all come out at your trial! They will try to establish that you have a pattern with youngsters! They kill men in jail for that!" His voice cracked with increased anxiety. "And let's not even mention your drug history. You'll be all over every motherfuckin' news channel in this country! *What happened between you and Andy!*"

Water poured from Emil's eyes. "He drugged me, Xavier! I couldn't tell anyone. I'd just completed all of my steps. My employers were watching me like hawks. We would've both faced so much public embarrassment. I didn't want any old issues to resurface at work, so I just buried it. Ask Kari – she'll confirm my story."

Xavier sat down and became quiet for what seemed hours. Emil had never seen this side of him. He seemed to have entered a meditative state. Is this what he did when working a case? Was he contemplating whether he would he defend Emil, or deny him?

"Emil, I am still your friend. And I've seen a lot in my career, so I understand how things can happen in the heat of the moment. But I am going to ask you one last time, and I want a straight answer. Did you, or did you not, kill Ramon Del Peral?"

Emil knew that his entire future now rested on the next few words to leave his mouth. "Alright, Xavier. I…"

A clerk walked in. "Officer Twostones would like to see you. She says it's really important."

Xavier demounted his chair and followed the clerk into the hallway.

"Hey!" Twostones said. "How's it going in there?" She noticed that he looked quite dejected, and led him into a private room twenty-five feet down the hall. She then locked the door behind them.

"Belinda, this just isn't a good time, OK? I'll catch up with you la-…"

"Care to make a trade?"

Xavier squinted. "What?"

"Some info on your client, fire-boy Theodorio Beals, in exchange for… a little assistance with your friend's case?"

"You've gotta be kidding me!" Xavier lashed. "Now you're trying to bribe an attorney to violate lawyer-client privilege just so you can jump up to sergeant! You know, I've had it with your games. You have stepped into very dangerous territory here." Xavier didn't admit it, but he liked Twostones' gall. No, he *really* liked it.

261

"Are we making threats now?" she countered. "Well, let's consider how all this'll go down on CNN: your best friend, a highly lauded professor at a top North American university – and a Baptist minister to boot – on the chopping block for the murder of a teenage college football star, whom he was fucking."

"Speculation." Oooh, this woman was hot.

"We both know that if Emil is convicted, he'll go up the river and won't come back until he's a senior citizen – that is, if he's not shanked to death while inside. He's a recovering drug addict who's been seen in public at least twice with the fallen victim. In addition to all the evidence at his apartment, we now have testimony from your firm's cleaning lady which confirms a screaming match last night, as well as heavy objects falling. Fluids are being tested right now at the lab, and if they match up... well you're a smart guy, Xavier. You can figure out the rest."

"OK... What precisely would you need me to do?" Xavier asked.

"You know exactly what. I need Beals's mental health records, his journals – and before you say he doesn't have any, spare your breath: all the crazies keep at least one journal – as well as the name of the new woman he's seeing. I have a hunch about her."

"Are you sure you're not just obsessed with him? He is a charmer. Perhaps you just want his new girlfriend out of the picture?" Xavier teased.

"Oh, trust me, I've got my eye on someone else."

She had managed to titillate him even today, of all days. It was clear that this woman had special powers.

He argued, "Officer Twostones, you know I could be disbarred if I gave you any of that information, assuming that any of it actually exists. Everything: my job, my house, my future, they'd all be on the line. I've worked too hard to get where I am to mess up now." Xavier wasn't sure whom he was trying to convince, Twostones or himself. "And I'm concerned about what Beals might do if he found out. He can be a bit of a loose cannon."

"So help me take him down," she brazenly replied. "You know this is a big case for me. I wouldn't risk it by ratting you out. Your secret would be totally safe."

He tried to assess her body language in order to determine whether he could trust her.

"Xavier, I'm not a bad person. I told you: I just play to win, like you. Give me what I need, and I'll make a call to someone downtown who owes me big. He'll place a crackhead felon at the crime scene at the time of the assault, and get your friend back home in time for Oprah."

"I'm sorry, I don't know the name of Theo's new girl. Really, I don't."

"Ah, but he likes you," she said. "And he trusts you. Get him to tell you her whereabouts, and I'll take it from there."

"If I were to do what you're asking, I'm not sure I could live with myself."

"You'd be saving your friend from public persecution and inevitable imprisonment, as well as preventing another of our local businesses from being robbed bone dry then burned to the ground."

"Now, wait one minute," Xavier struck, "My client had nothing to do with those…"

"Yes, he did. Stop playing games, hotshot. You think I haven't been watching you? Your reputation for intuitiveness is becoming legendary in this town. You pick juries better than your bosses. So you must suspect that he's involved. How does *that* sit on your conscience? And by the way: before you write me off, you might wanna do a little research on me to learn who you're dealing with…"

"I already have," he informed. "Seven-hundred sixty-three arrests and seven-hundred thirteen convictions in just two years on the force. You're good. That's the only reason we're talking now."

"We could make a great team, you and I."

Though reticent to admit it, Xavier kind of liked that idea. But there was one problem. He was a great lawyer because of his uncanny ability to read people's personalities within minutes of meeting them. But try as he might, he could not read Belinda Twostones. He never knew from which angle she was coming. Was she lying to him now? Did she really have a high-powered friend who could bed this case? Was she even attracted to him at

all? Or would she say anything to get what she wanted, no matter whose face she had to step on? Though he had no answers to any of these questions, was he willing to risk everything on her anyway?

"So how do you know I'd follow through with your requests after you get Emil off?"

"Because you wouldn't want any of those bright-eyed young pre-law students who'll be reading your ethics textbook to find out that back when you were their age, you plagiarized a term paper... would you?"

Xavier was shocked. And impressed. And totally turned on.

"Plus, Xavier, you're honest," she said. "You don't screw people over. That's the problem with people like us. We could rule the world, if only we had it in us to be assholes."

"You're trying to blackmail me into screwing over my own client. From the looks of it, you're well on your way to becoming vice-president."

She laughed. "OK, look, do we have a deal, or does the professor fry?"

Xavier thought. His whole life would be turned upside down if Twostones was lying. She could in fact even be setting him up – he did have enemies – potentially creating a pit even too deep for the young master attorney to escape. What would he do then?

But his best friend was in brutally serious trouble, with very few prospects for survival. Emil might even die behind bars without some kind of help. Because of that potentiality, Xavier had no more time to weigh options. In fact, he had no options. He turned to Twostones.

"OK, let's do it."

February 17ᵗʰ, 2010: 3:18 p.m.

Emil retrieved his belongings at the front desk, then asked to go to the restroom, where he stayed for nearly forty minutes. Xavier wasn't altogether certain, but could've sworn that at several instances he heard him sobbing and muttering random phrases to himself – perhaps even praying.

Then he reemerged.

On the drive back to Baptist Hospital, Xavier noticed how silent he had become. He didn't even say thank you once released from police custody. Instead, he immediately called his new Parisian employer to confirm his moving and flight arrangements. Then he called his bosses at Vanderbilt and New Israel to inform them of his resignation.

He declined to share any of the specifics with Xavier. In fact, it seemed that he wished to keep Xavier from learning anything at all about his move. Why was he so hushed all of a sudden? Was he angry? Just tired from the long day?

Or had Emil actually murdered Ramon Del Peral? Emil had always been the one friend whom everyone knew the least about. And every piece of incriminating evidence did point directly at him. Was he actually capable of taking another life?

An increasingly discomforted Xavier began to have second thoughts about endangering himself to save someone he obviously did not know as well as he'd thought. Noticing a serene, statue-like Emil from the corner of his eye, Xavier wondered, had he done the right thing by risking it all? Or was he indeed chauffeuring around a cold-blooded killer?

February 17ᵗʰ, 2010: 3:49 p.m.

Though the intensive care unit was housed on the eighth floor, Xavier parked on the fifth. He wanted to give Emil additional time to break his silence. But Emil remained tight-lipped for the entire thirteen-minute walk through the throng of ravenous paparazzi and into the hospital. Finally, on the elevator, Xavier turned and stared mercilessly at Emil, hoping that it would wear him down. But an expressionless Emil still just stared right back at him, saying nothing. Xavier was beginning to get a little creeped out.

Then the door opened.

The men walked into Baptist Hospital I.C.U. to find Charmaine standing on the north end of the room. Karianna sat on the other. Both women's eyes were crimson red. They looked up at Xavier and Emil, now frozen in their steps. Something had just happened.

"He's gone."

8844027R0

Made in the USA
Lexington, KY
07 March 2011